With this issue, we've increased our
magazine width, column width, and page count,
making room for more great work.

While we've yet to break even,
what a marvelous way to live!
All of these fictional lives being led
(36,826 stories were sent to us in 2003),
as we lead our own lives, none of
these—fictional or real—ever quite following
the established course. The world swirls around us
and through us, and our steps move steadily forward,
side by side as sisters, embracing it all.

We are mightily glad for the company
of our writers and our readers. It is a pleasure
and a privilege, and enriching beyond measure.

To life!

*"In two straight lines they broke their bread
and brushed their teeth and went to bed."*
Madeline by Ludwig Bemelmans, 1939

PAST CONTRIBUTING AUTHORS AND ARTISTS
Many of issues 1 through 49 are available for eleven dollars each.

David Abrams • Robert A. Abel • Linsey Abrams • Steve Adams • Diane King Akers • Susan Alenick • Rosemary Altea • Julia Alvarez • Brian Ames • A. Manette Ansay • Margaret Atwood • Kevin Bacon • Doreen Baingana • Aida Baker • Russell Banks • Brad Barkley • Andrea Barrett • Kyle Ann Bates • Richard Bausch • Robert Bausch • Charles Baxter • Ann Beattie • Barbara Bechtold • Cathie Beck • Jeff Becker • Janet Belding • Sallie Bingham • Kristen Birchett • Melanie Bishop • James Carlos Blake • Corinne Demas Bliss • Valerie Block • Joan Bohorfoush • Robin Bradford • Harold Brodkey • Danit Brown • Kurt McGinnis Brown • Paul Brownfield • Ayşe Papatya Bucak • Judy Budnitz • Susanna Bullock • Christopher Bundy • Jenny A. Burkholder • Evan Burton • Michael Byers • Christine Byl • Gerard Byrne • Jack Cady • Annie Callan • Kevin Canty • Peter Carey • Ron Carlson • H. G. Carroll • David Cates • Brian Champeau • Vikram Chandra • Diane Chang • Mike Chasar • Robert Chibka • Chieh Chieng • Carolyn Chute • George Makana Clark • Dennis Clemmens • Aaron Cohen • Robert Cohen • Evan S. Connell • Ellen Cooney • Rand Richards Cooper • Lydia E. Copeland • Rita D. Costello • Wendy Counsil • Doug Crandell • Ronald F. Currie Jr. • William J. Cyr • Quinn Dalton • Bilal Dardai • Tristan Davies • C.V. Davis • Laurence de Looze • Toi Derricotte • Janet Desaulniers • Tiziana di Marina • Junot Díaz • Stephen Dixon • Matthew Doherty • Michael Dorris • Siobhan Dowd • Greg Downs • Eugenie Doyle • Tiffany Drever • Andre Dubus • Andre Dubus III • Stuart Dybek • Wayne Dyer • Melodie S. Edwards • Ron Egatz • Barbara Eiswerth • Mary Relindes Ellis • Susan Engberg • Lin Enger • James English • Tony Eprile • Louise Erdrich • Zoë Evamy • Nomi Eve • Edward Falco • Anthony Farrington • Merrill Feitell • J. M. Ferguson Jr. • Lisa Fetchko • Susan Fox • Michael Frank • Pete Fromm • Daniel Gabriel • Ernest Gaines • Tess Gallagher • Louis Gallo • Elizabeth Gallu • Kent Gardien • Ellen Gilchrist • Mary Gordon • Peter Gordon • Elizabeth Graver • Lisa Graley • Jo-Ann Graziano • Andrew Sean Greer • Gail Greiner • John Griesemer • Zoë Griffith-Jones • Paul Griner • Aaron Gwyn • L.B. Haas • Patricia Hampl • Christian Hansen • Elizabeth Logan Harris • Marina Harris • Erin Hart • Kent Haruf • Daniel Hayes • David Haynes • Daniel Hecht • Ursula Hegi • Amy Hempel • Andee Hochman • Alice Hoffman • Jack Holland • Noy Holland • Lucy Honig • Ann Hood • Linda Hornbuckle • David Huddle • Siri Hustvedt • Quang Huynh • Stewart David Ikeda • Lawson Fusao Inada • Elizabeth Inness-Brown • Debra Innocenti • Bruce Jacobson • Andrea Jeyaveeran • Charles Johnson • Leslie Johnson • Wayne Johnson • Allen Morris Jones • Thom Jones • Tom Miller Juvik • Cyril Jones-Kellet • Elizabeth Judd • Jiri Kajanë • Hester Kaplan • Wayne Karlin • Andrew Kass • Tom Kealey • Andrea King Kelly • Thomas E. Kennedy • Tim Keppel • Jamaica Kincaid • Lily King • Maina wa Kinyatti • Carolyn Kizer • Carrie Knowles • N.S. Köenings • David Koon • Karen Kovacik • Jake Kreilkamp • Marilyn Krysl • Frances Kuffel • Mandy Dawn Kuntz • Anatoly Kurchatkin • Victoria Lancelotta • Jennifer Levasseur • Doug Lawson • Don Lee • Peter Lefcourt • Jon Leon • Doris Lessing • Debra Levy • Janice Levy • Christine Liotta • Rosina Lippi-Green • David Long • Nathan Long • Salvatore Diego Lopez • Melissa Lowver • William Luvaas • Barry Lyga • David H. Lynn • Richard Lyons • Bruce Machart • Jeff MacNelly • R. Kevin Maler • George Manner • Jana Martin • Lee Martin • Valerie Martin • Alice Mattison • Jane McCafferty • Judith McClain • Cammie McGovern • Cate McGowan • Eileen McGuire • Susan McInnis • Gregory McNamee • Jenny Drake McPhee • Amalia Melis • Frank Michel • Nancy Middleton • Alyce Miller • Katherine Min • Mary McGarry Morris • Ted Morrissey • Mary Morrissy • Bernard Mulligan • Abdelrahman Munif • Manuel Muñoz • Karen Munro • Kent Nelson • Thisbe Nissen • Sigrid Nunez • Ron Nyren • Joyce Carol Oates • Tim O'Brien • Vana O'Brien • Mary O'Dell • Chris Offutt • Jennifer Oh • Laura Oliver • Felicia Olivera • Thomas O'Malley • Stewart O'Nan • Elizabeth Oness • Karen Outen • Mary Overton • Patricia Page • Ann Pancake • Peter Parsons • Roy Parvin • Karenmary Penn • Susan Perabo • Dawn Karima Pettigrew • Constance Pierce • Steven Polansky • John Prendergast • Jessica Printz • Melissa Pritchard • E. Annie Proulx • Eric Puchner • Kevin Rabalais • Jonathan Raban • George Rabasa • Margo Rabb • Mark Rader • Paul Rawlins • Nancy Reisman • Linda Reynolds • Kurt Rheinheimer • Carol Roh-Spaulding • Anne Rice • Michelle Richmond • Alberto Ríos • Roxana Robinson • Paulette Roeske • Stan Rogal • Carol Roh-Spaulding • Frank Ronan • Elizabeth Rosen • Janice Rosenberg • Jane Rosenzweig • Karen Sagstetter • Kiran Kaur Saini • Mark Salzman • Carl Schaffer • Libby Schmais • Natalie Schoen • Jim Schumock • Lynn Sharon Schwartz • Barbara Scot • Amy Selwyn • Catherine Seto • Bob Shacochis • Evelyn Sharenov • Sally Shivnan • Daryl Siegel • Ami Silber • Al Sim • George Singleton • Floyd Skloot • Brian Slattery • Roland Sodowsky • Scott Southwick • R. Clifton Spargo • Gregory Spatz • Brent Spencer • L.M. Spencer • Lara Stapleton • Barbara Stevens • John Stinson • George Stolz • William Styron • Virgil Suárez • Karen Swenson • Liz Szabla • Mika Tanner • Lois Taylor • Paul Theroux • Abigail Thomas • Randolph Thomas • Joyce Thompson • Patrick Tierney • Aaron Tillman • Tamara B. Titus • Andrew Toos • Pauls Toutonghi • Vu Tran • Patricia Traxler • Jessica Treadway • Doug Trevor • Rob Trucks • Kathryn Trueblood • Carol Turner • Christine Turner • Kathleen Tyau • Michael Upchurch • Lee Upton • Gerard Varni • Katherine Vaz • A. J. Verdelle • Daniel Villasenor • Sergio Gabriel Waisman • Daniel Wallace • Ren Wanding • Mary Yukari Waters • Jonathan Wei • Jamie Weisman • Lance Weller • Ed Weyhing • J. Patrice Whetsell • Joan Wickersham • Lex Williford • Gary Wilson • Robin Winick • Terry Wolverton • Monica Wood • Christopher Woods • Leslie A. Wootten • wormser • Celia Wren • Callie Wright • Calvin Wright • Brennen Wysong • June Unjoo Yang • Nancy Zafris • Jane Zwinger

CONTENTS

That's me and my mother on the couch. The picture was taken in September 1968. My father, the cameraman, must have just returned from Vietnam. The book is a giant Disney anthology. The images and stories from that book are clear in my memory to this day.

Clark E. Knowles lives in Portsmouth, New Hampshire with his wife Gail and his daughter Grace. He teaches writing at the University of New Hampshire. His fiction has appeared in *Black Warrior Review*, *Scribner's Best of the Fiction Workshops 1999*, the *Flying Horse Review*, and has been nominated for the Pushcart Prize.

THE SMALL SIDE OF LARGE

Clark E. Knowles

The furnace quits at three in the morning. Willard Dix's feet—
huge paddles of flesh—stick out from under the covers, growing
colder and colder. It surprises him, really—the temperature, his numb
toes, the stillness of the room. For a moment, he can't place himself in
the world. His wife is dead, of course. She's been dead ten years. Jesus
H. Christ, he's still confused without her. At the time of her death,
they said he would grow used to being solo, learn to accommodate
this universe of solitude; but he has yet to successfully traverse the
unrelenting gentleness of absence.

Gradually he recognizes his ceiling—the swirls of plaster, the crack
running diagonally from east to west, disappearing beneath the light
fixture, reappearing, trailing off into the wall as if being chased from
one end of the room to the other. He has slept in this room for close
to thirty years, Samantha and he preferring to keep their bedroom on
the ground floor on account of their size. He pulls himself upright in
front of his mirror. He salutes the reflection—instinct from his military days. Get up. Stand straight. Salute. Do your job. That was what
the military taught him. They told him they would make him a thin
man. In this they failed, but they had instilled in him an irreplaceable

work ethic. When someone tells you to get up and do something, get up and do it. Ask questions later. Just work. This lesson, one of continual productivity, has carried him through life—a fairly happy life, mostly, except for a few things. The shitty curveballs. Samantha being gone, for instance. That was a wicked slider, a spitball if he'd ever seen one.

He is a long man, deep in his bones, the sort of body that goes on forever. If one were to plunge inside somehow, they might get lost in the thickets, briar patches, and grouses. He weighs more than two regular-sized men. He shakes his head—big ears flapping—to clear the fog of sleep and trudges down the hallway, slipping his arms into a great tent of a shirt. He holds himself ramrod straight as he passes the photos of his dead wife and his grown daughter, Denise, who lives in St. Petersburg, Florida, and who brings her husband Mike and her children, Wanda and Randy, to visit twice a year. During those weeks, as he showers affection on his family, he often feels as though his heart might explode. He will be playing with his grandkids and become convinced that his heart is growing without control. If I don't get up, he thinks during those undeniable moments of chest expansion, there will be guts and blood all over this goddamned room.

Before they visit, he cleans the whole apartment from top to bottom, scrubs the floor beneath the bed, runs a Q-tip around the rubber gasket in the refrigerator. On normal days, he pays little attention to those details. His apartment—the first floor of the house he and Samantha shared for twenty years, the house now divided into three separate units—is not unclean, just occupied by an old careless man. The place is not the same as it was when Sam was alive, but is nice, respectable, honorable in its way. He thinks his dead wife might appreciate his attempts at cleanliness, but still shake her head at his tremendous failings on so many other levels—perhaps, even, his failure to move on, to live without her. Samantha had been quite beautiful— as big a woman as he is a man. Denise is a little less grand in stature. His son-in-law is quite small—about a quarter Willard's size, or so it seems. Because of these discrepancies, Willard predicts his grandkids will be the size of normal people.

Although it is a nuisance, this coldness, he knows the furnace just needs to be reset. Like so many other things, the unit comes equipped with a little red button for just such occasions. It seems so random, this resetting. Three times in the past two weeks, he has had similar problems. Each time, Lucy Morales had complained. Three months ago, she had moved into the attic apartment: a nice space with a ceiling angled to accommodate the rake of the roof. While signing the lease in the front office he built on the old porch, they had talked about the World Series. She had been strangely adamant that the Braves would win.

It is *just* their year, she said as she handed him back the signed copy.

Willard had not known how to answer this, for he knew her to be dead wrong. He had noticed her lopsided face—I have been hurt, it seemed to say. He knows little about her beyond her passion for the Braves. She seems clean. She pays on time. But she does complain about the cold; he can hear her voice already. Please, she will say in her wheezy way, isn't there *something* we can do to make this problem disappear? She is like that: gentle, odd, pleading her case. Can we have *more* salt on the side steps? I almost slipped off. Can you imagine me lying in the hedge all night? It would be the *end* of me. Can we have *another* outside light installed? Maybe some kind of motion sensor? Sometimes I walk at night and can *barely* see to get in the front door.

Jesus, she gives him a headache. He rubs his fat fingers over his eyes. Actually, they aren't so much fat, but immense. The size of pepperoni. He is a huge, meaty man. He shuffles a bit once he leaves his front door and enters the main hallway. As he opens the basement door, he pauses to adjust his sweat pants over the vast savannah of his ass.

Far into the basement, the furnace, a black hunk of a thing.

Willard pushes past the crates of old pipe fittings and O-rings and other plumbing fixtures left from the overhaul required to change his home into apartments. It wasn't like he woke up one day and said, Let's renovate this big old house. Let's invite strangers to live here. No, that wasn't it. The origins are muddled together with his first year without Sam, all that time and emptiness. First, he transformed the second floor into an apartment, hopefully for his daughter, but that never came to pass because of tiny Mike and the encroaching normal-sized offspring. The attic seemed like a natural extension of the project. The whole thing took two full years. He sold his half of the printing business to his longtime partner, invested some of Sam's life-insurance money, and devoted himself to the house.

There is little he can do with the basement. It is damp and he is certain the radon levels are sky high. He cannot bring himself to buy one of the home tests at the hardware store. He isn't really sure what radon poisoning does anyway. He assumes it levels some form of justice upon a body, upon the skin or spleen or brain. Some sort of cancer. He read once that by the year 2050, there wouldn't be anything anywhere that doesn't cause some sort of cancer. This is discouraging, not for his own fat self, but for the relatively normal-sized lives of his grandkids. He was sad for those kids—sad that they never got to meet Sam. He wrote them a letter once a month and described in detail how he fixed different problems in his house. He described how he had to climb under the sink in the second-floor kitchen, and how he had to take the doors off the cabinet so he could slip his shoulders through to reach the leaky pipe in the back. I had to swab butter on my shirt, he had written, or I could have never squeezed in. He loved writing those letters.

As he walks, he gathers cobwebs in his hair; they sit atop his head like a little silky crown. The reset button is popped and he knows he should have called his repairman the first time it happened, but that is life. He knows the radon is coating his lungs—feels it really, a powerful sealant. He pushes the button, but nothing happens. It is loose in its socket and he tries again. Nothing. He hates like hell to have to hear about this from Lucy Morales. Lord knows how she will take it, having to wait till morning, having to dig out a pair of wool socks, or extra sweater. He reaches down and pokes the reset button several times even though there is a sign on the unit that specifically states he only push the button once. It seems such a silly rule. But maybe his constant resetting has worn it down. He cannot tell.

The casing of the furnace motor is round, sort of like the alternator of a car. Before his death, Willard's father had shown him how
to knock a car alternator to life with a wrench. They get dead spots,
he had said. You got to whack it real good to get the damn thing to
turn over. What you are doing is whacking the dead spot until it
loosens up. And so Willard had whacked. A few years later, his
father gone and his mother suffering a nervous breakdown, Willard
was sent to live for a time in Harrisburg with Big Aunt Julie. About
a month after Willard moved in, Aunt Julie's car wouldn't start, and
Willard climbed out of the back seat and popped the hood. He
looked around for a wrench, but all he could find was a good-sized
rock. He picked it up and whacked the alternator good and hard,
just like his dad told him. The car roared to life when Big Aunt
Julie turned the key.

And that is what Willard decides to do now. Can't hurt, right? He
walks over to the little workspace in the corner of the basement and
opens the cabinet and sees his bottle of Old Granddad and screws off
the top and sips a little bit. He takes out a crescent wrench and walks
back to the furnace and whacks that motor good. And the damn
thing kicks in. Ain't that something? Of course, he still has to call the
repair guys. It was no panacea, this jarring of machinery, but it should
keep old Lucy warm for the night. He thinks this might be reason
enough to walk back to the cabinet and have another drink of Old
Granddad. He likes the name of the bourbon. The only time he ever
drinks it is here in the basement. Also inside the cabinet is a picture of
Sam. The Granddad gives her memory a healthy, distant sadness. He
imagines holding her in the night, their two big bodies filling the
king-size mattress. To them, a king-size mattress was nothing—a post-
age stamp on which they perched.

When he gets back to his apartment, he is glowing with Old Granddad.
He drank more than he thought, drank until he could feel the tickle
in his toes. The phone is ringing. He stares at it for a moment and
wonders if it might be one of those dreams he sometimes has when
Samantha is calling from the other side.

Clark E. Knowles

Sweetie, he says in his dreams, I was just thinking about you.

Willie! she says. Things here just aren't good without you.

Where are you? Willard says. I'll leave right now.

Although he knows Sam is in heaven, whatever that is, he has his doubts as to whether or not he will follow. It seems like such a long journey to speak with St. Peter. All those stairs.

Hello, he says, foggy.

It's me, upstairs, Lucy Morales says.

Yes, he says, wondering if maybe this is Sam—the Old Granddad whispering in his ear.

Well? Lucy says.

I'm sorry, he says.

So what? Do I have to freeze?

Oh, Lucy.

Who else?

Oh, no one. I just have these dreams.

He doesn't know why he says this.

He says, The heat should be back on soon. Sorry for the problem. I'll get the heat guys in tomorrow. Make sure it doesn't happen again.

My radiators are bone cold, she says.

Did you turn the knobs the wrong way? That sometimes happens. It happens when you are cold and tired.

Of course I didn't. Something is wrong. I wasn't sleeping. I'm not tired.

Well, I'll come up and look first thing in the morning. I think it might just take a few minutes to get the water running up that far again.

Can you come and check, she says. There must be something you can do.

He imagines this: lamp shades covered in red silk, wine sitting out on the table, gypsy music playing in the background. Maybe a crystal ball, a cloud of incense smoke. A stranger lurking in the shadows. When he walks through the door, Lucy Morales will mouth the word, Help. But that is where he stops the fantasy. How in the world had it started? It must be the bourbon, he thinks. He is too big to save

12

Glimmer Train Stories

anyone. Oh, what a lack he carries. His own useless body is a source of continual amazement and disappointment. When he was a small child, relatively speaking, he had fallen on a boy while trying to find a seat in the bus, and the boy had to be rushed to the hospital with fractured ribs. The rumor persisted for years that he had killed the boy. Broken ribs rammed right through his poor, skinny heart. Right there on the bus. That killer. The big fat guy. The fucking big fat kid with his big fat hog butt. All this despite the fact that the same boy shared nearly all his classes until graduation. Lucy Morales was skinny. What if he fell on her while he was trying to adjust her radiators? Imagine the rumors.

Well? Lucy says.

I'll be right up, Willard says. Give me two minutes.

Please, she says.

The mirror in the bathroom is cheap. The reflective surface is smudged with black streaks and pockmarks. It isn't revealed in the mirror, but his skin is really quite smooth. He rubs Oil of Olay on it every night. He spends a small fortune on the cream. When he finally sends his body to the grave, when they find the box large enough for his mortal remains, he wants a smooth corpse. Leaving the world his acres of soft, silky skin—*that* will be something. He runs his hands through his hair and the light from the bathroom flickers a bit. He opens a new bottle of Scope and rinses. He runs deodorant under his arms. Looks at his tongue. He doesn't know why. He wonders how in the world Lucy can possibly live all alone up in that attic.

Before he knocks, he stands still in the hallway and catches his breath. It is his heart, really, thumping there in his chest. He is huffing and puffing, leaning against the wall, embarrassed at his own body. Sam had once asked him if he thought they were too fat as a couple.

As a couple, he had said, we are just right.

Even thinking about Sam makes his heart shrink a bit.

When Lucy comes to the door, she is wearing a big terry-cloth robe over what appears to be several sweaters. A knit cap is pulled down snug over her ears, big furry slippers shaped like bunnies on her feet.

Honestly, it is not that cold. But there is no incense. No gypsy music. The apartment is bright, colorful, and full of multicolored Mylar balloons. When he and Sam first bought the house, the attic was full of bats and pigeons. So this is like a new world, but one built between familiar walls—like the dreams he has of Sam, strange but normal. Somehow he expects to see Sam sitting at Lucy's kitchen table—just like the dreams—her hands folded over her heart, as though to remind him how fragile that muscle is. She is soft there, in those dreams, bathed in silky white. Lovely, of course, big in her body, but obviously free, constructed of mist.

Mr. Dix, thank you, Lucy Morales says.

Hello, he says.

I'm sorry to have to bother you like this, Lucy says.

Is it getting any warmer?

Have you been drinking?

I suppose I have.

He dwarfs Lucy Morales. She is the smallest woman in the world. His heart expands. He might explode all over her apartment. His chest is rising and falling as the balloons in the apartment dance across the ceiling. In his haze, he imagines walking amongst the balloons, climbing higher and higher, bouncing and twisting, but safe, secure.

What's with the balloons? he says.

My birthday, Lucy says. My son sent these.

Where is he?

Tempe. He works in a Ford dealership there. He'll own it one day.

What are you doing all the way out here?

It's where I was born.

How can you have a son old enough to own a car dealership?

I had him when I was eighteen. I'm fifty now. And he doesn't own it yet.

You aren't fifty.

I am.

Call me Willie.

I'm sorry I had to call. Can you look at my radiators?

But by the time he gets to the radiators, the heat is beginning to

14   *Glimmer Train Stories*

pump again, the water bubbling through the pipes. Air in the pipes causes them to thump and clank and ring as the hot water expands. He'll have the furnace guy bleed the pipes while he's at it.

They're heating up again, he says. I thought it might just take a few minutes.

I'm sorry to call you up. Can I get you a drink?

What do you drink up here on the top floor?

Whatever. A beer?

Nah, he says. Water would be great.

The left side of her living room is covered in a wall of books, all kinds of books, every kind of book Willard can imagine. Heavy science books, pamphlets, paperback mysteries.

He says, My wife used to read a lot. She was big like me. She's gone now. It was her heart, just couldn't take it much more.

Lucy Morales gives him a cup of water. She holds a cup for herself.

I don't know why it was hers and not mine, Willard says. He is staring at the books.

I'm sorry, he says. I'm just babbling a bit.

It is worse in the night, he says.

He holds the tiny glass in his hand. It seems to disappear against the flat space between his nose and his lips. He inhales his water. Old Granddad will do that to a person, make him thirsty. That damn brown liquor. He will have a horrible headache in a few hours and will have to go through the morning with the shades pulled.

It's going to be a long day, he says.

I should let you go, Lucy says. I know you have a lot to do. My husband used to be driven crazy by my schedule. He hated that I never came to bed when he did. I stay up till three, four sometimes.

Where is he now?

Same as your wife, dead. Seven years ago.

Heart?

Lungs. He was a smoker. He died and I came back here. My old church, my old friends. I didn't know what else to do. I just didn't like the place I was renting before I came here.

I miss Sam every day. I can't even believe it.

I know. I know the feeling. Would you like something to eat? I have some leftovers I could warm.

Do I look, he says, like a man who turns down food?

At about ten o'clock, Willard takes the furnace man to the furnace.

That's it, he says. I think there must be a dead spot there somewhere.

Yup, the man says. He is a short man, but solid, a fireplug. He wears a green jumpsuit with red letters. Hoyle's Heating. *Hoyle's.* Sounds funny to Willard. Like a joke on the tip of his tongue.

What kind of name is that? he says. Hoyle.

Name of the guy owns the company.

No, I mean where's it from?

How should I know? My name is Danberg.

Oh. You see that little red reset button?

Yup. Right where it is supposed to be.

I've been punching that sucker.

Says to only punch it once.

That's what it says.

Willard sucks his teeth. On a normal day, he never would have wanted to come down here and talk with some surly bastard from Hoyle's Heating, but here he is, radon and all.

You ever worry about radon poisoning? Willard says.

Not particularly, Danberg says.

I guess I'll leave you to the furnace, Willard says. It occurs to him that he doesn't talk to many people. His conversation with Lucy the night before was maybe the longest he's had since Denise last visited. He doesn't remember much. Some potatoes. Some fried chicken. Some chitchat. He had somehow invited her to dinner—imagine!—most likely a result of his late-night imbibing. He walks over to his little cabinet and unlocks the door. He takes down his Old Granddad. It is an odd thing, holding this bottle so early in the day. But there is just nothing in the world that seems more natural. He takes a sip.

The room expands, but not because of the bourbon. Danberg has plugged in his work light. All the corners are lit up, all the dirty little secrets of the room. All the things he cannot keep to himself any longer. The picture in the cupboard calls to him. But he just lifts the bottle and sips again—embarrassed somehow to look at Sam's face. He watches Danberg's shadow play against the old stone wall. The road to his fat heart is paved with all sorts of self-inflicted rules. The light he has to shine inside himself is nowhere near bright enough.

He takes another sip and thinks of his grandkids. How wonderful it will be to have normal-sized relatives. Every member of his immediate family has been huge. At least the ones he can remember. There is fat Uncle Bub—né Darrel—and big and tall Harmon, and loud and big and fat Aunt Louise, and even Teri, the sort of retarded one; she is *large*. Oh, Lord is she large. There was a rumor going around for a time that the largeness was a factor in her being so slow. But the truth is that she is slow *and* large. And, of course, there was his Big Aunt Julie. She was the size of a fruit stand. His own mother had been just big—not terribly huge—on the small side of things, really. The small side of large. His father—that memory is too long gone. There is the memory of knocking the alternator to life, some hazy moments watching his father climb into a car, bound for the Korean conflict. But the man had been a Dix through and through. How in the world did Denise keep from being so damn big? How in the world did she meet and marry such a nice little man? In the wedding pictures, Willard looms over Mike like the Giant over Jack.

Where the hell is my golden goose? he seems to be saying, all dressed up in his tux. Sam is conspicuously absent from those pictures.

Shit. Shit. Shit. Oh, those poor grandkids, how much they are bound to suffer, the world of hurt that barrels toward us all. That charge of loss and pain, the wicked heat of life—a fastball right straight out of Roger Clemens's hand. All of it. That burden of loneliness. How it tears and tears at a man, at the very fabric of his goddamned heart.

You want a sip? he says. He holds out the bottle. Danberg comes over to him.

Now you're talking, Danberg says.

I keep this down here, Willard says.

I'll say, Danberg says. That's fine by me.

You married?

Eight years.

My wife is gone. Dead now close to ten.

That sucks, Danberg says.

Yeah, Willard says.

Something unspoken passes between them. They understand and yet cannot articulate this lithesome sadness. Maybe it is something passed down through DNA, some empathy. Poor Danberg and his wife. All the future.

Willard can stand upright in the basement only if he positions his head between the floor joists. After he sips, he leans his head against the old wood.

I don't know what I'd do if Missy died, Danberg says.

That's a fine name, Willard says. I had an Aunt Missy. She was on my father's side. A large woman. That's a fact.

All your people big?

Just about.

Missy is downright skinny. Skinny in all the right places.

I got a skinny woman upstairs. Lives in the top apartment.

Something going on with you two?

Not that I know of. I asked her to dinner at my place tonight. Can you believe it? She's the reason I called you. The heat was out and I whacked the dead spot and kept it going for a while. But I didn't want to take any chances.

The Old Granddad passes between them. They drink and talk like this for a few more minutes. Then Danberg climbs back upstairs and pulls parts and tools from the van. By noon, the furnace is good as new.

Willard cleans the whole apartment. He lifts the toilet seat and wipes beneath it with a clean rag, although he has already done this several times. He walks down the hall and dusts the tops of all the pictures. He knows he is lonely. He knows this because he some-times watches the afternoon talk shows. And he also knows that a woman—other than his daughter—is coming to his apartment. This frightens him. He has not had sex in ten years, since lovely Sam's death. He cannot help think about this, even though he is sick about it. Sam was round and fleshy and warm and all encompassing. He can only imagine falling on Lucy Morales and crushing her. He cannot imagine her skinny bones bearing up under his massive weight. As if that is something a man like him needs to worry about. In his whole life, he has only slept with one woman. Or, he thinks, only one woman wanted to be close to him in that way. Truthfully, he is in a tizzy.

She's just coming here for dinner, he says.

She's my tenant, he says.

This is the silliest thing, he says.

And yet there he is in front of his mirror, looking at his face, at his teeth, at his nose. He could sink a role of dimes into a nostril if he so desired. They are that big! How could any woman be attracted to a man with such a feature? What will he tell his daughter? How can he tell her that he is sleeping with another woman? And how can he even be thinking this far into the future? She is just coming over for dinner, for Pete's sake. It isn't as if he is asking someone new, someone skinny, to marry him.

He had asked Samantha to marry him in a crowded movie theater. Their knees had pushed against the seatbacks in front of them. They had a box of popcorn. Their shoulders were mashed together. Willard twisted toward Sam to ask for the soda, and she had looked so big and fine and regal—a word he had never even thought of before, but there it was, the most beautiful word in the world—and instead of saying, Hand me the Coke, would ya? He said, Sam, will you marry me? And Sam had said yes, of course, and they had held hands through the movie, and Willard didn't remember a darn thing except the excited thumping of his heart as her fingers danced with his in the popcorn.

He brushes off her picture again. In the soft dim light of his entryway, his face is reflected in the glass of the frame. Both their faces hover. In the tiniest of moments, when he moves to answer the door, his image glides over Sam's. He cannot tell where she begins and he ends.

Lucy Morales is wearing a fine dress, quite beautiful, dark blue, high collar, a simple chain hanging just below the curve of her throat. Her hair is pulled back tight against her head, and Willard can see the crooked twist of her right earlobe, as though it had been frostbitten, or cuffed one too many times. He is instantly sad for her, but he also knows that she is telling him something by wearing her hair back. What this is, he doesn't know. Of course, she might be doing this because she has lived so long with the twist that she does not even notice it. Sort of like Willard and his largeness. He is wearing regular pants, pleated khakis, as opposed to sweat pants, and he wonders what sort of message he is sending. The two of them move down the hall, and Willard points out everything to her, all the pictures, who everyone is, how important the grandkids are, how he writes to them once a month, how Sam used to work for the Department of Health and Human Services. They walk in and eat the cheese and crackers he has prepared. Later, they eat the salmon he has bought and broiled using Sam's special marinade recipe. They drink a few glasses of wine, and Willard unbuttons the top of his shirt, and Lucy puts her feet up on the coffee table.

Why in the world would you want to have dinner with me? Willard says.

Losing your wife has been so hard for you, hasn't it?

I have trouble sleeping, he says. It seems a trite thing to say.

You obviously love her very much. It is easy to see that.

Can you tell me about your husband?

What can I say? I think I've mostly worked through it all.

The night grows long and they talk, and when she stands up to leave, she thanks him for the nice dinner, and even though they are both lonely, or alone somehow, Willard thinks, he is warm in her company.

Lucy hesitates at the door, and before she leaves she says, Thanks again. Maybe we can do this, have dinner once in a while.

Yes, Willard says, yes.

And imagine! There is his heart—enduring, enduring—unsure of itself in its passage between large and small.

William Trevor, aged about seven.

William Trevor is the author of twenty-nine books, including *Felicia's Journey*, which won the Whitbread Book of the Year Award and was made into a motion picture. In 1996 he was the recipient of the Lannan Award for Fiction. In 2001, he won the *Irish Times* Literature Prize for fiction. Two of his books were chosen by the *New York Times* as best books of the year, and his short stories appear regularly in the *New Yorker*. He lives in Devon, England.

SOLITUDE

William Trevor

I reach the lock by standing on the hall chair. I open the hall
door and pull the chair back to the alcove. I comb my hair in the
hallstand glass. I am seven years old, waiting for my father to come
downstairs.

Our house is a narrow house with a blue hall door, in a square, in
London. My father has been away and now he is back. *The first morning, we'll go to the café.* Ages ago my mother read what he had written
for me on the postcard. "They're called the Pyramids," she said when
I pointed at the picture. And then: "Not long before he's back." But it
was fifty days.

I hear him whistling on the stairs, "London Bridge Is Falling Down,"
and then he hugs me, because he has come in the night when I was
asleep. He doesn't believe it, he says, how I have grown. "I missed you
terribly," he says.

We walk together, across the square to where the traffic and the
streets are. "Coffee," my father says in the café. "Coffee, please, and a
slice of Russian cake for you-know-who."

But all the time there is what happened and all the time I know I
mustn't say. A child to witness such a thing was best forgotten, Mrs.
Upsilla said, and Charles nodded his long black head. No blame, Charles
said, any child would play her games behind a sofa; all they'd had to
do was look. "No skin off my nose," Charles said. "No business of a
poor black man's." And, not knowing I was still outside the kitchen

door, Mrs. Upsilla said it made her sick to her bones. Well, it was something, Charles reminded her, that my mother wouldn't take her friend to the bedroom that was my father's too. At least there was the delicacy of that. But Mrs. Upsilla said what delicacy, and called my mother's friend a low-down man.

"You're learning French now?" my father says in the café. "Do you like French?"

"Not as much as history."

"What have you learnt in history?"

"That William the Conqueror's son also got an arrow in his eye."

"Which eye? Did they say which eye?"

"No, I don't think so."

In the café the waitress is the one who always comes to us. My father says that is because we always sit at the same table. He says our waitress has Titian hair; he says that's what that color is. My father is always commenting on people, saying they have this or that, guessing about them, or asking questions. Often he falls into conversation with people who enquire the way on the street, and beggars, anyone who stops him, anyone in shops. "Rich as a candy king," I heard someone in the café say once, and my father laughed, shaking his head.

All the time in the café I want to tell him, because I tell him everything when he comes back from a journey. I want to tell him about the dream I had that same night, all of it happening again. "Oh, horrid nightmare," my mother comforted me, not knowing what it was about because I didn't say, because I didn't want to.

"The picture gallery?" my father suggests when we have had our coffee. "Or the dolls' museum today? Look, I have this.'"

He spreads out on the table a handkerchief he has bought, all faded colors, so flimsy you can see through it in places. Old, he says, Egyptian silk. There is a pattern, and he draws his forefinger through it so that I can see it too. "For you," he says. "For you."

In the bus, on the way to the dolls' museum he talks about Egypt. So hot it could make your skin peel off, so hot you have to lie down in the afternoon. One day he'll bring me with him; one day he'll show me the Pyramids. He takes my hand when we walk the last bit.

I know the way, but when we get there the doll I like best isn't on her shelf. Unwell, the man says, getting better in hospital. It's his way of putting it, my father says. He asks the man: that doll, the Spanish doll, will be back next week. "Well, we can come again," my father promises. "Who's going to stay up for the party?" he says when we're back in the house.

The party is tonight. In the kitchen the wine bottles are laid out, two long rows all the length of the table, and other bottles on trays, and glasses waiting to be filled. Charles comes specially early to help when there is a party. There always is when my father returns.

"You sit down there and have your sandwich." Mrs. Upsilla's gray head is bent over what she's cooking; she's too busy to look up. Charles winks at me and I try to wink back but I can't do it properly. He passes close to where I'm sitting and then the sandwich I don't want isn't there any more. "Oh, there's a good girl," Mrs. Upsilla says when she asks if I've eaten it and I say yes. And Charles smiles. And Davie giggles and Abigail does.

Abigail and Davie aren't real, but most of the time they're there. They were that day, when the door opened and my mother and her friend came into the drawing room. "It's all right," my mother said. "She's not here." And Davie giggled and Abigail did too and I made them be quiet.

"My, my," Charles says in the kitchen when Mrs. Upsilla calls me a good girl. He says it so often it annoys Mrs. Upsilla. "Why's he saying that?" she asks me every time. "What's he on about?" And Charles always laughs.

I thank Mrs. Upsilla for the sandwich I haven't eaten because she likes me to thank her for things. On the way upstairs I remember that when the person in the café said as rich as a candy king I heard my father repeating that to my mother afterwards; he said that maybe what the person meant was he was rich to have so beautiful a wife. Or you could take it differently, Mrs. Upsilla said when I told her: the person in the café could have been referring to my mother's inheritance.

Upstairs, my father is standing at the door of their bedroom, my mother is tidying the bed. He has brought her a handkerchief too, bigger than mine, and already she wears it as a scarf. "So beautiful you are!" my father says and my mother laughs, a sound that's like the tinkling of a necklace he gave her once. The bath taps are dribbling in the bathroom, turned low for my mother's bath. "Who's going to help me take the corks out?" my father says, and my mother asks him to open the window at the top. Her lips are soft when she kisses my forehead, her scent makes me want to close my eyes and always be able to smell it. "Good darling," she whispers.

In the kitchen my father draws out the corks and I make a pile of them, and count them. The red bottles are really green, he says, but you can't see that until they're empty. He cuts away the shiny covering over each cork before he puts the corkscrew in. "Well, that's all done," he says and asks how many and I say thirty-six. "You take me to the picture gallery next time?" he says, and the dancing ladies come into my head, and the storm at the cricket match, and Saint Catherine, and the portrait of the artist. "That to look forward to," my father says before he goes upstairs again.

We play a game in my room, Abigail and Davie and I. We pretend we are in Egypt, climbing up a pyramid, and Abigail says we should be wearing our cotton sun hats because the sun can burn your head even through your hair. So we go down for them but then it's cooler so we walk about the streets. We buy things in a market, presents to bring home, rings and brooches and jars of Egyptian peaches, and Egyptian chocolate and Egyptian rugs for the floor. Then I go back to the kitchen.

Charles has gone out for ice. "You going to keep me company?" Mrs. Upsilla says, still busy with her cooking. "You'll trip on those laces," she says, allowing the electric mixer to operate on its own for a moment. A nasty accident there could be, and she ties my laces. Always double-tie a shoelace, she says and I go away.

In the drawing room the bowls of olives and tit-bits are laid out; the fire is blazing, the wire net of the fire-guard drawn down. I watch the raindrops sliding on the windowpanes. I watch the people in the square, hurrying through the rain, a woman holding an umbrella over her dog, Charles returning with the ice. The cars go slowly, the street lights have come on.

I sit in the armchair by the fire, looking at the pictures in the books, the old woman who kept children in a cage, the giants, the dwarfs, the Queen's reflection in the looking glass. I look out into the square again: my mother's friend is the first to come. He waits for a car to pass before he crosses the square, and then there is the doorbell and his footsteps on the stairs.

"Have one of these," he says in the drawing room, cheese straws that Mrs. Upsilla has made. "Time for your dancing lesson," and he puts the music on. He shows me the same steps again because I never try, because I don't want to try. "How are they?" he asks and I know he means Davie and Abigail; ever since my mother mentioned them to him he asks about them. I might have told him they were there that afternoon but instead I just say they're all right. Then other people come and he talks to them. I hate him so much I wish he could be dead.

I listen from one of the window seats, half behind the curtain. A man is telling about a motor-race he has taken part in. One of these days he'll win, a woman says. In his white jacket, Charles offers the drinks.

Other people come. "Well, goodness me!" Mr. Fairlie smiles down at me, and then he sits beside me. Old and tired, he says, not up to this gallivanting. He asks me what I did today and I tell him about the dolls' museum. He manages on his own, Mrs. Upsilla told me, since his wife died. My mother went to the funeral, but he doesn't talk about that now. "Poor old boy," Charles said.

You can hardly hear the music because so many people are talking. Every time Charles passes by with another tray he waves to me with a finger and Mr. Fairlie says that's clever. "Well, look at you two!" a woman says and she kisses Mr. Fairlie and kisses me, and then my father comes. "Who's sleepy?" he says and he takes me from the party.

It will be ages before he goes away again: he promises that before he turns the light out, but in the dark it's like it was in the dream. He'll go away and he won't come back, not ever wanting to. There'll never be the picture gallery again, our favorite picture the picnic on the beach. There'll never be the café again, there'll never be the dolls' museum. He'll never say, "Who's sleepy?"

In the dark I don't cry, although I want to. I make myself think of something else, of the day there was an accident in the square, of the day a man came to the door, thinking someone else lived in our house. And then I think about Mr. Fairlie on his own. I see him as clearly as I did when he was beside me on the window seat, the big freckles on his forehead, his wisps of white hair, his eyes that don't look old at all. "A surgeon in his day," Mrs. Upsilla told Charles the morning my mother went to the funeral. I see Mr. Fairlie in his house although I've never been there. I see him cooking for himself as best he can, and with a Hoover on the stairs. "Who'd mind being cut up by Mr. Fairlie?" Charles said once.

The music's so faint it sounds as if it's somewhere else, not in our house, and I wonder if they're dancing. By ten o'clock the party will be over, Mrs. Upsilla said, and then they'll go off to different restaurants, or maybe they'll all go to the same one, and some will just go home. It's that kind of party, not lasting for very long, not like some Mrs. Upsilla has known. "Here?" Charles asked, surprised when she said that. "Here in this house?" And she said no, not ever an all-night party here, and Charles nodded in his solemn way and said you'd know it. He'll stay for an hour or so when everyone has gone, helping Mrs. Upsilla to clear up. I've never been awake then.

Davie says it was some kind of game. Fun, he says, but Abigail shakes her head, her black plaits flying about. I don't want to talk about it. A Wednesday it was, Mrs. Upsilla gone off for the afternoon, Charles tending the flowerbeds in the square.

I try to think about Mr. Fairlie again, having to make his bed, doing all the other things his wife did, but Mr. Fairlie keeps slipping away. My mother's dress was crumpled on the floor and I could see it when I peeped out, her necklace thrown down too. Afterwards, she said they should have locked the door.

The music is still far away. The noise of the people isn't like people talking, more like a hum. I push the bedclothes back and tip-toe to the stairs to look down through the banisters. Mrs. Upsilla is dressed specially for the party, and Charles is carrying in another tray of glasses. Mrs. Upsilla goes in too, with two plates of tit-bits. Bacon wound round an apricot she makes, and sandwiches no bigger than a stamp. People come out and stand about on the landing. My mother and her friend are there for a moment, before she goes into the drawing room again. He stays there, his shoulder against the wall by the window, the red curtains drawn over. "The child's on to it," was what he said the day before my father came back.

I don't want to go back to bed because the dream will be there even if I'm not asleep, Mrs. Upsilla saying my father's gone forever, that of course he had to. When I look for it, the leather suitcase he takes on his travels won't be there and I'll know it never will be again. I'll take out the Egyptian handkerchief and I'll remember my father spreading it on the café table, showing me the pattern. "Our café," he calls it.

My mother's friend looks up from the landing that's two flights down. He waves and I watch him coming up the stairs. There's a cigarette hanging from his mouth but he hasn't lit it and he doesn't take it out when he puts a finger to his lips. "Enough to make them drunk," Charles said when he saw the bottles opened on the kitchen table, and I wonder if my mother's friend is drunk because he takes another cigarette from his packet even though he hasn't lit the first one.

When he sways he has to reach out for the banister. He laughs, as if that's just for fun. I can see the sweat on his face, like raindrops on his forehead. His eyes are closed when he takes another step. Slowly he goes on coming up, another step and then another and another. There's a fleck of spit at the edge of his mouth, the two cigarettes have fallen on to the stair carpet. When I reach out I can touch him. My finger-tips are on the dark cloth of his sleeve and I can feel his arm beneath, and everything is different then.

There is his tumbling down, there is the splintered banister. There is the thud, and then another and another. There is the stillness, and Mrs. Upsilla looking up at me.

I watch them from my window, coming separately to the table they have chosen for breakfast in the garden of the hotel. They place their gifts by my place. They speak to one another, but I never know what they say in private. I turn from the window and powder over the coral lipstick I have just applied. On my seventeenth birthday nothing of my reflection is different in an oval looking glass.

Downstairs, the salon I pass through is empty, the shutters half in place against the glare of sun that will be bothersome to the hotel guests later in the day.

"*Bonjour, mademoiselle,*" a waiter greets me in the garden.

Even in the early morning the air is mellow. Chestnuts have begun to fall; bright crimson leaves are shrivelling. The sky is cloudless.

"Well, old lady," my father says. There is a single rose, pink bled with scarlet, which he has picked for me. On my birthday he always finds a rose somewhere.

"What shall we do today?" my mother asks when she has poured my coffee, and my father remembers the year of the Pilgrims' Way, when he took me on his back because I was tired, when we met the old man who told us about Saint Sisinnius. He remembers the balloon trip and the year of the casino. Birthdays are always an occasion, my mother's in July, my father's in May, mine in October.

We live in hotels. We've done so since we left the house in the square, all kinds of hotels, in the different countries of Europe, a temporary kind of life it seemed at first, acquiring permanence later.

"So what shall we do?" my mother asks again.

It is my choice because of the day and after I've opened the presents they've given me, after I've embraced them and thanked them, I say that what I'd like to do is to walk through the birch woods and have a picnic where the meadows begin.

"*Moi, je suis tous les sports,*" a man is telling his friend at the table next to ours. "*Il n'y en a pas un seul auquel je ne m'intéresse pas.*"

I can hear now, thirty-five years later, that man's rippling voice. I can see the face I glimpsed, bespectacled and pink, and hear his companion ordering *thé de Ceylan.*

"It will be lovely, that walk today," my mother says, and we choose our picnic and after breakfast go to buy the different items and put our lunch together ourselves.

"Why do you always find a rose for me?"

I ask that on our walk, when my mother is quite far ahead of my father and myself. I have not chosen the moment; not because my mother isn't there; there's never anything like that.

"Oh, there isn't a reason for a rose, you know. It's just that sometimes a person wants to give one."

"You make everything good for me."

"Because it is your birthday."

"I didn't mean only on my birthday."

My mother has reached the meadows and calls back to us. When we catch up with her the picnic is already spread out, the wine uncorked.

"When your father and I first met," she says once lunch has begun, "he was buying a film for his camera and found himself short. That's how we met, in a little shop. He was embarrassed so I lent him a few coins from my purse."

"Your mother has always had the money."

"And it has never made a difference. An inheritance often does; but by chance, I think, this one never has.'"

"No, it has never made a difference. But before we say another word we must drink a toast to today."

My father pours the wine. "You must not drink yourself, Villana. That isn't ever done."

"Then may I have a toast to you? Is that ever done?"

"Well, do it, and then it shall be."

"Thank you for my birthday."

In the sudden manner he often has, my father says:

"Marco Polo was the first traveler to bring back to Europe an account of the Chinese Empire. No one believed him. No one believed that the places he spoke of, or the people—not even Kublai Khan—existed. That is the history lesson for today, old lady. Or history and geography all in one. It doesn't matter how we think of it."

"In German 'to think' is *denken*," my mother interposes. "And in Italian?"

"*Pensare.* And *credere*, of course."

"This ham is delicious," my father says.

They took me from England because that was best. I never went to school again. They taught me in their way, and between them they knew a lot: they taught me everything. My father's ambitions as an Egyptologist fell away. Once upon a time he went on his travels—always determined to make discoveries that had not been made before—he had scrimped and saved in order to be independent in his marriage, and in Egypt often slept on park benches. But after we left the house in the square my father had no profession; he became the amateur he once regarded as a status he despised. His books did not remain unwritten, but he did not ever want to publish them.

"Oh, how good this is!" he says, his soft voice hardly heard when my birthday picnic is over, the wine all drunk. We, all three of us, in the warm autumn sun, and then I pack the remains of the picnic into the haversack and think that my father is right, that this is good, even that it is happiness.

"I worry sometimes he does not get enough exercise," my mother remarks on our journey back, going by a different way, my father's turn now to be a little ahead. Often, it seems to me, it is deliberately arranged that I should always be in the company of one or other of them.

"Doesn't he get enough?"

"Well, it could be more."

"Papa's not ill?"

"No, not at all. Not at all. But in the nature of things…"

She does not finish what she might have said, but I know what follows. In the nature of things neither she nor my father will always be there. I sense her guessing that I have finished her sentence for her, for that is how we live, our conversations incomplete, or never begun at all. They have between them created an artifact within which our existence lies, an artifact as scrupulously completed as a masterpiece on a mosaicist's table. My father accepts what he has come to know—which I believe is everything—of my mother's unfaithfulness. There is no regret on my mother's part that I can tell, nor is there bitterness on his; I never heard a quarrel. They sacrifice their lives for me: the change of surroundings, constantly repeated, the anonymous furniture of hotels, nothing as it has been—for my sake, no detail is overlooked. In thanking them I might say my gratitude colors every day, but they do not want me to say that, not even to mention gratitude in such a manner because it would be too much.

"*Quel après-midi splendide!*"

"*Ah, oui! on peut le dire.*"

"*J'adore ce moment de la journée.*"

Often my mother and I break into one of the languages she has taught me; as if, for her, a monotony she does not permit is broken. Does she—do they—regret the loss of the house in London, as I do? Do they imagine the changes there might be, the blue hall door a different color, business plates beside it, a voice on the intercom when one of the bells is rung? What is the drawing room now? Is there a consulate in the ground-floor rooms, stately men going back and forth, secretaries with papers to be signed? All that I know with certainty— and they must too—is that the violets of my bedroom wallpaper have been painted away to nothing, that gone from the hall are the shipyard scenes in black and white, the Crisis of London too. They may even wonder, as I do, if the chill of the past is in that house, if the ghosts of my childhood companions haunt its rooms, for since leaving England I have never been able to bring them to life again.

"*C'est vraiment tres beau la-bas,*" my mother says when we catch up with my father, who has already begun to gather chestnuts. We watch a bird which he says is something rare, none of us knowing what it is. There is a boy at the hotel to whom we'll give the chestnuts, each of us knowing as we do so that this will become another birthday memory, spoken of, looked back to.

"Ernest Shackleton was a most remarkable man," my father comments in his abrupt way. "Maybe the finest of all those men who were remarkable for making the freezing winds a way of life, and ice a landscape, whose grail was the desolation at the end of the world's most terrible journeys. Can you imagine them, those men before him and all who followed later? Secrets kept from one another, ailments hidden, their prayers, their disappointments? Such adversity, yet such spirit! We are strangely made, we human beings, don't you think?"

It doesn't matter that he hasn't taken me to see the Pyramids, not in the least does it matter, but even so I do not ever say I understand why he hasn't. For that, of course, is best not said. I, too, prevaricate.

"We've never brought you to Heiligenberg," he muses as we walk on.

The last of the autumn wild flowers would still be in bloom at Heiligenberg, and the hellebores out all winter. The hotel they know—the Zeldenhof—would be grander since their day, my mother says.

We'll spend the winter in Heiligenberg, they decide, and I wonder if at Heiligenberg a letter might come from Mrs. Upsilla. Now and again, not often, one arrives at some hotel or is discovered at a *Poste Restante.* Once I saw what I knew I should not have: the cramped handwriting I remembered, the purple ink Mrs. Upsilla always favored. Such letters that come are never opened in my presence; once when I looked in my mother's belongings none had been kept.

"We stayed at the Zeldenhof when we were married a month," my father says. "I photographed your mother at the refuge.'"

I ask about that, and I ask where the little shop was where they met, when my father was buying a film for his camera.

"Italy," my mother says. "The front at Bordighera."

There is a photograph.

The ticket collector's beard is flecked with gray, his uniform in need of attention. I know him well, for often I travel on his train.

"*Grazie, signora.*" He hands my ticket back, reminding me to change in Milan and Genoa. In the early afternoon the string of little seaside towns will begin, the train unhurried then, slowing, halting, juddering on, gathering speed again. That part of the journey I like best.

I wear blue because it suits me best, often with green, although they say the two are difficult to combine. My hair's well tended, the style old fashioned. "You're an old-fashioned lady," my father used to say, not chiding me for that, his tone as light as ever. She liked my old-fashionedness, my mother said when I was very young. I'm in my fifty-third year now, a woman who has settled down at last in the forgotten Italian seaside resort where they met. In 1949 that was, I calculate.

They died, he first—in his eighties—she less than a year later; and I, who should have known them better than anyone, did not know them at all, even though my mother did not release my hand all during her last night. The second funeral was conducted with the same simple formality as the first, the coffin placed beside the other in the small graveyard they had chosen, the place remembered from the summers we often spent in the Valle Verzasca. I walked away from both of them through cold winter air, snow on the ground but no longer falling.

A month or so later, calling in at the *Poste Restante* at Bad Mergentheim, as we had always done in their lifetime, I found a letter from Mrs. Upsilla. Addressed as usual to my mother, it had been lying there for almost a year. *...I only write because it is so long now since I have heard from you. I am concerned but perhaps it is all right and you have been so kind to an old woman. The summer has not been good in Brighton but I struggle on, the season very poor. Several other landladies have given up and I read the writing on the wall and think how different life was once, those days in London! Well, I must not say it but there you are. I only write because I have not heard.*

I knew at once that my mother had paid Mrs. Upsilla all these years. Charles too, I imagined. The rich's desperate bid for silence: I think of it as that; but no, I do not blame my mother. I replied to Mrs. Upsilla, simply saying that my mother had died and asking her to pass this information on to Charles if she happened to be in touch with him. No acknowledgement ever found its way to me from either of them, but it was hearing from Mrs. Upsilla that first made me want to honor my father and mother. For Mrs. Upsilla would die too, and Charles would, and I myself in time: who then, in all the world, would be aware of the story that might be told?

In the hotel where I live, in Bordighera's Regina Palace, my friends are the dining-room waiters, and the porters in the hall, and the bedroom maids; I do not turn away such friendship and I have myself for company too. Yet when my face is there in the glass of my compact, or reflected in shop windows when the sun is right, or glimpsed in public mirrors, I often think I do not know that woman. I wonder when I gaze for a moment longer if what I see is the illusion imposed by my imagination upon the shadow a child became, if somehow I do not entirely exist. I know that this is not so, yet still it seems to be. Confusion has colored my life since my mother's death; and the waking hours of my solitude are nagged by the compulsion to make known the goodness of two people. Obsessively there, beyond my understanding, that has become the insistent orderer of how things should be. Not ever finding the courage to make it known in the corridors and lounges of the Regina Palace, for years I traveled from my shabby old town by the sea to distant cities where I might be anonymous. Again and again I searched among strangers for a listener who would afterwards pass on as a wonder the beneficence of those two people, a marvel to be repeated at family gatherings, at dinner tables, in bars and shops, interrupting games of cards and chess, spreading to other cities, to villages and towns, to other countries.

Each time I found my listener, each time across a teashop table or in a park, there was politeness; and moments later there was revulsion. Some traveler killing tedious time in a railway waiting room would look away and mumble nothing; or on a tram, or in a train, would angrily push past a nuisance. And the whisper of my apology would not be heard.

In my foolishness I did not know what I since have learnt: that the truth, even when it glorifies the human spirit, is hard to peddle if there is something terrible to tell as well. Dark nourishes light's triumphant blaze, but who should want to know? I accept, at last, that I am not to be allowed the mercy of telling what is mine to tell. The wheels of my suitcase rattle on the surface of the railway platform at Bordighera, and outside the station the evening is bright with sunshine. The taxi driver knows my destination without having to ask. I might say, in making conversation, that there will not be another journey, but enquire instead about the family he often tells me about.

"*Buona sera, signora. Come sta?*" The afternoon porter welcomes me in the empty hall of the Regina Palace, appearing out of nowhere.

"*Sto bene, Giovanni. Bene.*"

Small and pallid, an elaborate uniform dwarfing him, Giovanni keeps the Regina Palace going, as much as Signor Valazza, its manager, does; or the stoutly imperious Signora Casarotti, who knew it from her reception counter in its glory days. Fashion has long ago lifted its magic from what fashion once made gracious, leaving behind flaking paint and dusty palms. Masonry crumbles, a forgotten lift is out of order. But Camera Ventinove, the room I have always returned to from the failure of my journeys, has a view of the sea as far as the horizon.

"We will miss you always, *signora*," Giovanni tells me, practicing his English, as he likes to in our conversations. "Was fine, your travel, *signora?*"

"Was fine, Giovanni, was fine."

The door of Camera Ventinove is unlocked as that lie is told. Giovanni stands aside; I go in first. There is a little more to the ceremony of my return, not much: the opening of the shutters, the view again re-marked upon, the giving and receiving of the tip. Then Giovanni goes.

I hang some of the clothes I have traveled with in the wardrobe and write the list to accompany those that must be laundered. Unhur-riedly, I have a bath and, downstairs for a while, finish the easy book I bought for my journey. I leave it with the newspapers in case it inter-ests someone else.

I walk by the sea, my thoughts a repetition, imagining on this prom-enade the two people who have been rejected, who did not know one another well when they walked here too. The bathing huts of the photograph have gone.

"*Buona sera, signora.*"

It is not an unusual courtesy for people to address one another on this promenade, even for a man who is not familiar to her to address a woman. But still this unexpected voice surprises me, and perhaps I seem a little startled.

"I'm sorry, I did not mean to…" The man's apology trails away.

"It's quite all right,"

"We are both English, I think." His voice is soft, pleasant to hear, his eyes quite startling blue. He is tall, in a pale linen suit, thin and fair-haired, his forehead freckled, the blue of his eyes repeated in the tie that's knotted into a blue-striped shirt. Some kindly doctor? Schoolmaster? Horticulturalist? Something about him suggests he's on his own. Widowed? I wondered. Unmarried? It is impossible to guess. His name is d'Arblay, he reveals, and when I begin to walk on, it seems only slightly strange that he changes direction and walks with me.

"Yes, I am English," I hear myself saying, more warmly than if I had not hesitated at first.

"I thought you might be. Well, I knew. But even so it was a presumption." The slightest of gestures accompanies this variation of his apology. He smiles a little. "My thoughts had wandered. I was thinking as I strolled of a novel I first read when I was eighteen. *The Good Soldier.*"

"I have read *The Good Soldier* too."

"The saddest story. I read it again not long ago. You've read it more than once?"

"Yes, I have."

"There's always something that wasn't there before when you read a good novel for the second time."

"Yes, there is."

"I have been re-reading now the short stories of Somerset Maugham. Superior to his novels, I believe. In particular I like 'The Kite.'"

"They made a film of it."

"Yes."

"I never saw it."

"Nor I."

There is no one else on the promenade. Neither a person nor a dog. Not even a seagull. We walk together, not speaking for a moment, until I break that silence, not to say much, but only that I love the sea at Bordighera.

"And I."

Our footsteps echo, or somehow do I imagine that? I don't know, am only aware that again the silence is there, and that again I break it.

"A long time ago I lived in a house in a square in London…"

He nods, but does not speak.

"My father was an Egyptologist."

Taped music reaches me in the bar, where once there was the chatter of cocktail drinkers and the playing of a palm-court quartet. I order Kir, and when the barman has poured it he leaves me on my own, as every night he does, since he has other things to do. I guessed this would be so, and for company I've brought with me the temperate features of the Englishman on the promenade. "So much is chance," he said, and with no great difficulty I hear his distinctive voice again. "So much," he says.

I take that with me when I cross the hall to the struggling splendors of the Regina Palace's dining room. I take with me Mr. d'Arblay's composure, his delicate hands seeming to gesture without moving, the smile that is so slight it's hardly there. Royalty has celebrated in this vast dining room, so Signor Valazza claims. But tonight's reflection in its gilded mirrors is a handful of travelers, shadowy beneath the flickering chandeliers. There is a man with a yellow pipe on the table beside him, and a couple who might be on their honeymoon, and two ageing German *fräuleins* who might be schoolmistresses just retired. Little stoves keep warm *filetto di maialino* and *tortelli di pecorino*. But all reality is less than Mr. d'Arblay.

"*Si, signora.*" Carlo jots down my order: the consommé, the turbot. "*E Gavi dei Gavi. Subito, signora.*"

My mother gathered her dress from the floor, her necklace too, where she had thrown them down. The drawing room was heavy with her scent, and her friend put a record on the gramophone. The voice still sang when they had gone. And Charles came in then, and knew, and took me out to the square to show me the flowerbeds he'd been tending.

"*Prego, signora. Il vino.*"

The Gavi is poured, but I do not need to taste it, and simply nod.
"*Grazie, signora.*"

Mr. d'Arblay has walked through our square; more than once he remembers being there. It is not difficult for him to imagine the house as it was; he does not say so, but I know. He can imagine; he is the kind that can.

"*Buon appetito, signora.*"

A child's light fingertips on a sleeve, resting there for no longer than an instant. So swift her movement then, so slight it might not have occurred at all: that, too, Mr. d'Arblay can imagine, and he does. The unlit cigarettes are crushed beneath a shoe. There is the crash of noise, the splintered banister. There are the eyes, looking up from far below. There is the rictus grin.

The man on his own presses tobacco into his yellow pipe but does not light it. Ice cream is brought to the German schoolmistresses. The honeymoon couple touch glasses. Three late arrivals hesitate by the door.

"*Il rombo arrosto, signora.*"

"*Grazie, Carlo.*"

"*Prego, signora.*"

Three lives were changed for ever in that instant. Whatever lies my father told were good enough for people at a party, the silence of two servants bought. My mother wept and hid her tears. But some time during that sleepless night was she—my father too—touched by the instinct to abandon the child who had been born to them? Was it more natural that they should, and do no more than call what had happened evil?

"It is natural too," Mr. d'Arblay replied while we walked, "to find the truth in the agony of distress. The innocent cannot be evil: this was what, during that sleepless night, they came to know."

It was enough, Mr. d'Arblay diffidently insisted, that what there is to tell, in honoring the dead, has now been told between two other people, and shall be told again between them, and each time something gained. The selfless are undemanding in their graves.

I do not taste the food I'm eating, nor savor the wine I drink. I reject the *dolce* and the cheese. They bring me coffee.

"Theirs was the guilt," Mr. d'Arblay says again, "his that he did not know her well enough, hers that she made the most of his not knowing. Theirs was the shame, yet their spirit is gentle in our conversation: guilt is not always terrible, nor shame unworthy."

Petits fours have been brought too, although I never take one from the plate. One night she may, is what they think in the kitchen, and even say to one another, that one night when she sits down at this same table, as old as she will ever become, she will be lonely in her solitude. How can they know that in the dining room where royalty has dined she is not alone among the tattered drapes and chandeliers abandoned to their grime? They cannot know, they cannot guess, that in the old hotel, and when she walks by the sea, there is Mr. d'Arblay, as in another solitude there were her childhood friends.

*Evidence of early appreciation for extreme weather.
Minnesota, ca. 1950.*

N. Nye's work has appeared or is forthcoming in *Inkwell, bananafish, Writer's Forum, Women's Studies Quarterly*, and an anthology, *Higher Elevations: Stories from the West*. She lives in Green Mountain Falls, Colorado, and is an on-call reference librarian at Colorado College.

VICTOR'S BIRD

N. Nye

N. Nye

Frances wakes again to the sound of the bird next door. At the same time, Concha wakes Victor with a song of Cuba. Once he had two birds who sang to each other, but Benares flew off at the beginning of summer. Just flapped his wings and flew into the pine trees and up into the mountains, a flash of turquoise and yellow, bright against the Ponderosa. When the bird banked to gain altitude, Victor saw blue, the color of liquid seas on his underbelly, blue like the cloudless sky. He thought Benares just needed to fly and would return, but he hasn't seen him since.

Now Concha sings lonely songs, Cuban songs, because if you're Cuban but you're not in Cuba, you're lonely for Cuba. Victor is, and Concha is, and Frances, who has never been to Cuba, hears Cuba in the sound of the bird each morning. She lies in her bed in the house next door and thinks about color—orange, hot pink, turquoise, red like chilis, green that throbs. Outside her window, drought has dried everything to brown, a gray-brown that hints at mouse fur and lichen.

Next door, Victor's life is a mess. His sons are with their mothers: one in Florida, the other a few miles away. His daughter is pregnant and unmarried. His landlord is impatient for the overdue rent, and the drought means Victor can't grill hamburgers over charcoal out on the deck. In spite of all this, Victor is wildly happy. He has always wanted to live in the mountains, and now they rise outside his windows like all his hopes. He gets out of bed and walks to the front window which overlooks a canyon and a high ridge on the far side. He throws his arms out to embrace the dry mountains, the twisted pine that was dead when he moved into the house. He looks again for Benares in case he has come back in the night, but Victor thinks Benares has probably died by now. The nights are cold, and there must be predators that would consider Benares a rare and delicious alternative to mice. Victor keeps Concha in her cage where she sings good morning, good night, how are you, when are we going home? Meaning Cuba.

Frances wants to be angry at the bird for waking her up every morning, but when Victor takes the bird with him to spend the night at his girlfriend's, the mother of his second son, Frances misses the singing. She has had to tell Victor three times about the fire ban. The first time he called the marshal in town and asked if he could grill, the marshal told Victor to keep a hose handy. The second time Frances reminded Victor of the fire ban, he told Frances that the marshal had said it was okay as long as he kept the hose handy. The third time, Victor checked again with the marshal, and the marshal said he couldn't light a match outside, either to grill or to light his cigar. The tantalizing smells of charcoal and sizzling hamburgers are something else Frances misses, and she misses the sweet smell of Victor's cigars which he smoked on his front step as if he were in Cuba. She wants to be angry at Victor, but she can't work up the energy.

She is outside painting an old chair a startling color of blue when Victor comes over to borrow the hose. The water restrictions mean he isn't supposed to water in the middle of the day, or on this day at all since he lives in a house with an even number, but Frances isn't going to tell him this. Let the water police tell him. She hasn't seen the water police on the mountain, but down in town, they cruise the streets looking for offenders, people who are watering on the wrong day or at the wrong time of day. Houses that have wells post signs out front that say *Well Water*, meaning they can water whenever they want. Victor probably hasn't heard about the restrictions. Frances thinks that Cuba probably doesn't have rules about water, and if there is a shortage of water in Cuba, the water just gets turned off.

"How do you like the color?" Frances asks him as she strokes paint on the old chair. "It's a Florida color."

"As long as I don't have to live there," Victor answers. "The rudest of all people live in Florida."

"I hadn't noticed that. In Florida they all just seem old."

Victor looks at her, thinking she is no spring chicken, and Frances understands the look.

"Well, those old people make me feel young." She is in her fifties, which she doesn't consider old, not like half of the population of Florida, which seems to be over seventy. Victor is probably close to forty. It isn't like either one of them is Gen-X, Y, or Z.

"It's a pretty color," he says finally, although it makes him think of a nursery school. The blue she paints on the chair is a children's color.

"Every now and then, every few decades, I get a passion for brights," Frances tells him, just as she realizes this is true. "Once I painted my bedroom floor this blue, and about twenty-five years ago, I painted my daughter's room yellow like the inside of a marigold. This summer is so dry and brown, I need color. I've been dreaming about it." She doesn't tell Victor how the bird's singing makes her see color.

Victor attaches her hose to the faucet at his house and turns it on. Just hearing the sound of the water on the dry ground makes both of them silent for a while. The water bounces off the hard ground until Victor gets it soaked; then he moves to a new place in the yard where the water dances in beads that catch the sun like dozens of tiny rainbows. He wishes he had a cigar. He buys them in Miami at a little tobacco store owned by an emigré, an old Cuban with silver hair and dark nails stained from tobacco leaves. Victor sighs as the water agitates over the hard ground. He would be in Florida if everyone who lives there weren't so rude.

Frances bought the old chair at the Salvation Army. It's missing a rung, but it's a good, solid chair. Painted blue, it is turning gorgeous, like something underwater. She pictures the chair sitting on white sand in three feet of water, a relic of a world that sank on the edge of a continent. She's seen sunken cities in Turkey, whole rooms still intact, stone walls and benches, eerily ancient and still, submerged in turquoise and cobalt water. She swam from room to room and looked up at the sun from underwater.

Both Victor and Frances hear Concha begin to sing inside the house. Victor calls out some Spanish to her, but she ignores him. Her song is frenzied and insistent. A song of revolution, of parades and political rallies, Frances thinks. "Fidel, Fidel," with passion.

"Calla!" Victor calls, and aims the hose at the window where Concha sings in her cage.

At the same moment, Frances and Victor look beyond the arc of the water aimed at the window, up toward the roof line of the house, at the dead pine tree outlined against the sky. A flare of yellow, turquoise, and lime, thinner, songless, Benares sits on a bare branch with the blue sky behind him. Frances feels as if she is underwater again, looking up at the sun.

Victor drops the hose and precious water flows over the hard, baked earth. Concha goes berserk inside the house; water from the hose runs down the windowpane, blurring her colors. Victor holds his hand palm down toward the bird in the tree and clicks his tongue, then coos softly in Spanish. Frances watches as the bird plucks at his wing feathers, pretending not to notice Victor's outstretched hand. Then Victor is singing with Concha, a Latin rhythm, fast and seductive. The water gurgles out of the hose and soaks into the dry ground. When the bird takes off from the tree, it circles the yard, scorns Victor's hand, and lands on the back of Frances's blue chair. The scales on the bird's finely etched legs and feet perfectly match the blue of the paint. Benares looks directly into her eyes to be sure she sees how beautiful he is perched on the back of the newly painted chair.

Victor smiles. Benares transforms the chair from something in a nursery to something in a villa overlooking the sea. Victor whistles, and Benares flies like an arrow, straight and swift, to Victor's outstretched hand. Concha sings, no longer of revolution, but of water that reaches out to a horizon, an island.

VERY SHORT FICTION AWARD WINNERS

1ST PLACE

N. Nye receives $1200 for "Victor's Bird."

Nye's bio is on page 42 preceding her story.

2ND PLACE

Susan Messer receives $500 for "September Song."

He opens his eyes, and when he sees that both his daughters are beside him, here from the West Coast and the East, he gives them the mother of all eye rolls: taking in the full meaning of their presence, Renee thinks.

Susan Messer's stories and essays have been published in *North American Review, Creative Nonfiction, River Oak Review, Another Chicago Magazine,* the *Chicago Reader,* and on *KillingtheBuddha.com.* She has received awards for fiction and nonfiction from the Illinois Arts Council, the Center for Yiddish Culture, and Chicago Public Radio, and she has been a finalist in the *Chicago Tribune*'s Nelson Algren competition. One of her stories was performed and broadcast as part of Chicago Public Radio's Stories on Stage series. She works as a writer and editor and lives in Oak Park, Illinois with her husband and daughter.

3RD PLACE

Charlotte Forbes receives $300 for "A Cow in the Rain."

Clutching their cow blankets, they looked at each other with a sense of failure. Their chests had ripped open to reveal their hearts, and having exposed their hearts to the air, they scarcely knew what to do with them.

Charlotte Forbes's fiction has appeared in numerous literary magazines and in the *O. Henry Awards,* 1999. Her nonfiction has been published in national magazines and newspapers.

*We invite you to visit **www.glimmertrain.com** to see a list of the top twenty-five winners and finalists. We thank all entrants for sending in their work.*

INTERVIEW WITH ANDRE DUBUS III

by John McNally

Andre Dubus III is the author of a collection of short fiction, The Cage Keeper and Other Stories, *and the novels* Bluesman *and* House of Sand and Fog. *His work has been included in* The Best American Essays of 1994, The Best Spiritual Writing of 1999, *and* The Best of Hope Magazine. *He has been awarded a Guggenheim Fellowship, the National Magazine Award for fiction, the Pushcart Prize, and was a finalist for the Prix de Rome Fellowship from the Academy of Arts and Letters. Currently a major motion picture, and published in eighteen*

Andre Dubus III

countries, his novel House of Sand and Fog *was a fiction finalist for the National Book Award, the* Los Angeles Times *Book Prize, the L.L. Winship/PEN New England Award, Booksense Book of the Year, and was an Oprah Book Club Selection and #1* New York Times *bestseller.*

A member of PEN American Center and the Executive Board of PEN New England, Andre Dubus III has served as a panelist for the National Endowment for the Arts and has taught writing at Harvard University, Tufts University, and Emerson College. He is married to performer Fontaine Dollas Dubus. They live in Massachusetts with their three children.

Glimmer Train Stories, Issue 50, Spring 2004
©*2004 John McNally*

What's the first story you ever wrote?

I wrote my first piece of fiction about a year after graduating from the University of Texas at Austin with a degree in sociology. I was twenty-two years old and had been feeling the pull of fiction, of stories, of scenes, for a while without really knowing it. I was working construction in Salem, Massachusetts then and living in an apartment in Lynn, a tough town on the water. There's a famous saying about Lynn: *Lynn, Lynn, the city of sin, you don't come out the way you went in.*

Anyway, I was living there and working construction by day and training for the Golden Gloves at night, after which I would brew some tea back in my small apartment that had no furniture or radio or TV, and I would read social theorists like Max Weber and Engels and Marx, etc., till very late. I slept on a yoga mat and my pillow was a pillow case with two work boots in it. I was training myself to be a thinker whose ultimate goal would be to rid the world of social injustice everywhere! I'd been accepted at the University of Wisconsin at Madison's PhD in Marxist Studies program, and that's where I was planning to go in the fall of 1982. Then I met and dated a girl who wrote fiction, and I started reading fiction for the first time really. And one winter night, all dressed in my sweats for a run to the Lynn Boys Club where I boxed, I sat down at my kitchen table and wrote a scene, and never went to the gym at all. It was an overwritten, clunkily rendered portrait of a young woman losing her virginity on the hood of a car in the rain in the Maine woods. That one never went anywhere, but soon after that I started writing about the previous summer, when I took care of my mother's ailing parents in the woods of central Louisiana. It turned into the first short story I'd ever written. It took about three months, and was called "Blackberries." I showed it to my writer girlfriend, who justifiably tore it apart.

Did you show it to your father [Andre Dubus]?

I gave a copy to my old man and his third wife, Peggy Rambach, a writer who was my age but a lot more experienced at the craft of fiction. They both said nice things about it, and I remember my father telling me I should keep at it, that there were things inside me I should tap into. The truth is, I knew I would keep writing anyway; I didn't want to be a writer, but I loved how writing left me feeling: awake, alert, curious, passionate, and more like me than I could remember ever feeling.

Had you read your father's work when you were younger?

I think I first began reading my father's work when I was eighteen or nineteen, I'm not sure, really. I probably read one or two of his stories before then, but it was in my late teens, while visiting his mother in Lake Charles, Louisiana, when I read his first and only novel, *The Lieutenant.* She was shocked that I hadn't yet read it, and handed me her signed copy, which I sat down and read in one sitting. I loved it, of course. The language, the vivid images and sounds and smells, the arc of the whole thing—I remember sitting there on my grandmother's couch alone afterwards and thinking my father, who I hadn't lived with since I was ten, was special in some way, special in a way I hadn't known about. But also, though I didn't know it at the time, I felt moved and inspired artistically. I wouldn't begin to act on that for a few more years, however.

Do you have a favorite story by your father?

I don't know if I can point to one of his many stories as my favorite. He is one of those rare writers whose body of work is masterful at just about every turn. But I will tell you the one that comes to mind without my thinking too much about it: "A Father's Story." For its philosophical sweep, its veracity of characterization, and that incredible talk with God at the end! Also the fact that I read it in manuscript, hungover on a Sunday morning in my college girlfriend's dorm room, only weeks after trying to write fiction for the first time myself.

You lived in Iowa City when your father was a student in the workshop. Do you remember much about those years?

I was five and six years old when we lived in Iowa City on Brown Street. I have a lot of vivid memories of that time, most of them happy. We were very poor—my old man sold blood once a month for grocery money. We were on food stamps, and I remember the landlady—a lovely, obese woman who owned dozens of cats—driving up in her battered station wagon to give us homemade bread or some boxed cheese or canned beef. But this was before my parents' marriage started failing, and—flat broke or not—they seemed very happy together and with us and our lives so far. There were a lot of parties that we kids would listen to from our beds upstairs, the jazz on the record player, the loud talk and laughter, and we could smell the cigarette smoke and perfume and spilled beer. Every afternoon, their friend Kurt, who was probably forty and lived up the hill next door, would come over and watch *Batman* on our TV with us. He'd show up just before it started at three o'clock, sit on the couch with us, smoking cigarette after cigarette, laughing hard at all of it. His favorite character was False Face, he told me, this man we came to know as Uncle Kurt, who turned out to be Kurt Vonnegut.

Writing seems to be in your blood. You're also related to James Lee Burke [author of the Dave Robicheaux detective series], aren't you?

James Lee Burke is my father's first cousin, which makes him my first cousin once removed. His kids and my kids are second cousins; I just recently figured out what all those kin terms really mean! I'm a huge fan of his work and have been since I was sixteen or seventeen and first read his second novel, *To the Bright and Shining Sun*.

Did you have much contact with him when you were younger?

I didn't see much of him as I was growing up, mainly because all of my relatives from both sides are from Louisiana, and my mother and father had settled up in New England. I'm pretty sure Cousin Jimmy (as my family calls him) was living in Kansas for a while, then Florida. Raising his four kids with his lovely wife, Pearl, teaching, writing. I do remember him visiting once when I was about eleven or twelve. My parents had been divorced a year or so, and Pop and Jimmy had driven over with a U-haul to help my mother and us move from one rented house to another. It was a hot day in summer in a rundown neighborhood in this milltown on the river. Everyone was hot and sweating and we couldn't get the furniture through the doors, and then the big rental truck wouldn't start. My brother, Jeb, who was nine or ten, had gotten hold of a firecracker. While the men were looking under the hood of the U-haul—two writers who didn't seem to even know what they were looking for—Jeb lit the firecracker and tossed it into the back of the truck. With that echo chamber, the explosion was louder than it should have been. Both men jumped away from the truck like it was on fire and Jeb just stood there smiling. They could smell the spent firecracker then, and the old man started yelling, but Cousin Jimmy just laughed and laughed and called my brother The Dynamite Kid. "Shit, little cousin," he said, "I'm gonna call you The Dynamite Kid!" Some time that weekend, my father and Jim and some buddies went on an all-night drunk back at Pop's place and spent most of the night throwing a Mexican throwing knife at the newel post at the foot of the stairs. When I went over for a visit the next day, it looked like a beaver-gnawed tree stump. And this was a rented house!

When I published my first short story ["Forky" in *Playboy* magazine in February 1984], Jim sent me a handwritten and very generous letter calling me a writer and welcoming me as one more into the family. I didn't believe I was one, but it sure felt good hearing that from him, one of my literary heroes! Over the years, he's been very generous with me, calling now and then to see how we're doing, offering to help out in any way he can. I'm thrilled at all the hard-earned success he's had, and am proud to be of the same family tree.

Is there anything about the training or the mindset of a boxer that's applicable to the fiction writer?

Let me first clarify that I never fought any sanctioned amateur bouts, though I did have an AAU number for the Golden Glove tournament down in Lowell, Massachusetts, and boxed off and on for years in gyms and boys' clubs. I had a good jab and a lot of stamina, but I hated getting punched in the face, and so would "stick and move" too much and not plant my feet and try and throw a more damaging combination!

I know other writers far better than I'll ever be—Hemingway, Mailer, etc.—have talked about boxing and writing. For me, the only real parallel has to do with stamina and precision. Most of my life, I've run long distances to clear my head and feel good, anywhere from eight to twelve miles. As all those who do endurance workouts know, it can hurt! So, if you haven't boxed before, imagine running up the tenth long hill in the tenth mile of your even longer run, sweat burning your eyes, panting for air, all while somebody's hitting you in the head and trying to knock you down and out.

Writing fiction never approaches this degree of physical suffering, of course, though it can have its spiritual equivalent: the truth is it is hard to work at something for years that nobody ever seems to take an interest in, all while stealing the time to do it, enduring most people's belief that it's just a hobby and nothing substantial will ever come of it, and never mind how difficult it is to do that thing in the first place. Yet you still have to keep finding the right word—the truest word—in that sentence and in that paragraph and in that page—and even if you do that, you may have to cut it all anyway because it doesn't work for other, sometimes mysterious reasons.

What I'm trying to say, I think, is that it helps a boxer if he (or she) simply enjoys the inherent pain of boxing the same way it helps the writer if she likes, or can cheerfully tolerate, the inherent difficulty of trying to write well and alone, all while trying to be a normal person making a living and raising a family, too!

As someone whose modest goal it was to rid the world of social injustice everywhere, what role, if any, does politics play in your fiction?

That's a tough question about my politics, or political philosophies, and my attempts at writing solid fiction. Tough, because I don't really know the answer! I can tell you what I believe: the fiction I like to read and the fiction I try to write doesn't hit you over the head with any ideological point. I think art is about capturing the gray areas in us all, those that seem to be above or beneath politics. In writing classes, I quote a lot from Flannery O'Connor's masterful essay, "The Nature and Aim of Fiction." Just about every line of that piece is quotable. In it she says that the writer's beliefs are not what she sees, "but the light through which she sees." So if you're a white, working-class, Marxist twenty year old, then that reality cannot help but influence and shape your vision in some way. My hope is that my own political views do not show themselves in my fiction at all. Hemingway wrote, "The job of the writer is not to judge, but to seek to understand." That's an inherently non-partisan act, it seems to me, though the writer probably can't escape revealing her views a bit, whether she wants to or not.

How do you handle research? Do you do a lot before starting a story or novel, or do you research as you go along? How do you integrate it so that it feels organic?

I do find myself doing a lot of research. It's a tricky area for writers: How do you incorporate all you've learned without bogging down or killing the story? When do you do it? Should you do it? For me, I tend to research as I go along and only once I've written myself into a corner of life about which I'm completely ignorant. After *House of Sand and Fog* came out, I wrote what I thought was a new novel. My imagination, for whatever weird reasons of its own, brought me a character who had been raised on a dairy farm. Well, I don't know jack about dairy farms, and don't even drink milk! So I called dairy farms, visited one, visited a feed-and-grain store, learned a lot. Research material tends to give us a lot to work with and can even send the story down a much truer and deeper path. I got pumped up and wrote and wrote and wrote. After two years, I had over two-hundred handwritten pages and was feeling a bit lost, a normal feeling, like I'd stumbled off the trail and would never find it again. Whenever that happens, I stop writing and just read the whole thing from the beginning, telling myself I've never seen one word of this thing before, reading it like a reader and not the writer. What I found was eighty straight pages of the dullest prose ever about dairy farming! Elmore Leonard said once, "Try to leave out the parts the reader skips over." All that dairy-farm life I needed to know, but the reader didn't. I cut it all, except one page, and ended up with a forty-seven-page story called "The Bartender" [published in the Spring 1999 issue of *Glimmer Train Stories*]. So that's one of the dangers, but I do believe strongly it's something writers need to do. If I read of an east-coast birch tree in an Arizona desert, it's going to stop me and kill that dream the writer's working so hard to cast. I also think taking the time to find the real tree, if there is one, will help the writer go more deeply into the story in a way he or she could never have foreseen. I've just finished the draft of a new novel, and, for the first time, am spending weeks researching the next one because I know next to nothing about that world I'm about to step into. I'm getting all pumped up again, which means I'll probably make the same mistake as before and put in all this stuff I'm going to have to cut!

Wallace Stegner called the short story "a young writer's form," and went on to say that in his own writing "the novel has tended to swallow and absorb potential stories." Do you find that true for yourself? Do you find it harder to return to the short-story form after having written novels?

I don't agree with Stegner that the short story is a young writer's form. I tend to agree more with Faulkner who said that when we first start writing, we try our hand at poems, and when we fail at those, we try to write short stories, and when we can't do that either, we end up writing novels! I do think, in order for a short story to be *great*, that there cannot be one word too few or too many, and, to quote Coleridge, they all have to be in the right order, too. Would we look at Chekhov's body of work—or Katherine Anne Porter's? John Cheever's? Andre Dubus's, my father? Raymond Carver's? Tobias Wolff's? Alice Munro's—etc., and say these are the works of "young" writers? I doubt it. Maybe Stegner was referring to those writers whose natural form tends to be the novel in the first place. Because, yes, my first book was a collection of seven short stories that I wrote in the first six and a half years of trying to teach myself to write, and it did feel like I was first teaching myself how to build a box, then a table, then a dog house, then a deck, before I began to take on what felt like a house-building project—writing a full-scale novel. But I think I'm also more of a novelist, by nature, than a short-story writer. In other words, I don't know when to quit and can't shut the hell up! And yes, I have seen ideas for possible short stories come to fruition in novel drafts as scenes or parts of chapters. Though, in the last four or five years, I've seen two eighteen-month attempts at novels metamorphose into two fifty-page stories that, in my opinion, could only be those lengths. You see, ultimately, I think it's the work itself that tells us what it wants to be—novel or short story, poem or haiku, essay or letter to a dead relative. And yes, I do find it harder to return to the short story after having written novels—published and shelved—because I love the feeling of being completely absorbed and lost in a three-to-five-hundred-page narrative that takes years of my life to write. Which is another reason I suspect I'm more of a novelist than a short-story writer.

Whom do you consider your literary forebears?

By literary forebears, do you mean those writers in whose line I think I stand? If that's what you mean, then I have no idea, and the honest-to-God truth is that I never think in those lines. I still have a hard time even calling myself a writer at all. Maybe because I never set out to be one. Maybe because whatever abilities I have almost daily feel so inadequate to the task of trying to capture some semblance of human truth with any degree of artistry at all. And I know this kind of self-loathing can be just another side of narcissism. I can tell you that I love the naturalists and the realists, those writers who don't show off their craft but work hard at humbly listening to who emerges from their own pencils and pens. I love those writers who don't take refuge in detached irony and false world weariness, which I judge as chickenshit and easy! How's that?

Do you have any involvement with the film version of House of Sand and Fog?

With *House of Sand and Fog*, the movie [released in December 2003], I did get to be more involved than is usually the case with fiction writers. Vadim Perelman, who wrote and directed the film, sent me revisions of the script and was open to my editing suggestions right up until shooting began.

Russell Banks has a one-sentence role in the film version of his book The Sweet Hereafter. *Should we look for you in the movie?*

I did get a cameo. I have no lines, which is fine by me, but I play a cop in a scene with Ben Kingsley. I play Meyers, assistant to Lieutenant Alvarez in Internal Affairs. In my cheap suit, with a badge and nine millimeter strapped to my belt, I get to sit across from Kingsley and give him a cop's skeptical eye. It's a short scene but indispensable to the story, so I'm pretty sure I won't get cut!

Do you have any interest in writing screenplays?

No, I don't. I like movies, but for me the thrill and the majesty and mystery still lie in prose. It's those *sentences* I'm drawn to, the ones that yield the images and the sounds and the people in them that are a constant surprise to me. That's when it feels like it's going well, when it's all one big surprise.

You and your wife, who's a performer, worked together on the audiotape for House of Sand and Fog. *Was this an idea that you presented to the audiotape publisher?*

The idea to read together came from us, though it was really my wife who convinced me it would sound strange to have a male reader read both the male and female sections. I had already decided that unless they hired an Iranian reader that I would do it because I felt confident I could pronounce the Farsi words and knew pretty much how I wanted the colonel to sound. Whether I pulled that off or not, I don't know. But Fontaine's a wonderful actress, and I knew she'd nail Kathy, given the opportunity. The people at HarperCollins seemed to like the idea, too, so we did it.

Do you have any plans to collaborate on other projects?

Fontaine and I don't have any immediate plans to collaborate on other projects, though we've worked together in the past. I've been a "flesh prop" in some of her dance pieces, and we've acted in plays together. She and my sister, Suzanne, just finished writing a real strong screen adaptation of my dad's novella, *Voices from the Moon*, and I'll probably read one of the roles in an upcoming staged reading of the script. My wife, Fontaine, is a gifted woman, and our mutual yearning to try and create something good is a significant part of our bond.

When you first began writing, you were a single guy. Now you're married and have three kids. In what ways has having a family impacted your writing?

Yes, now I'm blessed with a family. And I do see it as just that—a blessing. I had no idea all those sweet old ladies were right all along, that when you meet the one you're going to marry, you just know it, and if you're fortunate enough to have kids, you'll feel more love in you than you ever thought possible. To answer your question, when I was single, my sole enduring thought from day to day was my writing. Now it is, and will forever be, my children. How to nurture them, keep them safe and healthy, send them out into the world as strong, loving, responsible people. This is not to say I no longer think of my writing daily. I do! In fact, because of the deep spiritual changes parenthood opens up in you—a greater capacity for love, vulnerability, fear of loss, acceptance of your place in the mortal coil, etc.—it has got to ultimately deepen the writing, too. And yes, the truth is there are more demands on my time than there were when I was still single, which makes time at the desk a bit lean sometimes, but so what! In no time at all, I'll be sitting on the couch in an empty house wondering why my children aren't calling me from their adult lives I'm no longer really part of; if I miss an occasional writing session to be with them, that's good!

According to your bio, you've worked as a bounty hunter, private investigator, carpenter, bartender, actor, and teacher. Have any of these jobs helped you, either directly or indirectly, as a fiction writer?

The weird truth is I have worked at all those jobs, though in my publicity packet with Vintage, it's implied I did that work before coming to writing; in fact, I took those jobs to support my writing, mainly because—except for the carpentry work—they happened at night, which gave me mornings to write. Also, the bounty hunting and private-investigation work was a six-month job with a guy who did both, and I was his twenty-two-year-old assistant with an alias. Because of his own scrapes with the law over the years, he only hunted down killers, which meant I hunted them down, too, which meant I did things like sit in my beat-up Subaru for twelve straight hours watching the house of a contract killer's girlfriend, freezing my ass off, peeing in an empty coffee cup, writing down all she did: watch TV, talk on the phone, watch more TV, etc. I don't honestly know if these jobs have helped, directly or indirectly, my efforts at writing fiction. Now that I think about it, though, they may have in this way: sitting in cars watching strangers taught me to sit still and wait. To look more closely at things. To try and listen more keenly. Again, I know there are solid writers out there who outline their tales before they write them, but for me, the whole writing process is an act of deep mining. I've learned over the years—and with far more creative failures behind me than successes!—to start trusting the details that insist on being seen or noticed in some way when I'm writing them. This is all much more an act of watching what unfolds and then waiting to see what will unfold next, rather than a massive effort at manufacturing something, like a big fat novel. So, the bounty hunting/P.I. stuff helped there, but bartending, which I did pretty steadily for ten years, did, too, because again I could just quietly serve drinks, and wipe down the bar and swab ashtrays and listen to all my customers open up their stories, one drink after another. Carpentry, on the other hand, after eight straight years of it, left me feeling more generally competent in the world, more capable of bold things. "You want that wall gone and a room built where there used to be a garden? No problem!" This hard-earned confidence (because I was a very inept carpenter for a long time) eventually seeped into my writing self. Why not write a five-hundred-page narrative that holds together? I just built a kitchen, bathroom, and new deck, didn't I?

The other jobs, the acting and teaching, probably influenced me, too. True acting makes you surrender to all the forces in you, whether you want to show them or not. It forces you to see and feel the difference between having an emotion and pretending or half-pretending to. It also, as a high art form, forces you to confront self-consciousness, probably the main stumbling block for anyone's potential creative struggle: how do I get out of my own way? How do I stop caring how this performance or this poem, etc., makes me *look*?! The teaching, on my good days, taught me to be more consistently curious, inquisitive, and compassionate. On my *good* days!

Your birthday is September 11th. Do you want to say where you were and what you were doing when you first learned of the attacks?

On that terrible day, I had just made my morning coffee and was heading up to my attic office when I overheard my wife on the phone with her sister, who'd just told her to turn on the news, that a plane had crashed into the World Trade Center. We turned it on, and like so many people, saw the second plane crash into the second tower. I ended up staying in front of the TV for most of that day, interrupted by my calling friends and colleagues in New York to make sure they were safe. They all were, thank God. A few people called me as well because I'd been flying quite a bit in and out of Logan Airport all year. In fact, I'd flown in on United the night before and was scheduled to fly out again on United a couple days later. I didn't write that day, and when my family came over to celebrate my birthday it was, as it should've been, a very low-key and quiet gathering, and if I could, I would've skipped it altogether.

I know what other writers mean when they say they felt as if their own "tinkering with a short story" was trivial in the light of all that, but I was spared that feeling by an editor at the *Toronto Globe and Mail* who wanted me to write a piece about the attack for that weekend's paper. Man, that was a tough one to write! I was still so full of rage and hurt and shock and grief, like everybody else. How in the world would I write anything with any clarity or insight at all? That's what I think Truman Capote was onto when he said, "A writer must write as cool and detached as a surgeon." Somehow I wrote and submitted the essay, then got back to work on the novel I've been wrestling with for years. While I hated most of what I was seeing on the desk in front of me—a normal feeling—it didn't feel trivial to be working on it. If the attacks of 9/11 have taught us anything at all, it's that life is horrifically short and precarious, sacred and fragile, and we should live as fully, deeply, and richly as we possibly can. Other than trying to be as good a father and husband as I can be, I can't think of a better way to live than to try and create something worth reading for someone you'll probably never even meet.

What advice would you give to the aspiring fiction writer?

Trust your imagination; don't try and figure out your stories ahead of time, because that's walking the high-wire with a big net under you. We were all born with the ability to imagine and dream endlessly, terrifyingly, gorgeously, wildly, etc. Our job, it seems to me, is to work mercilessly on finding the truest language to bring out whatever it is that needs to be brought out. Which is one thing a good writing class or program can do! And, much like having children, the writer (or parent) doesn't even get to choose what comes out, or how. So get in your daily sessions—if all you have is twenty minutes, then take it anyway; you're at least getting blood through the umbilical cord to that growing fetus. Don't think about the work or talk to anybody about it in any specific way; do other things in your life that make you feel good, because if you rely on writing to do that, it will disappoint you, especially if you're going deeply enough; and only quit writing if you find you can do that and still be you!

What about for the amateur boxer?

Don't neglect your jab or body shots!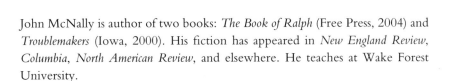

John McNally is author of two books: *The Book of Ralph* (Free Press, 2004) and *Troublemakers* (Iowa, 2000). His fiction has appeared in *New England Review, Columbia, North American Review,* and elsewhere. He teaches at Wake Forest University.

"Children can be told everything—everything."
—Fyodor Dostoyevsky

Daniel Villasenor lives in Italy where he teaches martial arts, and trains and shoes horses for a living. His first novel, *The Lake* (Penguin, 2001), has been translated into five languages. His first significant attempt at short fiction won *Glimmer Train*'s Award for New Writers in 1997. His next two novels take place in Italy.

TO A STRANGER

Daniel Villasenor

Winter in the east is good for thought, the student was thinking as he left the musty alcove of his apartment stairwell and crossed 4th Street to the neighborhood park. Each morning he followed the frozen, rutted paths through the park to the subway station on the opposite side. The brief walk enabled him to assemble his thoughts for the day. He knew exactly how much time it took for him to walk at a leisurely pace to the station, and he never missed his train. The Divinity School was in the center of the city, and often he did not return home until eight or nine o'clock in the evening. That morning he was thinking about the gray endlessness which characterizes eastern winters, a kind of protracted sobriety which holds within it a paradox: the sharp cold knife of each breath and at the same time a diffuse watercolor softness in the low even clouds and in the dun-colored air, in the grainy dissipations of buildings and in the quiet remove of trees. An impressionistic softness, not nourishing but its opposite, so that the frozen face of winter is really like a human face, like the unyielding and yet fathomless face of someone you have not seen in years, who has experienced more of life's pain and inconsolable joy than you have, who sits across from you and looks discompassionately at your mediocrity, and yet with a kind of surfeit pity for your inexperience—and thereby withholds. So winter in the east is good for thought, the student was thinking.

Not more than three weeks ago he had seen fall from the trees the last perhaps half-dozen leaves heretofore clinging to the top-most wind-raked branches of the last be-leafed tree, watching them loose on his way and feeling that incongruous lift of the spirit which the falling of leaves brings, as if death and gravity were pregnant withal with a bizarre levity. He remembered that although the park had not been peopled as it was in warmer months, he had seen a few sparse couples walking together on the Saturday, holding to each other in that intimate way that lovers do as if the ample, intertwined fabric of their coat sleeves was an electric charge upon their marriage. Upon marriage, he had then thought, if marriage was that endless lean of two souls in weather, two coat sleeves lost and yet supporting each other through the dark contracting months of the year, making the mouths whisper to each other where the bodies leaned, so that wish and dream and shame might thus be absorbed in the amplitude of wool and goose down, scarves and collars and hats. If, he had thought, that padded indivisibility was what marriage was.

The student, whose name was Peter, had hardly spoken a word to his wife in recent weeks. In truth it had been many months since he had come home in the evening from his courses and they had eaten supper without an almost unbroken silence, whereas once they talked quietly at table and by the light of the one shapely glass-ensconced candle which had often burnt down and pooled in the pewter before they had done with the elaborate meal. In the first year of their marriage they had sometimes made love in the evenings, before they were too tired, and in bed they were attentive and familiar with each other. The sex was uneventful, tender, and quick. Now he could not remember the last time he had made love to her, and the thought of that would enter him as a train approaches a tunnel and enters and rushes forth, blotting out the light of day, and with its insufferable clamor, all sound and sense and recognition, even the fact of the very train. So that it wasn't a thought at all, but a non-thought ushered upon the roaring back of a thought. He stood as the thought, in all its violent and remorseless inarticulation, entered and passed through him, rocked back on his heels by the wake of it. But then it would just as suddenly be quiet. Looking up, the day appeared blue and lit, just as in the depths of some all-but-entombed railway station light pricks the darkness again upon the passing of a train. And then there was somewhere to go, and something to do. Then the thought, the train, was like a forgotten bad dream which makes one feel all the day a gnawing physical weariness which is just barely untraceable to the stress and impasse and bitter confusion of the nightmare. He never said to himself, You have not made love to your wife. He merely watched the thought approach like an implacable apparition from the distance, even longed for it—longed to feel it smash its brute and inarticulate volume against the wall of his consciousness and the faintly effervescent numbness through his body after—almost a tenderness of absence. He longed for it as a depressed man longs for sleep.

That morning crossing the somber park he recalled again the Saturday just three weeks before when he had seen a few skateboarders trying to outdo each other with their tricks, and a theatrical young black boy wheeling his wonky bicycle in grand curves, speaking to himself without a care to the world's eyes, and earnestly debating something upon himself. There had been the gardeners cajoling each other, raking back the last pulverized leaves into the sallow grass. There had been children of all races about the swings, dressed and clumsy in their vibrant colors, alive in their voices. And walking then through the park he had been able to see the world moving in its turns, and thus turn himself back upon his world: his work, his studies, which were coming along fine. He felt that he was quietly impressive to all his teachers; that he was making headway; that in no long time he would command a similar quiet respect in the university, in the community, perhaps from within the pulpit. He felt confident of his destiny.

But over the course of the previous three weeks, as winter came on with a terrible finality, especially in the last fortnight, which was as cold as anyone could remember, so that people began to lose even that animation which accompanies the advent of terrible weather, so that their faces began to withdraw in their hoods as dust into the corner of a room, and they failed to meet each other's eyes, he had been plagued by a relentless sense of doom and purposelessness. Not just of his own life, for he was not habitually a self-absorbed man, but an unremitting sense of the folly and pointlessness of all human behavior, of all endeavor. That morning, looking at all the faces in the subway, he could see that there was not a spark of originality or intelligence on any face, that not a one had what could be called an internal life, a respectful conversation with oneself; that they stared blankly in stupefied un-wonder at their feet or each other or their own alienated jostling images in the darkly teeming glass; or that they traced with their thumbs spastic patterns along a briefcase handle or upon a thigh which itself jumped and twitched under the stress of some facile, visionless ambition; or they folded and refolded the day's newspaper not so much to learn of the terrible and innocuous repetitions of the news but simply in order to refrain from having a thought themselves to which they would be held accountable by some higher authority within. Because there was no authority. They had thrown away the authority with the rest of the refuse in which they waded. Or perhaps, Peter thought, it had never been there, the authority. And here he shuddered, because the line between an authority within and God without was a fine one. The disappearance of one meant, did it not, the disappearance of the other? He had never conceived of the divinity as an essence apart from human potentiality, and his sudden (or was it sudden?) misanthropy plagued his soul. And he wondered if his ostensible love of mankind was perhaps a fiction he had created about himself that he might have a path, a course of study and a position, lacking as he was in other gifts. Looking at the faces in the subway, he could see no innocence, nor complex awareness, nor honest grappling, nor that which was called suffering, if suffering was a clarity of grief. He could see only listless unconsciousness, so that people resembled nothing so much as cattle, and he even began to see or imagine (in his dreary state of mind it was nearly impossible to tell the difference) drool coming from out the corners of peoples' mouths. He considered what his own face might look like under the strain of such images and he shuddered again. Distraction, he thought, cease-less distraction and lethargy and the short-sighted mercenary pursuits which feed the pathetic and nearly homogeneous egos of modern people—this is what we call human life. He looked down at the floor of the subway, at the styrofoam cups, cigarette packs, sections of old newspaper, pamphlets advertising pornography, plastic shopping bags, the wrappers of fast food, and he thought, These people who must ride this same subway everyday, who throw down their trash only to look upon it the next day and the next; this heedless discard swelling about my feet is the measure of human life. We care no more than a cow does for his place at the slop.

He had gone through the day with an unshakable torpor. He had even opted to miss his early evening class, thinking that a swim in the lap pool, and a long steam after, would lift his spirits. The community recreation center was just six blocks from the Divinity School, and passing another park, this one even more humble than the one near his home, he could not help but remark to himself upon the terrible still-life of the little brown corner of earth. The hopeless attempt at an idea, an intimation of wilderness eked out within an urban zone the concrete of which stretched as far as a small sea. That too was some figure for the desperation of modern life, he thought, shrugging his shoulders so that his coat collar might cover the pale lobes of his ears (that morning he had forgotten his hat). He looked up at the trees against the monotone press of the sky and he could not help but see the branch tips as inkless writing implements dithering emptily upon the air. Just as in the subway car, the whole dead scene of the park seemed fraught with a terrible animism. Unwittingly he saw, in the large leaning trunk of a tree, in the knots and torqued runnels of the bark, the reclining figure of St. Peter as he is laid on the wooden cross in the crucifixion by Cara-vaggio, the complete incredulity of abandonment, the stake some-how bloodless through the left hand, the body rising up off the wood even as the men are carrying him inverted, the world-dead eyes of the man as if there has been some mistake, and there has, he thought. There has been a mistake.

In the pool he swam thirty-six lengths of crawl stroke, which was his routine. He dried off and did fifty sit-ups on the mat on the deck, and for a time lay flat on his back and listened to the electric hum of the lights high above like great fluorescent beehives in the vaulted space. He showered and returned to his locker and sat naked on the bench and absently mopped at his neck with the towel, feeling the quiescence of the body after exercise, thinking, If I could just sit here. If only I didn't have to move.

There had been only one other man swimming in the pool and presently he entered the small locker room. By chance, or by fate, of all the lockers in the room his was the one directly next to Peter's. He stood near for a moment, his hip at the level of Peter's bent head, until Peter, who was lost in thought, who was in fact thinking about Jesus, moved a few feet down the bench. He was thinking about the parable where the people are asking Jesus about access to the King-dom. *Whoever is shut out is shut out, Jesus said. And one of them was heard to say, O Lord, is this thing definite? And Jesus said, Listen: Insight, Knowl-edge, Obedience, Endurance, Mercy. These have slept in those who have be-lieved and acknowledged me. And since those who slept did not fulfill my commandment, they will be outside the kingdom and the fold of the shepherd; and whoever remains outside the fold will the wolf eat. And although he hears he will be judged and will die, and much suffering and distress and endurance will come upon him; and although he is badly pained and although he is cut into pieces and lacerated with long and painful punishment, yet he will not be able to die quickly.* How, Peter thought, could the bearer of magnanim-ity speak in the rhetoric of such punitive ultimatums? How, with an ordinary stone, could the Son of the Father of the universe draw in the sand such a sure line between right and wrong?

Could you help me with this? the man said.

His voice, though it came out of a silence punctuated only by the somnolent drip of a shower head, did not startle or even surprise. Even as it broke his meditation it seemed to Peter inevitable, faithful as a line delivered upon the stage. In fact directly upon the sound of it

Peter suddenly had an omniscient sense about the scene; that he was in a play, or that he and the man were thus composed in a painting of nudes and the one was standing quarter-turned while the other sat ruminating on a bench: Could you help me with this? And the voice! So calm, so light and quiet and sure; un-obsequious and yet blithely courteous. Immediately it made him feel lonely. No—it was not a sentiment. Something in the voice made even the possibility of its absence unbearable.

The man, turned thus, looked down at Peter, a silver bracelet dangling from his hand. Could you clasp this for me?

Again the voice! Even as Peter began to take in the man's features— the articulate shoulders, the long muscular limbs, the helix and the faint arch beginning in the low back and tapering to the neck so that his torso looked like a wet paint brush, and finally the quaint Renaissance face with the graze of a dimple in the chin, eyes the color of molasses in sunlight, the wet light-brown hair already beginning to lift up into waves of curls—even as he began to look at the man it was still the voice which disarmed him. Neither low nor high, it had within it at once some improbable conjunction of meditative introspection and mirth. And intelligence, wry but not ironic. And confidence—he had not even said so much as, Pardon me. And humility, as if he knew too well that part of human folly which asks of others what should not be asked, and yet here he was standing naked, asking this simple thing. Courtliness, Peter thought, out of nowhere. And then he met his eyes.

The man laughed, pleasantly, and turned from his locker to face Peter. This bracelet, I can't—

Sure, Peter said, standing. Yes, yes of course.

He took the bracelet and the man held out his arm, underside exposed. Peter brought the chain around the wrist and began to try and open the clasp and fasten it to the diminutive ring. But he couldn't do it. He tried several times but his manual dexterity had never been good, and his hands were damp from the wet towel and his thumb kept sliding off the catch just at the moment when it looked as if he had it. The man stood completely relaxed, his hand neither flaccid nor tense, as if in his open palm he held some invisible seed for invisible birds. Peter redoubled his effort, but the more he concentrated the harder the task seemed until his eyes were burning (he had lately misplaced his swimming goggles) and he could not properly see. The chain slipped off the man's wrist and fell to the bench, and from the bench it slid to the floor. They looked at it together as if it was some saurian presence somehow slipped onto the cold tile of human affairs. Peter rubbed his eyes with the back of his hand. He could hear his own breath, three breaths for every one of the man's. For a moment neither of the men moved to retrieve the chain. Then Peter bent down and gathered it in his hand. Do not look, he said to himself, Do not. But against all will power, as he stood his eyes grazed for an instant the tight balls and the clean, tapered shaft, flaccid and circumcised, the one vein traversing a diagonal and voluted along the relaxed curving beauty of it. Velvet, he thought, banishing the word from all future discourse even as he thought it. The man leaned closer to avail himself more earnestly to the task, and as he did so a current of what we call power—the quality of quality restrained—came off of his body or his breath, Peter could not say. Only it seemed he could not get enough air. He brought the chain once more around the wrist, but he could not even manage to pull back the tiny spring. I can't get it, he said.

He looked briefly into the man's eyes. He knew that those eyes had watched his body as it bent down. Even before he had begun to bend he had acquiesced to that, known that the eyes would follow him quietly and shamelessly, that he would for that time be blind to their gaze, helpless before it. He had bent to the floor as one bends back into a dream upon briefly waking, knowing that the conclusion might terrify and betray him, but unable to resist the sensation of the plummet. The man for his part looked at Peter evenly. His look was not prurient per se, but alive, abundant, and if there was the suggestion of sex in the flare at the heart of the pupils it was more the suggestion that sex might be where the intelligence places it, and that this might be such a moment, and it might not be. The eyes were simply interested. At which point Peter saw himself in his situation. He began to panic. The locker-room door swung open and a man entered and heaved his bag onto the end of the bench and looked at the two men standing there like some statuary of delicate communion, Peter's fingers actually grazing the other man's wrist veins as if he were poised to press some strings to the frets of an instrument. The man picked up his bag and went to the next row of lockers and coughed. I can't do it, Peter said again, whispering it fiercely as if it was some desperate secret between them. I'm sorry.

Just try one more time, the man said quietly. I think you've almost got it.

And so he did. With tremendous concentration Peter bent to the bracelet, his eyes leaking from chlorine, tiny sweat beads breaking out now upon his upper lip. He could barely see; he felt as if he were trying to thread a needle under water. And when the chain did finally clasp it was something of a small miracle. He breathed, straightening, pressing his eyes again with the backs of his hands. He looked at the man and smiled broadly, and the man smiled at him. Suddenly they broke out laughing together and clasped each other by the arms as if they had accomplished something perilous and of consequence. Thank you, the man said.

You're welcome, Peter said.

The man turned around and lifted his shirt from its hook and held it open in front of himself. He stood examining the shirt a long time, holding it thumb and forefinger each to the seam of a shoulder, like a mirror in whose draping folds he seemed to be noting the current of life in his own body. Peter watched him. Then they dressed in silence. Peter hurried. He could feel his clothes absorbing the dampness he had neglected and he cursed himself. It's the coldest day of the year, he said.

I was just thinking that I didn't want to go outside.

The voice! Again that resonant calmness! The paradox of it! The anchored levity of it! How did one live into such a voice? He was desperate to hear it again but he could think of nothing trivial enough, or important enough, to say to him. And he was equally as desperate to get away. He finished dressing and ducked his head under his satchel strap, but as he made for the door the man said, Wait, just a second.

Peter turned. The man was fully dressed now but his shirt was still open, and he held one sock in his hand. He stood looking at Peter a moment, and then suddenly he put the sock in his mouth—a gesture that should have seemed ridiculously childish, but with the man it was simply spirited, gamy—and bent, rifling through his duffel bag. He pulled out a worn paperback book and sifted through the pages until he found the one he was looking for, and then he carefully ripped the page from the welt. He walked toward Peter, folding the paper once before he placed it in his hand.

It hardly matters if you feel the same, he said, or even understand. It's just very rare, and Whitman says it best. And I happen to have him with me. It would trouble me always if I didn't tell you.

He spoke in the same easy, direct, and unaffected regal timbre. A voice that could incur no debt, Peter thought. Thank you, Peter said, not looking at the piece of paper. He turned and pushed open the door and walked echoing down the hall.

When he reached the far end and opened the door to the street he could not believe how cold it had become. And now there was wind. Debris flew down the avenue in fits and starts, and in the harsher gusts the street signs buckled. Outside, he pulled the door shut with difficulty and stood leaning against it, breathing as if he had been walking uphill. In the light from the sign above the lintel he examined the paper. It was a poem of Walt Whitman's entitled, "To a Stranger":

> Passing stranger! You do not know how longingly I look upon you,
> You must be he I was seeking, or she I was seeking (it comes to me
>   as of a dream),
> I have somewhere surely lived a life of joy with you,
> All is recall'd as we flit by each other, fluid, affectionate, chaste,
>   matured,
> You grew up with me, were a boy with me or a girl with me,
> I ate with you and slept with you, your body has become not yours
>   only nor left my body mine only,

You give me the pleasure of your eyes, face, flesh, as we pass,
You take of my beard, breast, hands, in return,
I am not to speak to you, I am to think of you when I sit alone or
  wake at night alone,
I am to wait, I do not doubt I am to meet you again,
I am to see to it that I do not lose you.

He read it twice, then he folded it and stuffed it in the pocket of his wool duster. He walked half a block and then he stopped: It would trouble me always if I didn't tell you. He repeated this last sentence of the man's over and over again, and then he laughed suddenly, a short, hard burst of submerged air. I have never in my life uttered a single true sentence, he said out loud.

He began walking again, his hands jammed into his pockets so hard the inverse pressure seemed to pump his feet lightly up out of the ground. The clarity of the man! And to preserve his dignity by telling a truth to a stranger, and yet to ask nothing of him! In word or tone or demeanor—to ask nothing of him. Where did such reserve come from? Peter silently screamed the question to himself. And he answered himself: He has no shame. And how much shame must one openly eat, he thought, until shame disappears?

He was walking rapidly with his head down. When he looked up he saw that he had passed his subway stop. Retracing his steps, he thought, If he has no shame, then his conscience must not thwart him. And if he spoke that way to me, to a stranger, naked and in a locker room, then he must carry himself always without fear, and he must believe what he thinks and think what he believes, and he must be at once undivided and variable, and the world must be full of endless possibility and mystery for him. And he felt, for a moment, what an adventure life must be for such a man. He was suddenly struck with a blow of nausea, and he wanted to go home. He stood in the walk and breathed and looked about the city, at the lights along the converging streets in their endless processions, and upward at the buildings and the sporadic yellow squares of light—so many fulgent paper cutouts upon the sky. And he thought that behind each window someone must be mulling over sentences, words in the mind that he or she was trying to shave closer and closer to truth, so that they might thereby untrouble themselves; that people everywhere, this very minute, were answering the terrible summons of their souls, together or privately, performing small acts of bravery which would release them from the prison of their fears. And he had a tremendous desire to go home, to open the door of the apartment, and to blaze upon his lovely wife these thoughts and words.

He got off the 6 train at 57th St. and walked up the station stairs into the freezing night, then crossed the street and descended the south-side steps and entered the F to Brooklyn, and sat, all the while talking to his wife. But by the time the train entered the 7th St. station he was growing numb. Words, revelations, and entreaties, which so immediately prior had been prompt and eloquent on his tongue, slipped from him now, down through his body like schools of dead fish sinking through a chemical sea. There was an acidic taste in his mouth. And by the time he was walking through the familiar paths of the park, abruptly he had nothing to say. The words were gone; he could not have found them to spare his life. And the warm woman he had pictured taking him prodigally in her arms, this anima-wife, this sibling figure of endless compassion, had become again the cold companion of his house. Even their friendship was dead. They could not please each other if they tried. He stood stock still in the middle of the park, as silent and as cold as one of the trees.

When he finally climbed the steps to his landing it was late, and he knew he had missed dinner. He stood freezing without the door, wishing he were wet with snow, wishing he could shake out some dampness in two or three snaps of his elbow, that the drama of the action might help him enter his house. Jennifer, he said, as he stepped into the hall and shut the door.

His wife did not say anything. He heard her rise from the couch in the living room and pad into the kitchen. He heard the refrigerator door open and close. She is laying out the cold brisket and the boiled string beans on a plate, he thought. She is lifting, as if it were the grossest impertinence to have to do so, a dead dollop of mashed potatoes and slopping it cold on a plate, and she is not even going to ask me if I want it heated up. She's put her hair up tight and her face is pulled back as if by wire, and her eyes are the color of gun-metal, and she is looking at the food right now wondering if she should heat it up, and she's not going to.

Baby, his wife called from the kitchen, I'm heating up your dinner. Do you want a roll?

He turned and leaned his forehead against the wall. Yes, thank you.

He walked down the dark hall to the kitchen and stood in the door looking at her back. She wore a faded midnight-blue silk nightgown and her old sheepskin slippers with the clumped wool lining. Her hair was not tied back but swung loose and pendular, dark blond, past her shoulders. He could see the remnants of auburn tint in her hair where she bent under the overhead light of the stove. I met a man today, he said.

Hmm, she said.

In recent weeks, nay, months, they had grown used to speaking to each other in short blurts of meaningless data, miserable non-attempts at conversation, such as, I met a man today who reminded me of someone, or, So and so's wife has an old Volvo, or, There are some students from the department meeting next week at that Cuban restaurant we read about last year. And these phrases lately went unanswered, as if they were fragments of some background broadcast of radio or television which interrupted the silence when the distant signal came in. She turned from the stove and set his plate on the table and turned back to the sink and started placing the not-yet dry dishes in the cupboard, loudly. In recent months she had become noisy whereas once she seemed to attend even inanimate objects as if they had a vulnerable sentience. This was one of the qualities about her which he had loved. Now she seemed to try to sound every object she handled and test its strength to the breaking point against another. In fact she had broken several dishes inadvertently lately. And her back, her body on the whole, as he sat now looking at her, moved in hard, jutting motions; her shoulders were high in a perpetual shrug. I met a man today, he said, not lifting his utensils.

She paused and moved her hair from about her face, but did not say anything or turn around. When she finished storing the dishes she stood looking down into the empty sink. She stood on her toes a moment and then she arched her back slightly, rising further on her toes, and as if her whole body was inflated with a single breath, she exhaled, slumping at the sink in sudden and profound diminishment, her body vibrating minutely as she braced herself to keep from falling to the floor. I can't go on like this, she said, her mouth hardly moving, as if she were cold. She stood and turned. I can't, Peter. I can't go on like this anymore.

She leveled at him terribly now, and she looked, Peter thought, gutted, like a house after a savage storm. That is despair, he thought— if you can just get up and touch her you will be her husband.

He rose and walked to her and put his arms around her. He wanted to tell her that he understood, that they shared a like despair, and that if they could just realize it together all would be fine. But he could not find those words. I met a man today, he said instead. At the pool, a swimmer.

Peter, are you listening to me, she whispered fiercely into his shoulder. I can't take another step like this. I'm dying.

Yes, he said. I understand. I am too. I'm trying to tell you something.

What are you trying to tell me?

I met a man.

For a moment they were in a complete unbridgeable privacy. He felt her falling a great distance, speeding through his arms. There was a muffled horn from the street, and laughter, a greeting, a door slamming somewhere in the apartment complex. She caught her breath. She leaned back and looked up at his face a long time. Her eyes were swollen and her mouth was a deeper bordeaux, and blowzy, and there was an almond glow about her skin. He realized that even before he had come home she had been crying. Are you saying—

Yes.

What are you saying?

Yes. I don't know.

When?

Today. I said so. Maybe all my life.

She looked into his eyes, one and then the other, as if she were measuring the yield of one truth against the other. Perhaps five minutes passed. She looked at him without reprieve. Peter, she whispered finally. She had never been so still, and yet it seemed to Peter that all the faces of her life, the oeuvre of her mien, her selves, those he'd heard of and seen in pictures, and the tidy array of faces he'd married, it seemed they passed across her face until they passed, or rather bypassed, the two of them as there they stood, and then she was unrecognizable. And he saw, from far in the reaches of her strange eyes, from the inscrutable underside of the world, he thought, a flicker, a flare begin to dawn as slow and circumspect as the day's dawn itself, until she seemed to shed and gain her innocence in a single stare, like a child who, with its finger along a blade or in a flame, experiences the first numb awareness of the ecstasy of pain. She was almost smiling; one corner of her mouth began to quiver and lift with that wry ascent to paradox that so quickly becomes a kind of irrepressible glory, and profoundly female. She began to walk him back to his chair, shaking her head back and forth slowly, her eyes wet and confounded and full of tragic resolution. When his calves pressed the edge of the seat he sat. Tell me about him, she said, and directly she had said it she clapped her hand over her mouth. With her other hand she began to loose the tie of her gown.

Are you laughing at me? he said.

Tell me about him, she said, sliding off her slippers.

I want to laugh, Peter said.

Her gown swung open. She squatted and unzipped his trousers and pulled down his boxer shorts and took his sex in her hand. Laugh, she said, looking up at him, her mouth trembling, expressions of indignation, seduction, and the spur to tears fleeing about her face like leaf-shadow. And rising now, laughing herself with a sound more like gasping for astonishment, or pleasure, she swung one leg over his thigh, and then the other, and then lowered herself upon his lap, her gown spread around her, his sex still in her hand. And he did fairly harden. And she placed him inside herself and began slowly to move. Tell me about him, she said.

Jennifer, he said.

Him, she said.

He was beautiful.

My God, she said, lifting up and angling herself the better to have him.

Not God, Peter said, moving into her now.

I don't care, she said.

Don't you? Peter said harshly. Don't you? Don't you?

God, she said. Just take me.

He thrust vigorously then, bracing himself with his hands and rising up off the chair.

Tell me, she whispered fiercely in his ear.

I'm going to come, he said.

And she stopped instantly, leaning back and looking into his eyes with some shifting admixture of compassion, arrogance, lust, pity, wonder, and terrible need. Let me watch you, she said. You never let me watch you. I've always wanted to watch you.

And she began to move again even as he started to come. He looked at her as long as he could and then he flung his hands over her face.

No, she said, knocking his arms away. She threw her arms about his neck, sobbing as his convulsions died into her.

He held her in stillness a long time after, listening to the house. At some point he shucked off his shoes and underwear and his trousers and stood and carried her into their bedroom and laid her down on the bed. He took off his shirt and moved naked alongside her, his body against her back, feeling her breathe. In the low light of the bedside lamp he studied her face. He looked at her skin, at the pores of her skin. He saw the faint sickle-shaped marks outlining her mouth, lines he had never seen before in repose, only when she smiled or frowned. Her mouth was dry; small flame-shaped flakes of skin rose upward on her lower lip like the peaks of spume upon ocean waves. He bent into her nape and inhaled her. It seemed to him that in a single breath he could imbibe her whole life, her childhood, her brief, rare, irrepressible moments of happiness, and her shattered dreams. It seemed to him that a multitude of lungs dilated throughout his body, that his body was a lung, that there was in him an infinite invitation to air. Her eyelids flickered, and he remembered the first time he had watched her dream. He leaned back and traced with his eyes the line of her neck from where it extended from the soft hair back of her head to her small, sharp shoulder. He looked at the wing of her scapula, rising and falling, or rather opening and closing in a breaking rhythm in time with her breath. Her skin—all human skin—seemed so frail, so thin, to house such subtle convergences. She seemed to him a delicate bird that had flown headlong into his care, given him her life. And it occurred to him with a resolute clarity that he had deceived her as he had deceived himself. It had so little to do with the swimmer, beautiful as he was. If they failed at marriage it would be because, undisguised, they did not help each other live. My god, he thought, marriage… marriage was not, as he had surmised just weeks before, some soft contract of mutual absorption, but something far stranger, and more harrowing. Perhaps it reached its shining significance only in the moment of its dissolution, like a god; perhaps it went on expanding, like a galaxy. His hand was poised over his wife's hair, not wanting to touch her lest he keep her from sleeping, and wanting all the same to stroke her into sleep. We can care for no one, he thought, beyond our ability to hurt them. And it was as if she heard his mind, for she turned and looked up at him and said, Peter, I'm so scared.

I know, he whispered. I am too. But I don't want to lie anymore.

Are you lying?

No, but inside.

Inside? Are you lying inside?

I don't know. I'm so glad it's winter. I need time.

Time for what?

Time to begin to think without lying.

I'm afraid, she said, that if I sleep when I wake up it will be like it was before.

It won't be, he said.

And he lay there with his arms around her, and she did finally sleep, and he felt that they were traveling, that if they looked out the window they would see earth and trees and cities moving by them, landscapes of places and peoples they had never heard of, or read about in the books of such things.

FICTION OPEN AWARD WINNERS

1ST PLACE
Daniel Villasenor receives $2000 for "To a Stranger."
Villasenor's bio is on page 62 preceding his story.

2ND PLACE
Jimmy Olsen receives $1000 for "Wormwood."

"Guess what else," she said, pouring two fresh rums. "They're all laughing at your legs because you keep wearing shorts after I've told you how many times men here don't wear short pants."

Jimmy Olsen is a native of Hoffman, Minnesota, and has degrees from St. Cloud State University and the University of Alabama. He's worked as a newspaper reporter, editor, and photographer. A life-long scuba diver (instructor since 1974), he lived five years in the Dominican Republic, where he taught English and owned a dive shop. He began writing fiction seriously in 1990, and since then has published short stories and the novel *Things in Ditches* (2000). His new novel, *The Poison Makers*, is scheduled for release from Capra Press in the fall of 2004.

3RD PLACE
John Stinson receives $600 for "Family."

They were one and the same squash, really, with that splendid name to catch them all, but the stores insisted on delineating them to create excitement, doubt, choice.

John Stinson, a graduate of Kenyon College, works for Teach For America in Baltimore. His writing has appeared in *Glimmer Train*, *Chicago Review*, *Berkeley Fiction Review*, the Baltimore *City Paper*, and the book *Split*, edited by Ava Chin.

*We invite you to visit **www.glimmertrain.com** to see a list of the top twenty-five winners and finalists. We thank all entrants for sending in their work.*

Here I express my obvious distaste for the new 1977 Ford LTD Country Squire Wagon. I am still haunted by the Energy Crisis. Barely visible here, our Pinto was much closer to my exacting environmental and safety standards.

Jonathan Kooker is a graduate of Syracuse University and the master's program in Creative Writing at Emerson College. A winner at age twenty-eight of the 1999 Virgin Fiction Contest from William Morrow Books, he works as a freelance writer in Chicago. "Vast Inland Sea" is his second story accepted for publication.

VAST INLAND SEA

Jonathan Kooker

Long before I think they're old enough to grasp the full scope of what I have to say, I begin telling Marie and Nellie of the vast Inland Sea that covered our area of the country millions of years ago. The sea was the richest, past or present, swarming with every single one of the earth's creatures at the time. All the elements and minerals were there—the building blocks—the same elements and minerals we can actually see in the rocks of our own gravel pit and in the walls of our own cellar. Without the vast Inland Sea, we wouldn't even be here. It was two months ago when I first began telling this story by sheepishly uttering the words, "Nothing lasts forever, but nothing can ever be truly gone."

Marie still looks confused, as if I'm her third-grade teacher introducing her to fractions. It's taken me four out of her ten years to understand her, to actually realize how she perceives the world, even though that changes every day. Suddenly it's all come into question—everything I say and promise—down to the frequency of meals to the nonexistence of a giant creature that may or may not live in the crawl space by her bedroom. I compliment her hair and she wants it straightened, fed up with her famous long black curls. Now she has stopped singing. Everywhere, all the time, Marie sang a soft tune, the intensity of which depended on the situation—loud and proud while playing on her bedroom floor or barely a hum when lying down to sleep. Now it's as if even singing out loud is too much of a risk.

But Nellie gulps my words like a goldfish on the floor an instant before I scoop her back up into her bowl. As her father, I have to admit I sometimes take an unfair advantage of my power over such a worshipful five year old. She has the only blue eyes of the family and the only straight hair. She can draw and there's a gift at work there. Her mind's eye seems wired directly to her hands, to her pencil, as my ear is to my hands, my guitar. This, her quiet voice, and her speculation on the world makes me wonder about the magnitude of her inner life. This makes me panic; everything she can look forward to—beautiful and horrifying—as a person of such vast sensitivity. She will need armor.

Of course, I've saved every drawing she's ever done. She draws with colored pencils now, with startling emotion. The one of the red house and the fantasy family of two-legged dogs I magnet to the refrigerator. The one of the farm underwater, the people floating askew amid sea monsters I do not. It's as if she already knows everything and can't bear to tell the world.

As Nellie became a little person, a thinking, cognizant entity that understood I and Other—as she became a challenge—I wanted more and more to hold onto the way in which I could become her whole world at the turn of a phrase and with the right mysterious tone. Whereas Marie bristles at the thought of a resplendent salinated pre-world, or anything I have to say lately for that matter, Nellie's face still relaxes into the wonderment I intend.

"Imagine the vast Inland Sea." At the time, I think it's the right way to go. Now is the time to fill their minds with a flame of wonder before the wind of the world starts snuffing it out. Honestly it's probably more interesting to me. I find myself searching the web for more details, more knowledge with which to dazzle my already dazzling daughters. I research plate tectonics, marine biology, carbon dating, and botany.

"Imagine the vast Inland Sea," I say. "Everything here," I gesture toward the horizon, toward the woods and the paddock, "everything here is because of that sea."

Marie follows my gaze, but again, that puzzled expression.

"How do trees live underwater?" she says.

"Not the trees," I say. "But the soil that the trees grow from."

"Everything is in the ocean?"

"From the ocean, yes."

"Even us?"

"Even us!" I say this with what I hope is contagious enthusiasm.

"Even Mommy?"

My expression falls for only an instant, but it's enough to make Marie's face change, too. Something hits the brakes hard in her mind just as it does in my own and I know I'll get no further tonight with my tales of the vast Inland Sea. Suddenly it's bedtime for the girls. I usher them upstairs and monitor their tooth-brushings and play their favorite song on my guitar. Marie doesn't sing along. The mood of the world changed suddenly, but I think I caught it in time; made it better before turning out the light.

Downstairs in the dining room I pour Scotch. It's romantic and therefore necessary. It's been weeks since I last did so, three weeks since I last allowed myself. On a psychology web site, I read it's crucial to avoid alcohol in times like these when things can fall down on you. Especially when it's late or early, or when it's suddenly quiet when you can hear the ticking of the cheap wall clock or the bubbler in the fish tank or the toilet that won't fill; when you watch a moth flutter up toward the light that will consume him, or when you suddenly smell the soil in the potted plants from the supermarket and your own body odor. That's the vulnerable time when I've decided it's okay to let a drink take over for you.

After it passes, after I replay the last two months in my mind for two hours, I find another dramatic mission; something, anything for the girls, and I'm at the computer again, printing mammoth JPEGs of wooly mammoths, creatures that roamed the earth and maybe even waddled in the vast Inland Sea. All I need is something to be successful at for someone else, and if that's what it takes to make it through the night, so be it. When I think of Shannon and me, all roads lead to failure. There's no two ways about it. My failure is an empirical fact. I could have been more of a husband instead of a father. Maybe things would be different if I spent as much time adoring Shannon as I do Marie and Nellie.

The next afternoon, Saturday, a Greenpeace solicitor comes to the door asking for the woman of the house. That's when I realize I don't even know what kind of man I'm becoming. I tell him she's dead. "God, I'm sorry," he says and turns away. Not ten minutes later Shannon calls and proves me a liar. I hear her typing as we talk. Nothing has ever bothered me more.

"You sound different," she says.

"Different how?"

"Like you didn't get enough sleep, Parker. As in none at all."

"Hmm."

"Anyway, I'm on my way. Will Nellie and Marie be ready by one?

"Ready and willing."

"So what happened last night?"

"Dinner, 'Proud Mary' on the guitar, tales of the vast Inland Sea. Stuff like that."

I wonder if Shannon has had any time between the love affair with the boss and the twelve-hour days peddling pills to consider something as big in scope as the vast Inland Sea. I wonder why I'm talking to the adulteress in the first place.

"Vast Inland what?"

"I didn't think so. It's common knowledge that millions of years ago, most of the country, including our home state of New Jersey, was covered with a warm, shallow salt-water sea, only about three thousand feet deep, in which there lived huge prehistoric monsters."

The typing stops. "You told Nellie a story including the words *prehistoric monster*?"

"They get quite a kick out of it. It's fun."

"Parker, she's five years old!" The typing resumes.

"She likes the stories."

"Don't scare Nellie. Not when she's getting adjusted to our big mess."

"I think you're overreacting, Shannon. And when you think about it, this is really your big mess."

"Parker, there was no Inland Sea in New Jersey. Maybe out west somewhere. The Great Plains."

"You see, I'm running damage control for the girls. It's the only reason we're even talking. And the vast Inland Sea was something like ninety million years ago."

"Whatever. I don't think so, is all."

"It's all true," I say. "Trust me."

"Don't scare Nellie."

"See you soon."

Here's another thing about the vast Inland Sea; it never really went anywhere. Aquifers and water tables and everything come back to the Inland Sea. The Grand Canyon, the Black Hills, and even New Jersey where we live. Just like there's a Law of Conservation of Energy (I can't wait until the girls are old enough for that one), the waters of the sea didn't really go anywhere. They simply changed forms. Water and mineral turned to sediment. Sediment turned to rock. The vast Inland Sea awaits us underground.

I find Nellie in the backyard digging with a wooden spoon from the kitchen. Our house is a small white one not far from the highway. The trees are thick and it's hilly, so if not for the noise, we'd never know how close we are to Interstate 80. Once upon a time it was part of a dairy farm. It was split up and sold off in pieces, ours being the farmhouse and the horse paddock. The very rich neighbors recently converted the barn into a stylish victory of home design. It's featured in a magazine that's sits on our coffee table month after month.

You can find strange and interesting things in the dirt on an old farm. Nellie knows this and usually digs on Saturday afternoons for the aforementioned farm treasures. On her side of the girls' room lies the collection: an Orange Crush bottle from the thirties; buttons; some of those square nails; and a very small horseshoe, the peculiarity of which kept me up the night she brought it inside. Currently she's begun the excavation of what looks like a baseball bat.

"Daddy, it's wood. It's buried. But we could dig it up and burn it in the fireplace." Of course, Nellie is filthy—covered in dirt as to be expected when digging in the yard. The problem is she's wearing the dress her mother will expect to see entirely presentable in an hour. Shannon is taking the girls with her to the company picnic. Every one of the pharmaceutical reps from the East Coast gather there once a year. The boyfriend, Bradley—the regional boss—will be in attendance, but they're meeting at the picnic per my request. I will not allow Shannon arriving to pick up the girls with a strange man behind the wheel. The girls don't know about Bradley yet. It's part of our plan as Shannon explores her feelings for him before undertaking anything drastic like divorce.

"It's definitely wood," I say and kneel down to her level. My hand clears away more of the dirt to reveal metal. It's not a bat, it's a handle. Could be a shovel or an old plow. Marie calls from the house, asking if she actually has to wear a dress to the picnic. I say yes. In fact, I have her don her finest for the occasion. Then I tell her to come out into the yard and help us dig.

At first Marie will have none of it. But as always, Nellie's enthusiasm is contagious and soon even this most world-weary ten year old is swept away by her own imagination.

"Maybe it's just the tip," Marie says. "What if it goes down ten feet?"

This concerns Nellie. "Then we'll never get it!"

I have a good idea what we're dealing with—most likely a kitchen or camp implement of some kind—and that our work is most likely almost done, but it's important to keep a game alive.

"We'll get it out," I say. "Remember when we found the old washtub? That was a big sucker, but we got it. That's how people used to take baths. Outside in a tub."

"Sounds posh," Marie says. It's a catch phrase at her school this spring, always used in derision with an air of sophistication, as in, "Pretty posh bike you got there," if it's not the favored brand.

88   *Glimmer Train Stories*

"Want to know where that word came from?" I say.

An emphatic "No" from Marie.

"It's from when people from London sailed to South Africa." Nellie has uncovered the entire handle and has dug around a circular piece of metal, alternately digging with her hands and unconsciously wiping them on the back of her dress. Marie is much more careful, but she's sitting on her knees, which are black with dirt underneath where she can't see them.

"The richest people paid more money to ride Portside out and Starboard side home so they could always see the shore. P.O.S.H. Get it? If something's expensive or ritzy, it's Posh."

Nellie reaches deeper into hole, then makes the announcement. "It's a pot!"

With both hands she drags a copper pot from the ground like a sapling. It's a big, deep one with not one but two huge wooden handles. A stock pot, maybe. Nellie holds it aloft, where it wobbles above her tiny arms.

"It's the poshest!" she cries. "Let's wash it."

"I'll put it in the dishwasher," Marie says, then reconsiders. "But it might get broken. It's pretty old."

"To the kitchen," I say. "Marie and I will shine this pot up good by hand. Nellie, you call the National Association of Historical Pots and give them the full report."

Marie and Nellie stand and I see what I have done to their dresses, which makes my stomach jump. It's almost one, so we all convene to the kitchen where the pot truly does come clean, and even gets a quick polish so I can show Marie and Nellie the bright copper. They hear the car pull up in the driveway and run to greet Shannon while I finish washing up, then follow.

Shannon is on her knees in front of the girls alternately laughing in shock and trying in vain to clean their hands with tissue. I'm not surprised she can get somewhat of a kick out of this sabotage. I am surprised to see Bradley step out of the car. It's a nice car; the BMW he bought two years ago when he lost his last job. Who spends forty grand on a car the week he loses his job?

He's wearing khaki shorts with a braided leather belt dangling just the right way, a short sleeved polo, and loafers without socks. Sunlight glints from the brass buckles. It's a perfect stereotype Shannon and I used to joke about.

"Parker," he says. "Hope you don't mind me tagging along. Didn't make much sense to make two trips between here and home."

"This really makes it," I say as I shake his hand with my filthy one. "I ask for one goddamned thing."

"We're sorry. It didn't make much sense to make two trips."

"One thing. And I get this."

"I'm sorry," he says. "You've been a good sport."

I make sure the girls aren't watching. "What the *fuck* is that supposed to mean?"

Shannon stands and balls the tissues dramatically. Marie and Nellie stand side by side as if squished together by some unseen force. Again I have caused the mood of the world to turn on a dime and the tension makes colors more vivid and the smells earthier.

"Sorry, girls," Shannon says. "I can't take you to the picnic like that."

"But Mom," they sing. "It was an accident."

"And I'm afraid we can't wait for you to get cleaned up and dressed."

She says this to me, not the girls, and I panic.

"Don't punish them," I say. "I'm responsible. You know that."

"Sorrys all around, I guess. We're late already."

I recognize her expression from only the worst arguments we've ever had, the face that says she's prepared to drop a bomb and do whatever it takes to get at me. But this isn't about getting at me. I mutter a word under my breath.

"Witch."

"Don't call Mommy that!" Marie says.

"Yes," says Bradley. "Don't talk to her that way. Not in front of the girls."

"Give Mommy the pot!" Nellie cries.

Not in front of the girls. Is that what he just said?

"Marie. Nellie. This afternoon Daddy can tell you more stories about the vast Inland Sea."

"The vast inland what?" Bradley asks.

"Tell him, Parker."

He really did just say not in front of the girls.

All I can think of to say is, "It's something from a long time ago. From this part of the country a few million years ago."

"I don't think so, Parker."

"Hmm?"

"Not this part of the country," Bradley says. "I don't think it was even really a country that far back. I don't even think the Rocky Mountains were around then."

Nellie, even Marie stare with great interest. He's captured their full attention and I am speechless. Small. The roles have changed. I am on the outside.

"It was all one big land mass at that point," Bradley says. "And I'm afraid we're a little too high above sea level for any inland seas in this neck of the woods. Right, honey?"

"Daddy said giant fish bones might even be in our own back-yard," Nellie says. She's defending me and it's more than I can bear.

"Stop," Shannon says, sensing a threshold has been reached, that to go any further might cause irrevocable damage. "We've got to go."

"But, Mommy," Marie says in tears. It's the most emotion I've seen her express since she helped her own mother move boxes from our bedroom into the station wagon two months ago.

"I love you both," Shannon says, "but I have to go right now. I'm really, really sorry."

A hundred ten to a hundred eighty-five million years ago in the Cretaceous Period of the Mesozoic Era, a rise in sea level flooded what would become the North American continent with a shallow Inland Sea. The Colorado Sea was the greatest of the North American Mesozoic seas, and extended all the way from Mexico up into the Arctic, covering most of central North America.

At the eastern gateway to Yosemite is Mono Lake. Like many of the lakes in the Great Basin, including the Great Salt Lake, it has no outlet to our modern sea. The water is hyper-salinated with a high concentration of carbonates. They say it's bitter and slippery, that there's a lot of salt and baking soda in Mono Lake. That's where we're going; where there's still something left, where dark clouds shroud mineral towers and where John Muir said snowy swans line the dusty shore just like they did millions of years ago. We are almost there.

Of course Nellie shares my enthusiasm for such an impromptu trek across country. Marie worries over school days missed and the fact that we didn't lock the house. I tell them it will be safe with Mom and Bradley, assuming she called the house after the picnic to check on the girls. That would have been almost twenty hours ago now.

Shannon and Bradley drove away yesterday afternoon with that air of sophistication that accompanies pity. The shock with which I realized how much everything has changed caused me to float out from myself. It's the horror that comes with the mind fighting to process the unimaginable. That's when I knew we would get in the car and leave that instant. That's when I realized I seek redemption in the waters of the vast Inland Sea.

I'm not exactly sure what to do when we get there—how long we'll stay. Maybe we'll just observe. I'll show Marie and Nellie that the sea does in fact still exist. Here will be the proof, and we will glean as much wisdom from the ancient sea as possible. Maybe it will be a paradox—that the most important things don't really change even though of course they do. Maybe it will be some kind of collective internal epiphany—that the vast Inland Sea is the infinite longing in our hearts, the wishes that will never die, and the wants that may or may not be fulfilled. Maybe there will be no wisdom and that non-wisdom will be enough. Maybe the vast Inland Sea is one of those unchanging, unfathomable constants to take comfort in. These are things I must figure out before we decide how to proceed from here; how to keep going in the face of so much actual and assumed uncertainty with the same sense of hopeful transcendence that got us this far in the first place.

SILENCED VOICES:
ALI LMRABET

by Siobhan Dowd

Morocco, since it ceased to be a French protectorate, has boasted three kings. The longest serving of these, Hassan II, ruled the country for thirty-eight years, up until 1999. For most of this time, freedom of expression did not fare well. PEN, the writers' association, had several cases of important literary figures—Abdelkader Chaoui and Abraham Serfaty spring to mind—who languished behind bars for many years before they were finally released. However, toward the end of King Hassan's life, there was a thaw. Gradually the press became less fettered; cases against writers dropped off; human-rights groups found grounds for optimism. Hopes surged when King Mohammed VI succeeded his father. In a television address shortly after King Hassan's death, he pledged that he would institute a constitutional monarchy, allow political pluralism, and foster democratic freedoms.

Glimmer Train Stories, Issue 50, Spring 2004
©2004 Siobhan Dowd

This was followed by specific promises to protect freedom of expression. He described the press as "one of the pillars of our plan for a modernized, democratic society." Despite these words, the number of actions against journalists and writers have unfortunately mounted again. A new anti-terrorism law, passed in May 2003, is partly to blame. It provides for prison terms for certain kinds of expression, and its over-broad language allows for a wide scope. Any "attack on Islam, the monarchy, or territorial integrity" made in the press can land its author a jail term of between three and five years.

One of the early victims of the renewed tightening up is Ali Lmrabet. The editor of two weekly newspapers, *Demain Magazine* and *Douman*, he is serving a three-year prison term for "insulting the person of the king," and committing an "offense against the monarchy" and "an offense against territorial integrity." He has also been fined 20,000 dirham (about $2,300). His case has caused a storm of international protest.

A bespectacled, outspoken man in his mid-forties, Lmrabet is no stranger to harassment from the state authorities. In November 2001, he was convicted for "disseminating false information which undermines public order or is likely to undermine it." The charge was related to an article in *Demain Magazine* about an alleged plan to sell a royal palace to foreign investors for conversion into a tourist venue. The judge condemned him to four years' imprisonment: but, as is usual in Morocco, he was allowed to remain free while appealing the sentence.

Despite this earlier sentence hanging over him, Lmrabet continued to publish whatever he wished and campaigned volubly for political change. He serves as Moroccan representative for the international press-freedom group Reporters Sans Frontières, and regularly expresses his views in interviews to foreign journals. A few days before his most recent court case, he gave an interview to *El Mundo* in Spain in which he called Morocco a country with a "light" dictatorship that had no definite direction to offer Moroccans. He called for an urgent review of the constitution, and said Moroccans today want a king who is only a "symbol" of the nation. He noted that the powers that be are unable to tolerate satire, caricature, or any real criticism.

Siobhan Dowd

On April 17, 2003, Lmrabet was told at the Rabat airport that he could not leave the country, because a case was being prepared against him. Several articles and cartoons in his magazines were cited in the prosecution's case: one was an interview with a former political prisoner who advocates the right to self-determination for the

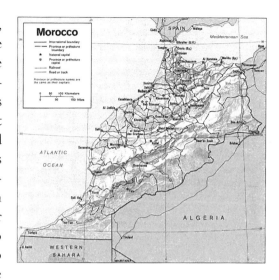

Sahrawi people in Western Sahara; another was a cartoon about the annual allowance that the Moroccan Parliament grants the royal family; a third was a pithy photomontage on Morocco's history of slavery, featuring well-known political personalities. In May 2003, he was summoned to answer the charges in court. In protest against the lawsuit, he began a hunger strike. However, on May 21 he was again condemned to four years' (later reduced to three years') imprisonment and arrested there and then. The court claimed there were "special circumstances" in his case that justified his immediate detention.

As soon as he was taken to jail, Lmrabet declared he would continue fasting until freed. On May 26 he was transferred to Avicennes Hospital in Rabat, apparently in a serious condition, with vision and kidney complications. He continued fasting until June 23, when Prince Moulay Hicham al-Alaoui, a cousin of the King, visited him. It is thought that the two arrived at an understanding, but whatever this understanding was, Ali Lmrabet remains in prison.

Concerns about his frail health persist, as he reportedly is without the full medical care he requires. His fiancée in Spain spearheads an active campaign for his release. In September she mounted an exhibition dedicated to him. His supporters worldwide have signed petitions and mounted internet appeals. Amnesty International has adopted him as a prisoner of conscience. His case was chosen by PEN to mark the Day of the Imprisoned Writer on November 15, 2003.

Letters politely requesting that Ali Lmrabet receive full medical care and that he be accorded amnesty can be sent to:

His Majesty King Mohammed VI
The Royal Palace
Rabat
The Kingdom of Morocco
Fax: 011 212 37 76 85 15

Siobhan Dowd of International PEN's Writers-in-Prison Committee in London writes this column regularly, alerting readers to the plight of writers around the world who deserve our awareness and our writing action.

Photo credit: Hank Meals

I think this is me, but each of my two brothers think it's them, too.
We are all close in age, and, at that time, spent a lot of time together,
playing and fighting. But I swear I remember standing in the little
alleyway on the side of the house where we stored our bikes and
garbage cans, and poking my head through the little window while
my dad's friend, a professional photographer, focused and snapped.

Frances Lefkowitz has published short stories in *Fiction, Hope Magazine, Passages North,* and *Northeast Journal.* Her essays, reviews, and journalism have appeared in *Poets & Writers, Yankee, Island,* and other consumer magazines and newspapers. Her books on Marilyn Monroe and David Letterman were published by Chelsea House in their Pop Culture Legends series. Awards include the Fellowship in Literature from the Rhode Island State Council on the Arts, the Martin Dibner Fellowship for Maine Writers, and a stay at the Hedgebrook Writing Retreat in Langley, Washington. Born and raised in San Francisco, she now lives in coastal Maine and works as an editor for *Body & Soul* (formerly *New Age Journal*).

FIGHTING WITH FIRE

Frances Lefkowitz (signature)

Frances Lefkowitz

My father was an East Coast Jew who headed west out of desperation and a romantic notion of finding himself by wandering amongst ranchers and riflemen. He left the gaggle of women who clustered about him in New Jersey, the aunts, sisters, grandmothers combing his hair, whispering in his ear, picking the lint off his sweater, and intended on working the railroad or maybe the waterfront, whatever he could do to get money for food and beer and a few hours now and then with a woman of questionable morals. He hitchhiked three thousand miles—this was in 1956, when you could still do that—to see how the Pacific differed from the Atlantic, and was all set to spend his young manhood in motion, sleeping in doorways and bus stations, waking up in towns he'd never heard of, holing up in the corner of seedy bars with the afternoon drinkers who'd come in for some relief from the heat and the emptiness of their lives.

Unfortunately for him, he hadn't even reached the ocean when he wandered right into my mother in what is known as the Great Valley of California, only three months after he left the east. She was something of a renegade herself, having left her family back in Abilene, but she was more Texan than not, and that was as exotic as Chinese to my father. It was his way of talking, which made him seem like he knew what caused the world to go round, that most charmed my mother, who had moved to Madrone to work as assistant to the local vet and whose knowledge was more practical. My father was so smart he forgot, as those afflicted with love often do, that he too was a slave to biology, and he watched my mother's stomach grow swiftly into a chain around his neck. But Carl's people had long admired sacrifice, so he did the right thing, snuffed out his dreams like baking soda to a grease fire, and settled himself and his new wife into a wooden house on top of a long slope five miles outside of town. As for my mother, she should have known better; she'd been watching animals mate, birth, and die since before she could talk.

Carl knew just enough about the world to make you think he'd traveled all over. But all he'd ever seen was nineteen of our own states before he settled down and tried to pretend that a bad seed can grow a good crop. If you ask me, he should have gone through whatever hardship, heartbreak, and moral or physical dilemma was necessary to have that baby taken out, or leave Ruth to birth it on her own. He should have gathered up his newfound hope and continued on to the coast or north to the Rockies, where men still make a living roping cows. Then at least, several years down the road, his tryst in the San Joaquin Valley would have been not forgotten, but over and done with, a spiny little memory.

That baby, of course, was me. And, as if the cry of a newborn could bring joy into a home, Carl and Ruth kept on having babies. Jason, two years younger than me, was a fragile boy who invited protection. Then there was Daniel, straight-haired like my mother, and the babies, Minnie and Rosa. The subsequent children were better received than myself, since, being the first, I was the one that put the plug in whatever small possibilities my parents' lives held. It didn't help that I came out a girl with the temperament of my mother and the looks of my father, with his dark eyebrows and black curls. They called me Jess, short for Jessica, though my mother used my name as little as possible. Whatever mothering Ruth had in her she reserved for the ones that came after me, and though Carl could see the unfairness in this he was accustomed to taking orders from women, and let it be. While my father had resigned himself that his youth had been snapped away from him, my mother never quite accepted the fact that her first love would be her last, and she used me as a sponge to soak up her resentment.

My mother was not one of those sentimental animal lovers who bring home stray dogs or birds with broken wings. She knew as much as Otis Dow, the large animal vet she worked for, and could have been a vet herself, if things had been different. There's a lot of divining to the medical sciences—not magic, but listening and watching for clues, knowing how to add them up. My mother had a gift in this; she had at least six senses and a clear, uncluttered mind that contrasted sharply with Otis Dow's, especially after his wife died and he got into the wine. He once killed a man's prize horse from giving it the wrong kind of shot, and from then on Otis Dow had my mother in charge of mixing the medicines. Most people would not let him tend to their animals unless Ruth was present.

When I was a baby, Carl got a job as a schoolteacher and Ruth, who wasn't about to let a child get between her and her work, brought me on her calls. The first time I remember seeing her work with an animal, I was four years old, standing on a pile of sawdust in the corner of a barn, minding my brother Jason. On the other side of the gate, Ruth was huddled over a cow with the farmer and Otis Dow.

The cow, pregnant and fat as a tractor, was on the ground with long wet strings of mucous spread on the hay all around her. My mother leaned down and put her whole arm inside the animal, which writhed like a car out of control. It looked like she was going to send my mother flying out of the stall, and I had to hold Jason tight to keep him from crying. But Ruth pulled her arm out, wiped the red mess on a towel, and told Otis Dow the calf was dead. Then they went out to the car.

The only sound now was the cow breathing, loud and desperate as wind. The farmer got on his knees and stroked her like she was his woman or his child. He said words to her that were so soft I climbed off the pile and walked over to hear.

"Sweet girl. That's my sweet, sweet girl." His hand rubbed circles on her big cheek and up to her temple. "You'll do just fine."

Ruth and Otis Dow came back in, carrying a case, and my mother uncapped a hypodermic as big as a plunger. The farmer did not move and neither did I.

"You're supposed to be looking after your brother," said my mother, watching the needle rise. I went back to the sawdust, put my arm around Jason, and listened as the farmer again whispered those soft, soft words.

Madrone is cropland primarily, and most of the livestock that Ruth and Otis Dow tended to were animals that farmers kept for their own or for selling locally. We lived in one of the largest fertile valleys in the world, five hundred miles long from the Shasta Dam down to the Tehachapi range in the south, though it wouldn't have been fertile if people hadn't figured out how to get it wet. Canals and aqueducts run the length of the valley, gathering water from streams and rivers, and feeding it into long metal arms that carry the water out to where it doesn't belong. It hasn't always been this dry. Before there were people, this valley was a part of the Pacific, an inland sea, with the San Francisco Bay as its isthmus out to the ocean. In winter, with the rains, it can look like it's underwater again, and I used to stand on our porch above the flooded fields like Noah on his ark.

The house, one story, low to the ground, was not the home my mother had dreamed of. It was made of grayed, unpainted wood that gave it a sour look, even on blue-bright days, and had a roof that sagged like a bad spine. There were six rooms with very few windows for all the sun that could have come in, and a little shed off the side of the driveway. But Ruth kept that house clean, and bent over backward to pay the mortgage every month.

Our house was built on sadness the way some houses are built on stone. Sadness filled the well and seeped in through the faucets, causing us to bathe and drink and soak our feet in that tepid water. There was the sadness of the marriage, based in poverty and carelessness, and the sadness of the land the house sat on, pale and brittle with soil that seemed forever thirsty. In the middle of this most fertile of valleys, surrounded by nut trees and orchards, we were perched on a long, grassy hill, green in winter, sand-colored in summer, with a lone tree, a sprawling live oak covered in Spanish moss. My father's people had made a history of being sad and chased and stolen from, while Ruth had it beaten into her by her mother, who she never talked to, and her father, who never talked to her.

It wasn't until I was old enough to go to school that I realized how quiet we lived. Mornings the bus, the same bright yellow as our pencils, picked me up at the end of the road and transported me to noise, colors, and perfect little desks in rows. At recess we were let out like bees from a jar, and my playmates, mostly boys, accepted me without question. But by sixth grade our differences could no longer be ignored.

One afternoon at Weston Arey's house on Nickel Bluff, a half-hour walk from my house, I was under the front porch shooting rubber-band rifles at anything that moved. None of them could aim, but I hit the neighbor's black-eyed mutt on the haunches and sent him yelping down the road. "Hey," said Raymond, the puniest of the three. "No girls can shoot like that."

It wasn't Weston who started it, but he joined in soon enough when they demanded proof that I wasn't a boy. Two of them grabbed my head and turned me over, pushing my face into the peach-colored dirt. "Know what else?" Weston said. "Her Pa is from New Jew-sy."

Then there was a hand reaching under me, grabbing onto my zipper, and a bunch more tugging on my jeans till they were at my ankles. I took my punishment in silence, which only seemed to aggravate them more. "Jewsy, Jewsy," they chanted. Then they turned me over and little Raymond took his rifle to my panties and pulled them down.

"What do you know, she's a girl after all," he said.

It took them less than a minute to get out of there and leave me alone, half-naked, with a mouthful of sand. But I stayed under that porch for hours, long after Weston's parents came home and the sounds of dinner filtered down through the wood. Finally night fell, I crawled out, and snuck home.

My father, though he was educated, had a naïve faith in the justness of the human animal and believed that respect would come to those who worked hard and lived honest. But you can't turn a pig into a cow no matter how hard you try, and so he learned not to see what he didn't want to. Ruth, on the other hand, had grown up proud, with fighting instincts, and was accustomed to the prairie justice of her home state. She refused to accept anything that she did not like, and she did not like being embarrassed by her children.

That evening when I got home from Weston's, she saw me coming in the door. "What do you got on your face and where have you been?" she said from the front room where she was reading to the babies. The lamplight circled them in a warm glow, like a painting. But she wasn't looking for an answer, and turned back to her story as I went down the dark hallway toward the room I shared with Jason. My father looked up from the kitchen table as I passed by. "I got a plate here for you, Jess."

I ate in the bathroom while I washed, and through the walls I could hear Carl whisper. "Ruth, please. She's a child. Won't you show some concern?"

"It's time she got some skin on her," said my mother. "She's too soft as it is, and things are not going to get any easier."

The secret to revenge is patience, something I had a lot of practice in. Acting rashly makes a person careless; besides, if you wait long enough you avoid being suspected. For most people, the sweetness of revenge comes from the accomplishment, the boasting. But my father's humility had infected me, and it was the justness of revenge, the way it righted things, that satisfied.

A couple weeks went by and then I went back to Weston's house and laid out a thin circle of brush kindling around it. I followed the circle with a quart of kerosene and a match, then crawled into the bushes off to the side and watched it light up like one of Saturn's rings. By the time the Areys came streaming onto the porch, pouring water from kitchen bowls, the fire was mostly gone, leaving just a fine black line etched into the dirt. Most people like the look of a fire at night, but I prefer to watch it in the daylight, the colors melting into the air so you can't tell where exactly the fire is or where it's headed. A day fire looks wild, limitless, and there is nothing so satisfying as watching pale tongues of fire lick, then swallow, whatever is in the way.

I didn't go out looking for reasons to set fires—they're all around you if you pay attention—I paced myself and exercised caution. The power of a lit match inspires respect and I tried not to get distracted by pettiness. That fall I made my second fire, in Principal Scanlon's office, after he put me in the dumb class because I didn't like to talk. It was just a little wastebasket fire, but it got him uneasy, which was all I wanted to do. By the end of high school, I had made eleven fires, but I never so much as singed anyone. It's sleeping people who get hurt by fire, and setting them in the daytime I caught people awake or gone.

It was always the same: the weeks of planning filled me with a throbbing, like I was touching the core of the earth, while everything around me faded. Then the colors, the shapes bold and sharp, the sheer heat of the fire. Flame, smoke, and, afterward, the sad line of ash. Climbing the long slope back home, the reds, oranges, yellows still glowing inside me, I'd reach the crest, see the house, gray as ever, and fall back to the ground with a thud.

Fire, in farming country, is a serious matter, though it is not always dry and flammable in the valley. I grew up amongst people who hoped everyday for rain, then cursed it when it came down, for it had no-where to go. Just under the topsoil is a shallow but impermeable layer of clay that can keep the fields saturated to the point of rotting. It was only after the aqueducts were built that the engineers realized that getting the water to leave was as much a problem as getting it to come. Much of it remains on the surface, and when the cool air of winter arrives, it mixes with the surface water to make a thick ground fog, what we call tule fog, white as smoke and almost as dangerous. But the water, when it got into the earth, produced wondrous things. All around us the land was carved into rows—narrow, unnatural shapes— with cauliflower, lettuce, and spinach growing low to the ground, and trees that blossomed into plums and pistachios. You could drive all day in any direction and not escape the rows or the brown bodies hunched over them.

When I was twelve, I snuck down to the fields on a Saturday in picking season. The sun had not yet risen when I got on line with the Mexicans, who were drinking chocolate out of metal cups. They paid little attention to me and we worked the rows, bending over, tugging, shaking the dirt free, till the sky was bleached with light, and sweat was dripping into our eyes. The truck came around and we threw our sacks in the back and climbed on to get out of the sun for lunch. I had brought only an orange and water in a canteen, but a man in a red bandana gave me a thick tortilla and a hard-boiled egg. "*Comida para segar la comida*," he said, cracking another egg against his knee. Food to harvest the food.

My hands, stained green, gave me away, and after a few weeks my mother figured out what I was doing. Otis Dow's was not a thriving business, and my father seemed to work all the time with nothing to show for it. But, as Ruth reminded us nearly every day, my parents owned their house and kept us fed and respectable. The last thing she wanted was for people to think we were poor. One night when she got home, she called me onto the porch.

"What are you doing acting like a field hand with the Mexicans and transients and God knows who else?" It was dusk but there were no lights on in the house. Jason and the children were inside, their faces against the window.

"What the hell do you need money for?" she asked. "Don't you know your father and I work hard so we can live decent?"

I kept my eyes to the floorboards and my mouth shut.

"I should tan your hide," she said, raising her hand. My mother rarely hit me, but the threat of it was always there, especially if Carl wasn't around. I braced myself, but through the purple air I made out her face, worn, weary. She'd done all she was going to do to me.

"Go on, now," she sighed, like a candle going out, and I backed into the doorway leaving her invisible.

My father, in contrast, could care less what I did with my time so long as I wasn't harming anyone. "I just want my children to be happy. That's all I could hope for," he used to say, as if burying his own desires could somehow cause his children's to flourish. How could he not know that everything he and Ruth did to themselves they did to us; that for every desire they squelched, they put out one of ours as well.

I would have loved to have seen my mother as a young woman, her hair long and straight, her hands strong from reaching inside animals and pulling out their reluctant calves. Even with her thick riding legs there must have been a softness there, an opening. I pity my father, dark, full of thinking, but overcome with a rash of optimism, running up against a headstrong beauty like Ruth, whose very footsteps demonstrated how solidly she was planted on the ground. She had no schooling to speak of, but she knew how to do things, and it was this concreteness that must have attracted him as much as her tanned skin, brown eyes, and full bosom, which she tucked into a man's button-up shirt. It was only after they married that he watched her words dry up like a summer rainstorm and all that strength turn against him. What little optimism the West had bought him dried up as well.

Even the cautious stumble, and it happened to me the spring I turned sixteen. John Carey, who owned four hundred acres of fruit trees in our area, had found Jason building a fort out in the northwest section of his land. John Carey didn't like us; he thought my father was womanish for wearing glasses and teaching school. He called the goddamned sheriff, who drove up with Jason, green, shaking, in the back of the squad car. My mother was filled with a shame that quickly turned to rage, and though she didn't blame Jason, she kept us out of school for a week.

Out on the Carey property, about forty-five minutes by bike, there was a decrepit old barn with a small outbuilding in even worse shape. I got there on a Saturday about eight in the morning and started pouring kerosene. I didn't want the barn, just the shed, but I wanted a small explosion, a pop, a ball of fire. I hadn't taken the matches out, but the air was thick with fumes when Bradford Carey, John's son, came out of the barn. He looked like he just woke up and we stood there for a moment like two cats wondering who'd caught who.

"Well, well," Carey said. "Little Jess Miller. This how you spend your weekends?" He was in the doorway, shadowed, and he started toward me.

His face, now that I could see it, looked like it had been kicked; there was green and purple around one of his eyes and a fresh scab along the temple. He felt me looking at it and reached up to touch the scab. Carey's father was a drinking man, and it was not uncommon for Carey to miss school, then show up with the leftovers of a bruise. It was odd to be on equal footing with him; he was a senior, three years older than me, and his people owned land and hired people to work it. He had a car and he dated Connie Downs, though her parents did not approve. But it would be embarrassing if anyone found out that Carey had been beat so bad he had to spend the night in one of his father's barns.

"You ain't too bad," he said, lifting the fuel can out of my hands, then rubbing a clump of my hair between his fingers like I was a horse he was thinking about buying. "Kind of foreign looking."

His fingers traveled down the back of my neck to the triangle between my shoulder blades and I felt my footing slip away. "How about if we go inside," he said, nodding toward the barn, "and work out a bargain." Then he took me by the elbow, almost polite, and led me in.

It was the opposite of fire, dark, wet. He pushed me into the ground and underneath it, till my body went numb and couldn't feel a thing. He sounded like a bull running, and he looked like one, too, his mouth loose and slobbering, his eyes pulled up and back. When he was done, he held me still and closed his eyes, and there was a moment of breathing before the sound of zippers and gates and footsteps.

I stayed there, eyes closed, till there was no sound at all. Then I went back out, picked up the can, and continued dousing the shed. I walked the sweet line of fuel over to the barn, inside the doorway, around the stalls, on the pile of straw where we had been. The flame made the outbuilding sputter and fizz, then followed the fuse to the barn. There was no wind and the fire ate its way leisurely, in thick orange waves.

We lived alongside a crack, even longer than the valley, where the earth is trying to break away from itself. But the two pieces, the size of continents, are welded together, and can only move sideways, one heading north, the other heading south. Every year this seam rips a few more inches, causing spasms, often gentle, sometimes fierce. But the coming together of continents is as violent as the breaking apart. Millions of years ago, when the pieces collided, the earth erupted into mountains. The Central Valley is surrounded by these mountains, and, depending on the weather, I used to be able to make out the peaks of the Sierra Nevada, the great range that runs the length of the valley, protecting it from the desert. To the west, the humbler coastal ranges kept us from the ocean, which I had seen only in pictures.

The barn fire made the paper, but Carey kept his mouth shut. Still, I was relieved when school ended and he left to join the service. That summer I was allowed to work, and I got a job at the coffee shop on Route 38. Gray-haired Mavis Knight taught me how to start the brewer and pour from the glass pots without getting burned by the wet clouds of steam. I spent as much time there as possible, clearing the chrome-edged tables, wiping them down, and setting them up again with white napkins and shiny spoons.

The shop served locals as well as those who traveled alone, driving to Salinas to pick lettuce or down to Barstow for the olives or what-ever else was ripe. Some craved conversation, and their talk was full of the names of places and the roads that took you there. I liked being the link between the customers and what they wanted, and I liked the smell of coffee, sharp, sweet, that stayed on me long after I got home. Every week I put my paycheck in the bank and watched the numbers grow like inches marked on a wall.

Because I was earning money, something Ruth now approved of, she stopped insisting that I have supper with the family. I could work as many hours as I wanted, even after school started, as long as I got my chores done. My father tried to get me home most Sundays for dinner, and, after the dishes were done and the younger kids in bed, we often sat up together at the kitchen table.

One day, about two years later—I was eighteen and about to graduate high school—Brad Carey came into the coffee shop with two of his buddies. He was on leave and he looked smart and citified compared to his friends, who worked as foremen on his father's land, and were covered in dust. He didn't make much of seeing me again, just winked on his way in and out. But an hour later he was back.

He strolled up to the counter and ordered coffee, black. I didn't know what states or countries he'd been to, but something was different about him. He walked lighter and his ears, made plain by the haircut, were pale and tender as shoots.

"Hey, Jess," he said, pouring sugar from the jar. "I've been thinking about you." I avoided his eyes and went back to stacking glasses under the counter.

"Yeah, there was something I always wanted to ask you," he said. I went on stacking, hoping he'd stop right there. "Is Jess your real name?"

I stood up, but didn't say anything.

"Come on," he said, his lips curling into a smile. "That's a boy's name. What is it really?"

"Jessica," I said, taking a sponge to the little white grains he'd spilled on the counter. "But no one calls me that."

"Well that's what I'm gonna call you." He brought the cup to his mouth. "Jessica."

There were two old men in the corner booth, the only ones in the shop, and I was afraid they'd heard us. Still, it felt good, him leaning on his elbows and calling me by a new name.

After my shift I met him at the café down the highway and let him buy me dinner and tell me about where he'd been and what he'd seen. The way he talked was like the world was open and waiting for him to come visit, and I wouldn't have minded if some of that attitude rubbed off on me. We went for a drive in his car, out to his father's orchard, where small green plums were turning to purple, and we slid down under the branches. The breeze washed over us, warm and quiet, as we undid our clothes and helped ourselves to each other, touching skin to skin, muscle to muscle, bone to bone.

Some seek pleasure while others just hope for relief. Brad Carey, he was not like people I knew. He had been away and he smelled of the ocean, clean, moist, salty. He helped himself to what he wanted and moved swiftly on. He was back at the base long before I realized that

I had made the same mistake as my mother and forgotten that desire did not exempt you from the laws of nature. But unlike my mother I did not see the baby as the end to a courtship that had just begun, and I intended to get rid of the thing before I started to show.

One evening in late June, we were standing in the kitchen, Ruth and I, scraping off the dinner plates. Doors and windows were open to discourage the heat, and the sounds of my brothers and sisters yelling drifted in.

"Have you seen a doctor?" she asked.

"Uh, no."

"It's time you did," she said, pushing bread crusts into the garbage. "I know one in Cordova you could see." My mother was not an evil woman; she was strong, decisive, and I am grateful to her for passing some of that fortitude along to me. But she had a blind spot, and that moment I saw that it was not going to go away. All my life I had been waiting for her to turn tender toward me, but it was never going to happen.

"But you better do it soon," she said, turning on the water and loading the dishes into the sink.

"Do what?" I asked, though I knew full well what she was talking about.

"Have it taken out."

A new idea caught hold of me right then and it made me feel thick and powerful, like I was full of money. I had something that was mine and she couldn't take it from me. "I'm not going to," I said, plunging my hands into the water. "I want to have it."

"What the hell are you thinking?" She threw a handful of silverware into the sink. "You'll do no such thing."

But everything around me had faded, her voice, the heat, and all I could feel was warm, silky water on my hands and the sweet sensation of things being righted.

There's not much in this world you can count on, least of all seeds, and toward the beginning of August I began to get sick. It came on fast, and I was retching five or six times a day till one morning I sat on the toilet with my head against the cool sink, afraid to move. The pain seared through my gut till finally I looked in the bowl, saw blood, and knew I had lost it.

I had missed a week of work and all I wanted to do was to get back there. The next day I went in, but I was weak and flimsy, and Mavis made me go home. The house was empty. I slipped into bed and fell into a sleep filled with sweat and fever dreams. It was still light when my father's voice, through the walls, woke me up.

"What are you doing with that stuff?" He was in the kitchen, but I didn't know who he could have been talking to in that voice.

"Does Otis Dow know you have that over here?" he said, with an anger I'd never heard from him.

There was a long pause, then a scuffle, glass against glass, metal against metal. Then quiet.

"You made her sick, didn't you?" he said.

"It's for her own good," said my mother.

"Since when have you cared about that?" he said. It got quiet again. "You could have killed her."

"I know what I'm doing."

"That's what I'm afraid of, Ruth." He'd lost the anger and his voice receded. "That's what I'm afraid of."

The rains come in November and stay till March. By summer, the rivers are dried up and the land is parched, the grass brown and crackling. Early one morning that October, it was clear, still, what we call earthquake weather. I left the house and hid in the shed with the door opened slightly, then watched my brothers and sisters tumble out of the house for the school bus, and Carl get into the Vega and drive away.

Kerosene stings the nose and makes the eyes water, but it's a good hurt, full of promise. It took two cans to make a wet trail around the house, and one more to cover the door frames, the porch, the railings. All sound seemed to evaporate into the air along with the fumes, and though Ruth was inside, I couldn't hear her. My intention was to frighten her, something I'd never been able to do, and make her cry for help. I put the can back in the shed and struck a match. Every five feet around the base of the house I lit another match, and soon the yellow tufts of flame were reaching out to each other. Once they touched, they formed a thick orange rope that scurried up the steps and erupted into a sheet of fire.

It was like my mother to calmly open the door and attempt to walk through flames. But Ruth didn't know about fire; she didn't know that as soon as she opened the door, the flame would swoop in on her like a bird of prey. She jumped back inside and slammed the door. I wish I could have seen her as she ran—no, she would have walked—to the back of the house, only to find another blaze locking her in. I waited for her to break a window and climb through it, but my mother approached fire like she did everything else, and she was not going to give in.

The flames lapped up toward the roof, and I began to wonder if my mother was stubborn enough to die. I had thought I was fierce, like her, but this fire scared me: It had no beauty, just urgency, and I was afraid of what it might do. I got my bike out of the shed and rode down the hill toward the Tandy's house, to call the station. But Ruth must have already called; the sirens were on their way, and I turned around and headed back toward the house as two water trucks passed me.

When I got to the top of the hill, they were carrying my mother, coughing, sputtering, from the back of the house. They put her on the ground and stuffed a bunch of padding under her feet. I rushed up, I had to know, but one of the men grabbed my arm.

"That your mother?"

I nodded.

"She'll be all right. You step back, now."

The fire had become a new creature, unrecognizable, and it was hard to believe that I had something to do with its birth. Around me the men were uncoiling hoses and then the water came on so violently it hardly seemed like a fair fight. Thick gray pillows of smoke gushed out the windows. But the flames, healthy, orange, had speed and agility on their side. They were cunning where the water was simply bold, and they multiplied and escaped in tendrils.

I sat down by the shed and watched the men, like soldiers, fall in line. They barely spoke, and we were surrounded by the awful sound of fire and water fighting each other. Then the Vega pulled up and my father ran toward the house. He, too, was stopped by one of the men, who pointed to where Ruth was resting on the ground. Carl bent to his knees and put his hand to her forehead before he got shooed away.

I imagine Carl's mind, which until that moment had only had room for worry, began to open up again, and wonder start to seep in. He looked up at his house, covered by a screen of smoke and dust, then looked beyond the house, at the yard, the giant oak tree, the fields in the distance. It was then he turned around and saw me. He went from wonder to knowing and his face got a look on it that I will never forget. He stepped toward me, and the horror began to melt off his face, in long, slow tears. I stood up to meet him and he put both hands on my shoulders and shook me, hard, then gentle. He kept one arm around me, and we turned to watch the fierce blades of color eat up our home.

Rain came early that year. It came in pellets, and the earth, which was not ready for the rain, repelled it, made it wait in pools on the roads and in the fields. But the water was persistent, and finally the earth relented, opened up and let it in. We salvaged a few belongings, wet and ash-covered, and went to stay at Otis Dow's, while he moved in with his sister. His was a square house, two stories, painted creamy white inside and out, and my family seemed oddly at home there, with shelves full of books, and little flowered cups hanging from the cupboards.

There was nothing for me to do but leave, and they let me go, my father playing chess with Daniel in the living room, my mother in the kitchen shelling peas. "You'll make out, Jess," she said, sticking her thumb in and splitting open the spine of a pea. She looked up from the bowl and into my eyes. It was the first time since the fire, maybe the first time ever, that she looked at me like that. "You'll do just fine." She nodded real slow, in approval, or assurance. Then she went back to her peas.

And so I gathered up my money from the bank and bought a map and a bus ticket. Then I began my climb up the mountains and out of the valley, heading west toward the ocean, to continue the journey my father had started, to see the things my parents had not seen.

The grin tells me that this picture was taken either in the summer or on a Saturday.

George Fahey graduated from Virginia Commonwealth University in Richmond, where he studied history. He has traveled extensively abroad, lived in Paris, London, and, since, in an assortment of cities in the U.S. For several years he taught English as a second language in the Los Angeles Unified Adult School Program. He is currently living with his wife, Mary, in San Francisco, wrapping up work on a novel.

GEORGI'S MOVE

George Fahey

The more Georgi Timofeyev watched his ancient country chug and wobble along its new silver-gray, wide-gauge track into the Twenty-first Century, the greater was his calling to sever blood ties and just go: West to where his clever friend Dimitri had emigrated three years earlier, before rosy cheeked, fun-loving Yeltsin anointed wan, serious-minded Putin. Peering from a lead-framed, six-quarreled window inside his father's extravagantly appointed dacha, watching a flurry of snow dust a line of naked black trees, he wrote to his longtime companion. "This fledgling so-called capitalist democracy is even more corrupt than things were under our old so-called comrades, where, yes, the nefarious underground economy, in truth, certainly had its roots. No, now you see, my old friend, I can't help but be struck by the thought that if this child is in this condition now, what can we predict he'll be as man. Everyone's got his palm out, ready to be greased, as you once put it. The government is nearly broke, if you ask me. To get a driver's license test, my friend Alexi was forced to pay two hundred U.S. dollars to some dew-eared, corrupt functionary who splits it up, no doubt, with the rest of his surly pals. It's a fact of life, you see, even worse than before, because now everyone dreams deliriously that he can get rich. And, of course, our little family continues to do well. But father has a shadow over him that gets darker each time we meet. I despise him, as you know. That shadow falls over everything in Moscow, and now that we have this grand house behind tall mossy gates, as it were, I suspect my father—no, I accuse him of cheating his fellow countrymen. His greed, you see. Wretched materialism where such a paucity of goods is here for the taking! It wrenches my heart to see our land, which, of course, produced Tolstoy, Dostoevsky, Tchaikovsky, Gogol, etc., etc., turn into a dollar-worshipping, soot-caked has-been. Is this all so ingenuous of me, Dimitri? Am I, have I become a man not eligible to live in modern society? Of course, I do not accuse my father with words. We only trade expressions at the long, polished cherry-wood dinner table. He knows I detest him and I know that he despises me. We don't need words. It occurs to me—forgive me for saying it, I know you don't have an appetite for such thoughts, but it is my letter, and I remain a man whose pen is driven and maintains aspirations—so then, it occurs to me that the greatest hate has love at its roots. The man who sows seed dreams for one crop, gets another, and then the field, as far as his wishes go, can starve or be deprived even a ray of sunlight until death. Add to that the pervasive shadow…"

Dimitri, who had been urging Georgi to come to America, read the letter sitting on his fancy, lushly puckered couch, only delivered a few days earlier from the huge Levitt's warehouse, and, though he actually loved Georgi, his philosophic friend, he thought as he read that his friend's laments were only amusing, entertaining at best, part of Georgi's attractive naïveté.

He took out his favorite ballpoint and scribbled that in America it was different, that "Everyone has the chance to swim in money, and therefore it is only a tyranny of the fittest, the way of the real world. Paucity is replaced with abundance. Even there is room for your philosophic musings, Georgi, but you have to beat out the other philosophers who universally think that they are better than the rest. One idea might be more right than another, but if you have placed yourself close to a publisher or in a big-time university position, then your chances of success are greatly increased. Oh well, like they say, everything is location. You see, yes, of course materialism is running rampant here, but so what, Georgi? People want to feather their nests. It's the nature of the beasts we happen to be. But here you can do it with or without corruption, if you see what I mean; there is the choice which you so sorely miss in Russia at the moment in history you describe to me with such anguish."

Georgi's father barely looked up from his dinner when his twenty-three-year-old son announced in a low, uncertain tone that he was going to find his fate in the mythical corridors of New York City, with the help of his old pal Dimitri. The large, wide-faced man struck a familiar pose, appeared to be chewing on a piece of gristle between two of his square front teeth as his son spoke. Finally, he took his slightly starched napkin from his lap, wiped his sliver of a mouth, and stood. "Where will you get the money for this adventure? Are you going to sell the books and the car that I bought for you with my money you so plainly despise?"

"I have a loan from Dimitri," he announced with some pride. "I need sell nothing you have bought me nor borrow a ruble here, Father. Dimitri has connections, has a job for me at a hotel where I can make one hundred dollars a day, opening car doors. Then, when I am on my feet, and he is paid back, who knows?"

Still standing, his father, not looking at Georgi or his diminutive wife, who always was ready with an expression she desperately tried to glean as correct around her husband's moods, thrust his index finger against his narrow bottom front teeth, picked at some morsel, dismissing any interest, found something wedged between a crack in the phalanx of gold-plated and tarnished enamel, chewed it with his molars, and said only, "Bon voyage." He turned and left the long, high-ceilinged room under the dappled glitter of a rather large and somewhat garish chandelier.

When the day arrived, his mother shed thick gray droplets from eyes which otherwise revealed no particular torment. She didn't go to the airport. His father was in Saint Petersburg on a two-day business trip. When the huge jet passed through the gray soup that lay across the cold sky above Moscow and broke out into the sunny blue sea above, Georgi wasn't sure he really wanted to land ever again. He looked into the cloud cover beneath, and thought that man's earthly schemes were shameful, that man had taken the world and made it, with all his misguided ingenuity and jealousy, a sullen rock where a hard, cruel man like his father held fast to his unhappy dominion. New York, America, lay ahead. Dmitri had exaggerated, of course, he thought with a smile of friendship, but how much?

At JFK, though he held his suit jacket tightly buttoned and valise close to his side, he felt like a man finding himself among the multitudes without his trousers. There were families and businessmen and announcements that, though he had supposedly learned to speak English, in his jet-lagged state he didn't begin to understand. He got through customs, had all his papers, but he couldn't help but flush across the forehead and cheek as though he were smuggling in some drugs or dirty pictures. He was surprised how the air of his chosen land seemed to constrict him. All some official had to do was confront him and he might confess to being a spy. He could feel his armpits dripping like the spigot outside the apartments where they'd lived when he was a small boy. Maybe he should never have come, he thought. Maybe he was putting his foot into a vortex that would swallow him up faster than the slow-moving, turgid, sewer-bound waters he had just fled.

Dimitri and Yelena, along with their small runny-nosed boy, Yakov, showed up in colorful outfits, a welcome sight. The boy's eyes were narrow and he rubbed them with his tiny finger after what had, no doubt, from Georgi's perspective, been crying. Yelena, though she wore a short, tight dress, low cut, still wore a rather bristly expression, even if she allowed her dark painted lips to spread and show her white, slightly gapped teeth. Yelena was a dental hygienist these days where a trio of Russian dentists practiced. She later boasted of having been on TV in an advertisement for the friendly triumvirate. "Come on down." Dimitri had become far richer in girth. His pink cheeks puffed jovially with good humor, almost laughing to see his friend finally walking self-consciously on American soil. The two men hugged, kissed cheeks; each had tears in his eyes. Yelena also kissed Georgi, leaving a dark red smooch mark on his long, usually serious jaw. Yakov was forced to hold out his hand for a shake. You'd think he was to be branded from the look on his little face. Unused to children, Georgi displayed a certain diffidence toward the five year old, which made Dimitri laugh with utter joy.

Dimitri owned a big car and lived in a brownstone with a small backyard in Flushing. Georgi watched as they pointed things out to him along the rather dismal route, the direction of the distant skyline of Manhattan he'd seen from the plane. For some reason he couldn't match his friend's robust joy at the reunion; his cheeks felt heavy, hard to lift. He imagined he presented the picture of a sullen immigrant who had not yet been able to wash away his Old World dismay regarding the future. He felt not himself at all, and apologized for his awkwardness.

"Well, Dimitri," Georgi said rather formally for his new home, "the long trip has no doubt taken a toll on me. Please don't mistake that for the feeling of joy I hold inside myself, finally seeing you again and being here where you so kindly invited me."

"We have a room for you, set up, near the kitchen," Yelena added soberly.

"I hope I won't be a bother. I certainly will look for other accommodations at the first…"

"Nonsense," Dimitri responded, nearly bubbling over despite his deep, booming voice. "No bother. There's lots of room. Besides, I have something to discuss with you. A plan. But not this moment, Georgi. We have blinis and caviar and bottles of vodka waiting for us to restore you from your triumphant journey. Don't worry, my friend, don't worry. We'll have you dancing and singing "Star Spangled Banner" before we slip you into your new room tonight. This much," he said, raising his thick index finger in a practiced gesture, "I guarantee."

Dimitri's house was full of Russians, full of food, full of drink and smoke. Stories of success punctuated by howling laughter vied as the night progressed with tales of failure colored by sad hues of tearful longings for Mother Russia. Georgi, his head swimming, nearly fell into Yakov's little wintering plastic pool in the tiny backyard before the night ended in a swirling sea of blurry profligacy.

All the next day, which was a Sunday, Georgi could not recover a healthy blush. His face looked bloodless except for the sliver rivulets of red coursing across the whites of his sad eyes. Yelena was as grim as ever, but Dimitri, after a gulp of ice-cold vodka he'd placed as medicine in the freezer the night before, was absolutely beaming. Yakov again seemed to be either just finished crying or ready to begin again, rubbing his eyes with that sticky index finger which never seemed to leave the vicinity. Looking on the youth, Georgi wondered to himself if Dimitri's family tree would ever really take permanent root in the New World. When Yelena gathered up Yakov to go off to the blue-domed Russian Orthodox church they'd pointed out on the way from the airport, Georgi and Dimitri, two lifelong atheists, were left alone but for the constant intrusion of the thirty-two-inch television, just now filled with acerbic faces and reruns of Clinton waving his finger at the "American" people. Dimitri made a few compulsory quips about the president's dilly-dallying, and Georgi shook his head in response, though, he was not entirely interested in the issue.

"Now tomorrow I take you to the hotel," Dimitri told him. "We'll get you the uniforms that fit. I'm bell captain," he reminded him. "Boss. In French hotel, believe it? Your French is still good too, I know, even though you won't need it much. Mostly Americans and celebrities. Cher. I carried her bags myself. Gorbachev. You believe it? I opened door for him in New York. Crazy world. But I wrote you that."

"You can just give me a new job just like that?"

"I fired Romanian doorman. It's difficult. The unions. Anyway, the general manager caught him drinking on job. Idiot, but right away I said I had intellectual émigré to take his place, and I told them you are hard worker and speak French beautifully. I remember that our dear old French teacher Miasnikov said you had great nasal accent. I remember that. You wanted to move to Paris," he laughed. "How you used to swoon about Left Bank," he smirked. "So, anyway, I'll show you how to take tips. You get used to it."

"Yes. I hope so, Dimitri. You say I wear white gloves. It's hard for me to visualize, taking money in white gloves."

"Money's money. But this is only first step. This is what I wanted to talk to you about. I've been thinking day and night about my next step." Dimitri eyed his friend carefully. "I want you to listen to me. I could not allow myself to even email you about this subject."

"Yes, yes, Dimitri, tell me. You can't think you have to be suspicious about me. I want to hear your idea. You don't think I want to be taking dollars even with white gloves for very long, though I'm very grateful, of course."

Dimitri offered his friend a cigarette, which was declined, and lit his own. "Okay. You know Internet, I know. Well, you have also heard of gold rush in California?"

"I read something, Comstock or something that…"

"Georgi, there is new gold rush in California. May I tell you what it is? Listen." He cleared his throat, his face was no longer confident but as apprehensive as a poet walking a tightrope over a snickering abyss of embarrassment. Rubbing his palms he finally whispered the two words as someone on making the discovery might have said: Dead Sea Scrolls. "Dot coms."

Beside himself, blushing with excitement and trepidation, Dimitri stood and rushed into the kitchen and returned with a frosty bottle of Stolichnoya which he poured, his hands trembling slightly. Georgi listened to his friend, feeling now and then that Dimitri repeated himself over certain aspects of his plan, making them seem a little unsure, like someone adding a third coat of paint where a second was enough to achieve the color.

"Pockets of Russians exist now all over United States. You yourself witnessed it last night. We are a sentimental people, Georgi. You are writer, you must know this. This transplanting, growing of slender, fragile roots in this new soil, has caused us to regard wistfully the thick roots from which we came. It's not us only. Irish, Italians, even French, for all I know, Spaniards, like to talk sentimentally, exaggerating about their origins, and are willing to spend money to have their family trees researched. This is where RussianRoots.com comes into view."

"Don't people know their roots already?"

"No. Not at all. They left them behind. Like when you have a kid, are you going to tell him all about your hated father and docile mother?

No. But, your kid is going to want to know. I've heard them, always asking, because they are curious and maybe their parents have already given up the ghost, or even the kids just want to find out what was wrong with their parents so they can have excuse if things aren't going well. Everyone wants to take pride or at least blame ancestors. It's all part of life in the New World."

Dimitri was not allowed to see, but his big plans didn't find a welcome at the threshold of his friend's careful ears. Given to fits of depression as part of Georgi's general makeup, this business of selling memories of the land he had just left for a new life might even reveal that he and his old friend had evolved, would indeed evolve into people, by his count, two steps removed. Loving his friend, and careful not to discourage the impulse which animated such an animated character, Georgi suffered his misgivings in silence.

Meanwhile things did not progress according to plan. The Romanian doorman accosted the general manager, a man renowned for having a soft spot here and there, with thick eastern European tears followed by mea culpas and oaths. His position was restored leaving Georgi up all night on the graveyard shift wearing a bellman's uniform complete with pristine gloves rarely corrupted by the filthy surface of a dollar bill. His duties amounted to taking late-arriving guests to their rooms in the huge, fancy complex, and getting things for the guests when they called down to the front desk, where his new acquaintance, Amardeep, saw to things between eleven P.M. and seven in the morning. Usually, after he got his footing those first few weeks, the sad-faced immigrant could be found down in the break room savoring some elaborate chocolate creation supplied by the chefs of the fancy French restaurant, leftovers from the restaurant. He'd wash that down with cup after cup of coffee, sampling American novels to improve his English, even reading some translations of Russian novels, confusing himself one moment and amusing himself the next. Amardeep was linked to the night bellman by a radio that hung on Georgi's belt.

"Georgi, there's a fish on your line. Better hurry. I can see his cab out front."

"Yes, I will be right there," Georgi said, stiffening up and fumbling with the radio. He stood and straightened his coat, pulled on his gloves, all this while his feet sped to the stairway leading to the opulent, sparkling, marbled lobby. He burst out the huge thick-glassed doors and took this tall man's valises from him, and with all due dedication he opened the door. The man, obviously well traveled, barely looked at him, but strode up under the lofty lobby ceiling to Amardeep, taking his wallet from his jacket pocket which was open under his long tweed overcoat.

The man's name sounded vaguely familiar the way that Amardeep said it. Georgi stood back a few paces at parade rest, as Dimitri called it, holding one gloved hand in the other behind his back, full of alert alacrity, still tasting a mix of tiramisu and coffee on his tongue. In the elevator he read to himself the man's name on the little envelope which contained the fancy card key to the room: Christopher Mahler. Not, he thought, the Christopher Mahler who wrote serious plays, whose play was in rehearsal just blocks away, the one Georgi had read about in the paper and whose collection of plays he'd taken out from the library, one of which he admired enormously. Georgi was ashamed to feel his heart react by pumping foolishly, as though his companion on the mirrored elevator ascending weightlessly to the forty-third floor had turned from a tall, rather gaunt man into a tiger growling and dripping at the mouth. Sheepishly, but impelled, Georgi forced himself to say the name of the play he liked. "*Across the Boulevard.*"

The man's head jolted just perceptibly; he drew himself from what had obviously filled his mind back to the elevator, and looked at his uniformed companion. "Oh, you saw it?"

"No. I read it. From the Flushing Library."

"Hmm." He paused. "Did you like it?"

His face went red. "Yes. Of course, my English isn't good thus far. I stumbled on some of the, what to say, colloquialisms. Do you understand me? I…"

"Perfectly." The man paused, thinking a moment. "Are you a writer, or an actor?"

"Oh, well, for right now only an actor: a bellman."

"And the hotel is your stage," the playwright smiled. "Well, everyone has to act. I have to act like a playwright."

"I do write, though," Georgi said after a moment, catching a cold wind that blew across the pause in the conversation, giving his backbone a chill.

"Really? What kind of writing?" he asked graciously, at least feigning interest. "Short stories, novels, screenplays…?"

Georgi forehead must have been crimson by now. "Observations. In letters. Nothing important."

They arrived on forty-seven with the tasteful plink of a muted bell. The man followed behind as Georgi led the way down the silent, narrow hall to his room. Georgi could feel that Christopher Mahler's mind was regathering its former thinking, leaving *him* to write "letters"—how quaint. Georgi's anxious heart began to beat a tune that incorporated a certain resentment mixed with a natural nervousness one feels in the presence of another human whose accomplishments tower above one's own. But he was surprised by what Christopher Mahler said next.

"Letters can be beautiful things, intimate, and, if you've got the nerve, full of unfettered honesty."

Georgi made a mental note to look up the word "unfettered," but because it was spoken with a breath that sounded like praise, he could not help but to beam as best his worried countenance could manage. Georgi put one valise on the stand, the other neatly next to it. One hands the guest his card key, and this is when the transaction occurs, according to Dimitri. It's at this point that the guest, the rich guest, since anyone who can afford to stay in this hotel is rich, slips a crisp, folded bill of a nice denomination, or several of inferior pedigree, into the gloved hand in exchange. Georgi did not want to stoop to this rather vulgar transaction on this occasion, but was conflicted, thinking in a split second that by not taking the money he might somehow insult this capitalist man of talent. His worry proved needless as Christopher Mahler's face flushed as he went through his pockets for a tip, and ended saying, "I can't believe this. I wasn't thinking. I gave the last of my cash to the cab driver."

126

"It is okay, because you see, really…"

"No. No it isn't," he said looking around, clearly unnerved. "Wait. Would you like to see my play? It opens in two weeks. You could write me a letter afterward and tell me what you think."

"You owe me nothing," Georgi replied in a friendly voice. He turned to go, leaving the man slightly awkward. But then—perhaps it was that a grain or two of his new land, America, had entered his blood unseen, or just a bit of the tiramisu and caffeine—he turned to look at the playwright just for a moment as he reached for the shiny door handle. "This is not to imply that I would not enjoy to see your play."

Christopher Mahler took down Georgi's name, spelling carefully, Timofeyev. Georgi explained anxiously that one ticket was sufficient since he was not long in New York. All Georgi had to do was show up on opening night and tell the man at the box office his name; then he could, if he chose, send the letter of his observations to the theatre whose address would be printed on the playbill. The playwright seemed a moment later to wonder if he'd been overgenerous with this morose-looking young man from Moscow, but the hesitation disappeared as though a switch were turned back on in his head, relighting his original intention, which Georgi thought later surely lived in the place where the playwright found his reason to be an artist.

Amardeep, on hearing of Georgi's theatrical gratuity, suggested without a blink that he scalp it and turn it into an amount of cash that would diminish the daytime bellmen's boastings to proverbial nickels and dimes. Back up in the break room, Georgi could not concentrate on his reading. He wanted to be a reasonable capitalist in one part of his complicated makeup, while a larger slice of himself was fully dedicated to art, written art specifically: what might be conveyed by one to the many with a stroke of a pen. On the one hand, how Dimitri would beam for Georgi at his promising gratuity before the assembled bellmen at the bellstand. How, on the other hand, Chekhov might be somewhere awaiting Georgi to evolve to a point where the beloved author might deign to inspire him. Finally, Georgi slammed his book shut, hid it in a narrow gap next to the Pepsi machine, and hurried to the lobby.

"Amardeep," he said, finding his friend doing some of the night audit in the little room off the front desk, "I want to speak with you regarding the playwright, Christopher Mahler."

"If you think I will want to purchase your little trip to the theater," he smiled, "forget that idea, Georgi. I have nothing to do with scalping. I'm not an Indian, you know. I'm from Pakistan."

"No, I meant…"

"I wouldn't spend good money to go see people walk around pretending to be somebody else in the first place. Better to spend money on food and shelter, if you want my opinion, or even a television set."

Georgi steeled himself. "I don't want you to tell anyone about my ability to get the ticket on opening night, Amardeep. I've decided that I must go to the play as Christopher Mahler intended me to."

Amardeep looked at him, narrowing his dark eyes in a mix of sarcasm and incomprehension. "You might get hundreds of dollars. Are you crazy? To see a bunch of actors walking around shouting a lot of baloney at each other? The playwright will forget the whole thing, if he even remembers to leave a ticket for you at the box office. You don't owe him anything."

"Not everything is worth only money," Georgi said with a hint of self-mockery in his laudable truth. "Money, money, money. It's a funny word if you say it ten times over."

"Maybe a funny word, but it's why I sit here all night away from the woman my parents sent me and the children I've fathered. It's why you sit in the break room all night. It's why you came to the United States."

"No."

"Then why?"

Georgi's traitor of a forehead flushed. "To observe the world, to escape seeing my homeland descend into…" He stopped himself before his amused interlocutor. "Look, Amardeep, you are my friend. Can you keep this secret for me? Will you? I'll bring you fresh coffee whenever you want. I don't want bellmen to know, and most of all Dimitri. Please? Do me this small favor."

Amardeep shook his head incredulously. "I don't need to tell anyone," he said, pausing with his dark eyes on his nocturnal inn-keeping associate. "I thought you might be an *artist* of some kind, Georgi. The thought certainly did occur to me."

"I am not an artist."

"You have that sad face of an artist. Why are artists so sad, anyway? I suppose because they give up opportunities so they can spend their lives being miserable," he laughed. Georgi turned to leave through the narrow door. "Hey, Georgi, where's my coffee? Hop to it. Not too strong."

It snowed that night, piling up on the entranceway to the hotel. Georgi was more than happy to shovel it as dawn crept up, subtly illuminating the flakes as they rushed to cover the sidewalks and sleeping streets. The aroma of the snow mixed with exhaust from the passing taxis, and those forming a line for the morning rush at the front door of the hotel made Georgi feel a real sense of nostalgia for Russia, and especially his youth, which was punctuated with many moments of sublime happiness under a heavy, inescapable pall of melancholy. All the sadness in his heart created such vast pressure that a beam of hope emitted from its center. America, by some stroke of its infinite luck, perhaps, had given him an opportunity to pour out his heart and intellect on paper to someone who might recognize his talent. He was scolding himself about not being able to contain such an arrogant thought when the bellmen started to arrive, sliding down the street, throwing snow balls, laughing, ready for a day when people, for some reason, while squinting through the falling flakes and swerving about, were more generous to one another generally and to bellmen and doormen specifically, in their case, in ways that one could count at the end of the day.

Occasionally, Dimitri would drive in and hand his car over to Georgi so that he could drive it home, and this way Yelena, on a day off, would have access to it during the day. On this snowy day, Dimitri had called to tell Georgi that this would be the method, since after all he liked to drive in the snow, and little Yakov had an afternoon doctor's appointment to get some childhood inoculation. The snow had clearly swept to the background any interest in letting slip the generous tip from the sleepy, well-known playwright.

Georgi drove the car carefully, especially on the bridge, where cars were swerving right and left, the steamy New York skyline disappearing behind in snow which seemed to turn to soot before hitting the pavement. Georgi was tired, but the thought of rubbing shoulders with a successful man of letters and the snow combined to exhilarate his senses. He even found himself daydreaming that one day he, too, would be a celebrated man; a man, the thought came out of some loneliness, that women might also admire with some subtle passion.

Yelena had not dressed. Georgi had not begun to conquer an awkwardness he felt around her when they were alone or even with the rather silent child. In this particular nightie, with its pale pink flowers and flecks of green, leaves perhaps, the abundance and contours, both soft and more abrupt, of her breasts were as evident as the fallen snow. Averting his eyes was difficult, for they were like little mice darting back and forth in the struggle between fear of the trap and delight in lovely pieces of cheese. This whole business revealed in him an impulse he found to be vulgar, something that shamed him, but proved difficult to contain.

"Oh, well, the dentists say that people are more afraid of a snowstorm than a toothache," Yelena explained, breaking some eggs for a breakfast she would share with little Yakov and Georgi.

"And the doctor?"

"Doctor?"

"Yakov's inoculation."

"No, no. No, little Yakov is safe from the needle today. I called. Is closed too." Yakov's natural sullenness was outwardly unaffected by the news. Sometimes Yelena seemed to wear a hint of a triumphant smile on her lips as she moved about and Georgi averted his eyes. He wondered if she might be toying with him, or worse, tempting him into a move that would certainly prove disastrous regarding his friendship and more importantly his lodging; clearly the latter would be her motive. When he looked at her he tried hard to keep his eyes focused on her lips, allowing the effect of her natural expression to stifle any base animal desires. Before he finished his toast, Yelena went into the bedroom, leaving the door, which was in sight of the kitchen, slightly ajar. She readied herself for her shower, and in the periphery of his vision Georgi noted the passing back and forth of a woman's silhouette which, inside his dark thinking, could well be naked.

When finally he fell into bed, Georgi, for the moments left to him of morning consciousness, allowed the dismal thought that the playwright had been overly tired, and more generous than he might feel looking over his note to the box office as he chewed his morning croissant and strawberries.

Before the snow was melted from the sidewalks of their Flushing neighborhood, Dimitri announced his great, good news. He was going to transfer to the brand-new hotel opening in San Francisco. "You see, there I will find many people, even investors of like mind who are ready for RussianRoots.com. It is my dream coming true." Georgi would stay at the apartment with Yelena until Dimitri sent for her a month later.

Not a day passed after the announcement before Georgi began to detect whispers in their little house in Flushing, and noted that he seemed not privy to certain conversations. His suspicions and natural paranoia in another man's home got the best of him finally. "I detect something in you, lately, Dimitri," Georgi said on his night off, while the two men sipped vodka and watched Jay Leno.

"What? What do you mean?" he wanted to know, looking uncomfortable before his old friend's tone.

"A distance," Georgi said carefully. "I suspect that you are holding back some feelings from me. I know that Yelena has not been pleased having me for a guest, but I do not want you to think for even a moment that…"

"What are you talking about? No, no, no. You stay here. Is my house. I pay rent. I need my month alone to set things up in San Francisco, then you can move in with Alexander, on Second Avenue, until I can invite you to San Francisco. I don't think Yelena dislikes you as much as you imagine."

Things became silent but for the TV. But Dimitri's eyes didn't leave Georgi. Instead they held on him for a long moment, appraising, blurrily, in a foggy if familiar, vodka-induced melancholy.

"Okay, I admit," Dimitri said when Georgi met his gaze quizzically. He went on to surprise his friend with an entirely unexpected thread, "You are very observant, Georgi. Look, you must know that I will need to have a connection, several, in Moscow, in order to get started, even attract investors for the dot com. You must be aware of that. Well, please, don't be angry, but I haven't told you because I know… I just know. Okay, look, Georgi, I've been in touch with your father. And, he has agreed to not only help me, but to invest on the Russian side of my RussianRoots.com." He paused, smiling with unsure enthusiasm as he noted Georgi's astonished face. "Don't look so, please. He has all the connections. He is very well placed. Georgi, he even asked how you were. I told him that it was just a matter of time before I send for you in California."

"My father? You can't mean my father," Georgi gasped. "And to think I was feeling guilty because I saw Yelena getting undressed. All the time you were plotting…"

"Yelena?"

"Oh, just a glimpse, an accident. She hates me. I thought she was trying to drive me out. Now I find that you have betrayed me and pushed a stealthy knife into my ribs."

"Don't overdo with your choice of words."

"You worked behind my back because you knew you were betraying me."

"Untrue. Untrue," Dimitri protested angrily. "You are not a businessman. Sometimes I think I should leave you here permanently."

"And what will my father do for your ridiculous dot com, if I may ask?"

"So, you think my idea ridiculous? The truth finally comes out," Dimitri accused bitterly. His bloodshot eyes glared at his friend for long, insane moments.

"Oh, please. I didn't mean ridiculous. I said it in anger, but nevertheless I demand to know what you think my father will do for you. He's a thief. He's a scoundrel. You know this very well."

Dimitri gathered himself, took a drink, and offered one to Georgi who pushed it away, then accepted it brusquely. His own eyes were already pink rimmed. Dimitri cleared his throat. "He has agreed to head up the family research division."

"What? Don't make me laugh! This is the biggest joke of them all."

"Your father has worked out a method, is ready to put people in place…"

"You'll be selling lies, family lies. Histories created in some basement under a dangling light bulb."

"That's a lie. Every piece of information will be authenticated." He stood in a rage. "Authenticated. Guaranteed. You are an artist. You know nothing about business. Dreamer!" he accused, and with that grabbed the bottle from Georgi and exited the dim little living room.

Over the next days silence soon became punctuated by the muted, if thunderous shouts of domestic inclemency. Yelena glared, accused with her eyes, never wore the nightie with the pink flowers in front of Georgi again. Finally, three days prior to Dimitri's departure, the two men found themselves alone but for some Louis Vuitton luggage and a rudely scuffed, brown briefcase that had been there forever in the luggage room.

"Alexander has said that I may move into his place right away, Dimitri."

"Oh, Georgi," Dimitri said gently, "this is not right. I leave very soon. How can we not be friends? I want you to stay at my house. Yelena does also. Little Yakov has become very fond of you, though he's not one to display such emotions. Stay another month, watch out for things before I send for Yelena, please."

He paused a moment. A smile invaded his face from nowhere. "If you wish."

"Good. Good," he chuckled. "I shall certainly send for you soon enough if you will agree to come." He looked at his friend with a vulnerability rarely displayed. "But tell me the truth, Georgi, don't you wish me well?"

"I do. Of course I do." Both men smiled, shaking their heads ironically, Dimitri slapping Georgi on the shoulder.

"And now you will come to my Bon Voyage party? Say yes, Georgi."

Georgi looked away. "I cannot. I have plans."

"What plans?" Dimitri laughed amiably.

Georgi paced around the little room, looking at the nametags on the Louis Vuittons. "Theatre. I have theatre tickets, or one ticket to a play. Opening night."

This news made Dimitri's face reveal a sadness that Georgi was hard pressed to look upon. It was as if the news let some air out of Dimitri. "I see. I shall miss you at the party. One party is like another anyhow, really."

Just then Amardeep poked his head in from the door leading to the front desk. "Fish on the line. Fish on the line." Georgi pulled on his gloves, grabbed the luggage cart, and went to answer the front. When he returned, Dimitri was gone.

Georgi suffered with his intention not to pass up his big literary chance in the New World. He didn't dare tell Dimitri the story of Christopher Mahler; not just because it wouldn't help Dimitri understand, but because he was deathly afraid that there might not be a ticket left for him at the theatre, and then he would be made to look like a fool, made to look like a Dreamer, be put into the position of being laughed at by, perhaps, not only the likes of his father, but indeed by his father himself. So he would take his big chance in silence, even if it hurt to disappoint his friend to whom he owed so much.

The two men passed among each other in a sort of reverent silence as opening night and the party approached. Georgi kept mostly quiet but to say now and then how he was always lost in parties, that no one could ever miss his presence; and Dimitri would make little of the party in an effort to appear humble and to let Georgi off the hook gently.

The night finally arrived. Georgi had arranged to have the night off, had bought himself a suit, and shined his shoes. He also, in his breast pocket, carried a notebook and new pen to take notes at intermission. He patted Dimitri, who himself was in a slight sweat in anticipation of his Bon Voyage party, on the shoulder and told him that he'd join him in the morning-after vodka.

All the way to and inside the subway the lump in his throat worked to hold down the butterflies in his stomach. He paced before the theatre, thinking that he should just rush off and be by the side of Dimitri, who, however, had certainly been reckless and deceitful in recruiting his father. Nevertheless, were they not lifelong friends? He was torn as he paced. But in the end, a man so close to, perhaps, an opportunity of a lifetime, begins to move in its direction like a drowning man heads for the shore. He waited nervously on line, assuring himself that the ticket would be there, and a moment later that surely it would not. The man in the booth first told him to speak up. Then he looked through the tickets without luck. "Timofeyev," Georgi repeated with foolish tears waiting behind his eyes.

"Oh, I thought you said Simosayev," the smarty-pants sort of fellow told him. In a moment, the man, whose fingernails seemed long, handed him the ticket the playwright had promised. With his heart wobbling in his chest, and though feeling a little dizzy, Georgi held his head high and entered the theatre.

I've always loved the water.

Adam Schuitema's work has appeared or is forthcoming in the *Cream City Review*, *Washington Square*, the *Rio Grande Review*, and the *Spoon River Poetry Review*. He lives in Grand Rapids, Michigan and is a recent graduate of the MFA program at Western Michigan University.

SAND THIEVES

Adam Schuitema

Uncle Lucien spent the summer surrounded by horseflies. They left the rest of us alone, except my mom, who blamed the scent of Aqua Net for luring them into her hair. During Memorial Day weekend, my two cousins and I kneeled in the sand at the top of the beach. Terry and Caleb had dug a wide hole and filled it with water to hold the turtle they'd just caught. I'd dug a narrow but deeper hole that swallowed my arm up to the shoulder. The underground sand was cold and moist. It was older than the soft stuff on the surface, and had probably been brought to the cottage years earlier.

Uncle Lucien walked slowly in our direction, swinging his old double-edged weed cutter with the long wooden handle, slicing dandelions and tall grasses along the top strip of beach. We were in his way.

A swarm of horseflies circled his shoulders and head, and a few other flies buzzed around his ankles, scattering and returning with each low swing of the blade.

Caleb looked in his direction. "You got a fly on your foot," he said.

Uncle Lucien stopped and picked up his can of beer from where he'd set it in the sand, then lazily waved his hand over his ankle, the way a cow in a pasture swings its tail. "They're lookin' for protein for their eggs," he mumbled. He stood still and took a long sip. The fly landed on his foot again. Uncle Lucien didn't move, but watched it out of the corner of his eye. A tear of blood slowly swelled and somersaulted off the side of his big toe, darkening a small circle of sand like an old penny.

"They got some teeth if you let 'em use 'em," he said. He took another long sip of beer, swished it around in his teeth, and then spit it onto his foot, scattering the fly again. "Get," he said. He set the beer back down and returned to swinging the blade, making it hum against the air and the grasses. My cousins and I reluctantly stood and let him pass.

He was my mom's uncle, and I tried not to think about him unless he was in my field of vision, within earshot, or unless Terry was making fun of him and I was chipping in. Uncle Lucien was bald as a dolphin and always wore a beat-up Tigers cap to protect his head from the sun, but the flies still stuck close to him. He never seemed bothered. As long as we kids didn't disturb him while he worked on the beach, he moved steadily through the day, with horseflies bouncing off his head.

"Like dog shit," said Terry. "He's like a big, steaming pile."

Terry was fourteen, two years older than me and ready to enter high school the next fall. His parents had been the first to divorce, and though his dad lived just three blocks down from his house in Fruitport, Terry rarely saw him. Terry showed up that summer of 1985 with a thin, black mustache and black tufts of armpit hair, which I noticed the first time he took his shirt off to swim. He and I and our ten-year-old cousin Caleb spent most summer weekends up at our family's cottage in New Era. The three of us were close. None of us had any siblings. We all lived alone with our moms after our parents divorced. We could have been brothers, except Caleb had bright orange hair—his dad's orange hair—and he didn't look dark like the rest of the family.

Uncle Lucien once noted this. "He's the only red-head fruit in our Polack family tree."

Weekends at the cottage were a time for us to breathe a little easier, to be relieved of the strange dynamic that results from single moms living all year with only their sons. That summer was the first without Grandpa, and though none of us talked about it, we seemed to keep busier and closer. The three of us boys joined up and disappeared for entire mornings or afternoons, and our moms gave us that freedom, happy, it seemed, to be back in their own clique for a time. They acted girlish when they were together, laughing, whispering, pointing at the young, shirtless men who put shingles on the Drysdale cottage across the street. They smoked cigarettes and drank wine coolers, cassettes of Dionne Warwick and Neil Diamond providing the soundtrack. Sometimes the three of them would recline on the beach, passing around a can of cashews—one of their weekend luxuries. Aunt Dee Dee, Terry's mom, wore a leopard-print bikini that I tried not to look at, but sometimes did. She, my mom, and my Aunt Tess sunned themselves in the early heat of Memorial Day, lying next to each other on their stomachs with their eyes closed, speaking dreamily about vacations they'd never take. They fell silent when we boys came near. Sometimes I think they were talking about men. Maybe the shirtless men across the street. Maybe our dads.

The cottage rested on a hill above Lake Tahoe, with a small lot of land—beech trees, moss, and a root-choked trail—bridging the cottage and the water. Lake Tahoe was a small lake. A big pond. All comparisons with the more famous lake out West end at the name. Instead of casinos there were trailers. Instead of mountains there were asparagus fields. Dogs without leashes chased kids through ferns and old leaves, around charcoal grills and propane tanks. Motorboats weren't allowed by ordinance, only quiet fishermen in rowboats and loud families churning away in paddle boats which—for all their rocking and jostling—couldn't manufacture any waves. In the morning, the lake looked still. At dusk, it looked stagnant. And if we stood close by the dirt road when cars or pickups drove by, dust filled our eyes and grit scraped our teeth. The cottage doesn't sound like much, but we loved the place, in large part because of Uncle Lucien's beach.

I call it *his* beach because it wasn't a natural geographic formation. He was a sand farmer. He farmed sand in the sense that he tended it every morning of every summer weekend, nurturing it so that it could thrive in the warm months and be consumed by the family—though he wasn't thinking of the family when he set out to work. To farm sand, however, he had to first become a sand thief.

Terry, Caleb, and I all lived within thirty minutes of each other, but I only met up with them on summer vacations and some holidays. It was the same with Uncle Lucien, only I didn't miss him like I did the rest of the family. None of us did. And that summer of '85, Aunt Dee Dee's indifference ran deeper, into layers of resentment. A few years earlier, my grandma had died at the veteran's nursing home in Grand Rapids after years of living in the haze of Alzheimer's. Grandpa went to the same home after he suffered a stroke in 1984. He died later that year.

But even though Uncle Lucien only lived about five miles away from the home, he never went to visit Grandpa, and never explained why. Our moms tried not to talk about it in front of us boys, but they avoided him during that whole three-day weekend, looking down at him from their perches on the deck while he raked the sugary beach.

I stumbled out of the road, and the firecracker exploded behind me. Caleb's fingers were in his ears. Terry was off looking for dry leaves to ignite. It was early June, still a month before Independence Day, but the three of us were already lighting Black Cats with a magnifying glass. I focused the white beam of light on the tips of the wicks, but staring at it was like staring at the sun. I had to rely on the hissing sound to know it was lit, and then blinked away the black, floating spots in my eyes as I got out of the way.

"God, my eyes," I said, rubbing them. "We need a lighter."

"Our moms said no," said Caleb.

"Do you know how many lighters they got inside? The junk drawer's filled with 'em. They're not gonna miss one more little plastic lighter if you just stick it in your pocket while they're out on the deck."

"*You* do it, Lance. You want it."

"Fine," I said. I began walking through the trees to the cottage.

Terry ran toward us with an armful of brown leaves. "Guys," he said excitedly, "you should hear the old man down there."

"What?"

"He found some more four-wheeler tracks on our property. Messed up his ferns. He was down there all yellin' to himself, 'Four-wheeler cock beaters!' It was great."

Uncle Lucien did this often. He raked the sand on his small beach with his shirt off, his thick shoulders and arms flexing with each motion. He hunched over slightly with age, still carrying the burden of his own, lasting strength. Early in the summer his skin burnt red under the curls of white chest and back hair. By mid-June, he would be tan. While he worked, he would find things that angered him: four-wheeler tracks, dog shit on the beach, loud or lazy children. He shouted and swore to the sky, spooking robins out of trees. Voices of swimmers on the other side of the lake would carry across to our side, so I can only imagine what nearby property owners thought when they heard the words of this crazed old man—parents on other shores clasping their hands over the ears of young children, carrying them indoors where the windows were closed and the radio turned on, the volume high.

I tossed the magnifying glass at Terry's feet. "That thing sucks. I'm frickin' blind. We're gonna get a lighter from inside."

"*You're* gonna get a lighter," said Caleb.

"Shut up," I said.

When I returned with it, Terry pried it from my fingers and picked up a new Black Cat off the ground. "Check this," he said.

He jogged to the crest of the hill and looked down at the beach. Then he crouched against the smooth, gray skin of a beech tree. "Wanna scare him?"

"Terry, don't," said Caleb.

"You chicken?"

"Don't do it," I said. I turned to my left to look at the deck. Our moms relaxed in lounge chairs reading paperbacks. "They'll see you."

"So what? They don't care."

"He'll kill you."

"No he won't. He'll forget about it five minutes after it's over. He's nuts."

Terry peeked around the tree trunk. Uncle Lucien was resting and looking out at the lake. His left hand held the rake, and the right tipped back his can of beer. Terry flicked his thumb over the lighter several times, but it only sparked.

"Shit, how old is this thing?"

After a few more tries, a short flame rose up from it. Terry touched the wick to the flame until it started to hiss. Caleb turned to run, and I followed him as Terry stepped around the tree and tossed the Black Cat in Uncle Lucien's direction. I didn't watch where it sailed, but I heard the blast as I sprinted toward the back of the cottage.

"Goddamn it!"

Caleb and I ran all the way to the shanty at the back of our property. Terry was a few strides behind with a smile on his face, mimicking Uncle Lucien. "Goddamn it! Goddamn it!"

We stopped running. "Did you hit him?" I asked.

"God, no," said Terry. "It blew up way above his head. But he probably pissed his beer right out of himself."

Our moms never said anything to us. And later, when Uncle Lucien confronted us and called us all no-dick sissies and a waste of our daddies' sperm, they didn't say anything to him, either. When they were our age, they'd heard similar words, what Aunt Dee Dee called his "oral flatulence."

Terry wasn't deterred. The following weekend he found an old UAW baseball cap in the kitchen junk drawer, along with a pair of enormous plastic gag glasses that resembled Uncle Lucien's. With Uncle Lucien out of sight, Terry grabbed a rake from the shanty, pulled his shirt off, and scooped up handfuls of wet dirt from under the leaky garden hose. He smeared it over his chest and shoulders. I noticed that he looked stronger that summer, but his muscles were still lean compared to Uncle Lucien's.

"Check this out," he said. "Little bit of chest hair. I'm like the great gorilla himself."

"It needs to be white to look like his hair," I said.

"Nah, brown's cool." With the dirt stuck to his body, Terry stooped over and shuffled around, raking lines in the sand and sometimes looking up through the gag glasses, speaking to the sky.

"Come here, girl!" he yelled. "I got some protein for your eggs."

I laughed, my face instantly red and my eyes wet. Caleb was reluctant and embarrassed, but he laughed the loudest.

"Dude," I said, "you got problems."

"Come here, goddamn it! I said I got protein for your eggs!"

Terry had started swearing more often that summer. He squinted and bunched up his face to make it look old, and Caleb and I laughed so hard that our voices evaporated into a pure, silent laugh that shook our bodies.

"Let me give it to you, baby!"

The wet sand dried and fell in clumps from Terry's chest. As I wiped my eyes with my hands, he turned the hose on and began to wash himself off, still wearing the huge pair of plastic glasses.

My grandparents bought the New Era cottage during their retirement, and as my grandpa's only living sibling, Uncle Lucien had been invited over every summer weekend. When I think of the two men together, I remember them storing warm cases of Pabst in the rotting wooden shanty, never facing each other during conversations, but moving through words carefully, settling into them. Grandpa sometimes smoked a pipe, and once I saw the two of them leaning against a parked car in the driveway and passing the pipe back and forth—their eyes never meeting—and puffing up clouds that floated between them. Their conversations were like that, too: Grandpa could speak to Uncle Lucien with the ease of smoke, the words slipping back and forth amid their breath, inhaled and exhaled. It was a skill or a trick the rest of us never figured out.

Most Saturday afternoons, Uncle Lucien would turn the key in his car, roll the window down, and from the front steps of the shanty the two of them would listen to Tigers games on AM radio. They could patiently sit together through a fourteen-inning pitchers' duel, standing only for more beer or to piss in the ferns by the horseshoe pit. The only other time either of them sat so still was around the fire after dark. Otherwise, they were in motion, my grandpa playing flag football with us boys, taking us on errands to Jack's Market, or letting us sit in the back of his pickup and driving down the two-tracks, tree branches whipping us as we laughed in the wind. Uncle Lucien was tireless in a different way, tending the beach, pruning the trees, pulling the weeds.

He married and divorced before I was born. He didn't have any kids. When I was about five or six, Uncle Lucien had a string of relationships with young, obese women. He occasionally brought them to the cottage on the weekends. I remember playing tetherball with one of them. And I remember Aunt Dee Dee speaking to my mom through unmoving lips in the kitchen while stirring a new pitcher of cherry Kool-Aid.

"I don't even want to *know* my uncle has a fat fetish, let alone witness it every week. If he's here to plump her up on my potato salad, tell him to just leave now. I'll give her a doggie bag for the trip back to Fat Rapids."

He worked for years at the GM Metal Fabricating Division in Grand Rapids, living in an apartment without a yard or a garden. He drove a Plymouth, feeling no loyalty to his company or union or anyone else. In the winter, he hibernated. In the summer, he returned to the sand. He woke early every Saturday morning when it was still dark, driving his baby blue Duster to Duck Lake State Park before the rangers arrived. The park was on Lake Michigan, and he brought four plastic buckets with him that were so large I'd once stuffed myself into one of them during a game of hide-and-seek. When empty, they bounced against Uncle Lucien's knees as he clumsily trudged along. He kept an old army hand shovel in his trunk, and I can imagine him kneeling in the sand, digging during the hour when shadows and stars share the morning. I imagine him lugging the heavy buckets over to the car and dropping them in the trunk so that it sunk a few inches. The big lake was probably starting to glint like an unsheathed blade as he left for the cottage. By the time the rest of the family arrived around nine o'clock, Uncle Lucien had already poured white Lake Michigan sand over the small square of beach at the east end of our property, pouring it like sugar over our coarse, inland dirt. He raked and tenderized it, making crisscrosses in the ground so that it seemed new and perfect. We kids never dared to step on the beach first. We waited for our moms to ruin it with their dirty yellow flip-flops.

When Grandpa died in December of '84, my mom spoke to Aunt Dee Dee on the phone, arranging the funeral, but also arranging the aftermath, trying to resolve the Uncle Lucien situation. In other words, was he still welcome now that the sisters owned the cottage? Aunt Dee Dee said they should cut him off for abandoning Grandpa at the veteran's home.

There was a blizzard the day of the funeral. I'd never seen Uncle Lucien in the snow. I'd never seen him wearing a stocking cap and gloves. During the service, he kept his eyes closed and his head bowed, like in prayer, but also like when he'd bury his face in his hands as Willie Hernandez took the mound for the Tigers with two on and two out in late innings.

I sat apart from the adults at the luncheon that followed the funeral. But afterward, as we walked to our cars, my mom called, "We'll see you Memorial Day, Uncle Lucien."

His future was secured. He returned that summer.

It didn't surprise me. Even if they did mock him behind his back and ruin his sand with their flip-flops, I think our moms felt he needed to keep coming. Terry thought it was because they wanted the sand. It was as if Aunt Dee Dee had sat across from him at the luncheon, piercing kielbasa with a plastic fork and scribbling a barely legible but completely binding agreement onto a prayer card or dessert napkin, outlining each party's terms, asking him to sign the deal that would keep him in business at the beach.

But no such words, if any, were exchanged. They wanted to fulfill Grandpa's wishes and keep inviting his brother up every weekend. And they wanted Uncle Lucien there for our sakes. He wasn't Grandpa, but at least he was a man. As for all the bizarre displays and "oral flatulence"? They were things to ignore, like horseflies circling our heads.

A cardinal landed on a tree stump a few feet from where Uncle Lucien sat. It was the Fourth of July, and I was by myself on the other side of the beach, reading a baseball-card price guide. I looked up occasionally at Uncle Lucien and the bird.

"Hey, sweet thing." He stretched his arm out at the cardinal. "How are you?"

The cardinal cocked its head and took two quick hops in his direction.

"Pretty bird," he whispered. "Pretty bird. Pretty bird."

The cardinal flew away. I'd seen this before. Uncle Lucien spoke to animals more than he spoke to the rest of us. He said he read the minds of birds and fish. When Terry and I were real young, we used to think he was a wizard. Then I saw a falconer at a Renaissance festival near Detroit and thought they shared the same gift. As if Uncle Lucien could extend his right arm and horseflies, big ones, would land on his wrist. As if he could send them on command to hunt cats and black squirrels.

Once, Uncle Lucien emerged from the lake, where he had been pulling weeds offshore, and leeches were stuck to his thighs. He took his time removing them, walking up the sandy trail to the deck where the rest of us sat at the picnic table eating hamburgers. He wanted us to see the leeches, to be both sickened and enlightened by the truths of the natural world. He picked up a plastic knife from the table and plucked the leeches from his skin.

A year or two later, when my parents split, he took me aside.

"Come here, Lance."

My name sounded raw coming from his old mouth. Uncle Lucien held a humming coffee can in his right hand with air holes poked in the plastic lid. He lowered his voice.

"Bees."

He led me by the shoulder into the cottage and closed the screen door behind me, while he remained outside. Down on the beach, Terry and Caleb dug trenches in the sand. Our moms read magazines beside them. I was seven years old. And Uncle Lucien was the only person with me, bending down to look at me through the other side of the screen, his eyes at the same level as mine.

"Get closer."

I leaned slowly forward until my nose brushed the filthy metal mesh of the door. Uncle Lucien removed the lid and pressed the open mouth

of the can against the screen. I couldn't see the bees, but I swear to
God I heard each wing slice the dark coffee-can air. They seemed to
kiss my lips. But the fear of stings was less than the fear of moving
from where I was told to stand. I kept my nose to the screen.

"Some people run like hell from bees," he said, "and others tell you
to stay still because they only sting in defense. Just stay real still and
they'll leave you alone. And I say fuck the little prick of a bee sting.
Don't worry about an itty-bitty boo-boo here and there. Some things
are dangerous. Some just hurt for a second."

He removed the can from the screen, and the bees diffused into the
sky. Uncle Lucien's eyes never left mine. "Divorce is like a bee sting,"
he said.

He took down Grandpa's American flag without asking our moms.
It was the first weekend after the Fourth of July, and he replaced it
with a blue state of Michigan flag. Grandpa was a proud patriot who
fought in Europe during the war. Uncle Lucien never talked about
his own time in the service. He'd been a mess cook stationed in Goose
Bay, Labrador.

"A cook," said Terry.

I took the old globe from the cottage coffee table and searched all
over Europe for about fifteen minutes before Terry, sitting across from
me, pointed at his side of the globe.

"It's here," he said. "Christ, it's all the way over here."

I turned the globe on its axis and saw the word stretched over north-
eastern Canada, an ocean from the closest German tank. Labrador.

The blue Michigan flag slapped against the front door of the cottage, pressing its nylon skin against the kitchen window when the
wind blew hard. An elk and a moose stood tall on their hind legs in
the center of the flag. A river ran to a pretend horizon.

Uncle Lucien was a Michigan jingoist. Later that weekend, while
the family lounged on the beach and he took a break from his work,
he explained that we—meaning the entire state—could secede from
the Union and survive on our own.

"We got everything we need." He extended a hard, knotted finger with each word. "Lumber. Fruit. Iron ore. Fish. Christ, we could send tankers filled with fresh water down the St. Lawrence. Swap it with the Arabs for oil."

That, of course, was horse shit. He wouldn't give the water to any outsider.

He then quizzed us on Michigan history, geography, and wildlife.

"What's the state fish?"

"I don't know."

"Brown trout, you dope. How about this tree, right here?"

"Pine."

"*White* pine. State tree. Ever look away from the TV to see one in real life?"

He hated how the suburbs had ruined us. He hated our surprise when we overturned rocks in the woods and found insects in the cold dirt. He hated our grimaces when we swam in the lake and brushed against the submerged weeds. Even when we were younger and still followed him around, he wouldn't let us travel to Lake Michigan when he loaded his sand-thieving tools into the trunk of his Duster. The big lake was his shrine, and he protected it from the ignorant— from us.

Later in July, he sat in his green lawn chair and read an article in the *Chronicle* about how the state of Arizona wanted to run a pipeline and pump the lake's water to the desert. Uncle Lucien didn't shout like I expected, but shook his head and exhaled deeply as if suddenly exhausted.

"If we ran low on sandstone, would we take a jackhammer to the goddamned Grand Canyon?"

In early August, on the northbound highway headed for New Era, my mom told me that Aunt Dee Dee had been dating a guy named Pete.

"I wanted to let you know," she said, "in case you overheard anything this weekend. But you got to promise not to say anything around Terry. She's waitin' till it's right to tell him, and it's not right yet."

I nodded and knew what she meant. He was still angry about things.

I didn't say anything to Terry all summer, and I wished I hadn't known at all. It got me thinking about my own mom. She wasn't the youngest sister, but she looked like it since she never permed her hair, choosing to leave it long and straight. I started thinking about her with other men on those nights when I went to a friend's house to sleep over. Maybe Terry was keeping something from me, too.

August was a sad month. The weather was hottest and time passed the quickest, seeming to accelerate as the school year approached. Weekend tumbled over weekend. The three of us played a lot of horseshoes, Frisbee golf, and tetherball. We drank Pepsi with sand in it. Since Terry was the teenager in the family, our moms asked him to man the grill. He let Caleb pour the charcoal, and I could spray the lighter fluid, but he always lit the match. The warm, blue rush of flame made Caleb and me step back, while Terry stood as still as a soldier guarding his post. He flipped chicken breasts and poked at bratwursts with the two of us looking over his shoulder or playing close by in the sweet smoke. Our moms joked and talked loudly inside while arranging condiments, slicing tomatoes, and boiling corn. Uncle Lucien was waist-deep in the lake, pulling weeds from the water that he heaped into a compost pile. He was clearing the lake, but back then I only noticed the stench of the rotting weeds.

On a Saturday night in mid-August, when the sun set and the lake darkened, Uncle Lucien gathered logs and placed them just so in the fire pit. Terry had drawn a large circle in the sand for us to hold wrestling matches in, and he and I were trying to pin one another before all light left the sky. At one point he rolled on top of me and sunk his knee in my chest. He was definitely heavier than he was the previous summer.

Uncle Lucien walked over and rolled Terry off me with one hand. "You, get some dry leaves." He pointed at me. "You, little sheep shit. Twigs."

He turned back toward the fire pit, while I scrambled in the dusk for kindling. Terry sat in the middle of the circle, his legs bent and his arms resting on his knees. His hair was messed up. His T-shirt was stretched out. In the failing light, he looked confused and frustrated.

Aunt Dee Dee, Aunt Tess, and my mom came down the sandy trail after dark with marshmallows and the sticks to roast them on. We picked our places around the fire, Uncle Lucien already settled in his chair, wordless and still, staring at the flames with huge eyes behind huge glasses. Our moms talked until they tired, and we all eventually fell silent like Uncle Lucien, entering his world for a few brief moments when the shared space of family felt comfortable, when it seemed like Grandpa was sitting with us again, the quiet moderator between generations. The lake was black glass and broken only by the occasional splashing lunge of a fish. I sometimes jumped from the splash in surprise, but Uncle Lucien remained unmoving. I remember wondering once if he had died, he was so still. Maybe he had died with his eyes open like people sometimes do, and the cottage would feel more like ours with him gone. Terry and I would become the family sand thieves.

And then he moved, making me jump again.

Our moms were the first to yawn repeatedly and then stand up from the fire to say goodnight. My cousins and I could have fought fatigue longer, but we didn't want to sit alone with Uncle Lucien. We hiked up the trail, stubbing our bare toes on roots and piercing our heels on acorns. We left him there in his green chair, which, as the hours passed, seemed to slowly sink into the week's fresh batch of white sand. An orange light glowed over the cottage door, and moths and earwigs clung to the screen. We opened the door quickly and ran our fingers through our hair to make sure no bugs had landed on us.

And when we woke Sunday morning, Uncle Lucien was shirtless and barefoot on the beach as always, raking the damp sand. I wondered if he'd slept the night before. He and my grandpa used to share one of the bedrooms, while all the women shared the other and we boys slept on the living-room floor. But I hadn't seen him go to bed that entire summer since Grandpa had died.

I imagined that Uncle Lucien did hibernate—saving his rest for the winter, returning full strength in the summer like the flies. Maybe, in those times I thought he had died open-eyed by the fire, he was sleeping. Or maybe, long after the rest of us had gone to bed, he slipped inside the house like the spiders we'd always find, and then slept on the couch without making a sound. Our suburban eyes probably couldn't adjust to see him in the darkness of country nights.

I had started thinking like a young kid again, about wizardry.

The next day when I spoke to Terry about this, he just shook his head. "It's nothin' magical." He turned and looked at the Duster parked in the gravel driveway. "He wouldn't share a roof with just us. He sleeps in his car. And our moms are cool with it."

"No way," I said. "They wouldn't let him sleep out here."

"Sure they would. They hate him."

"Yeah, but not that much. They let him keep coming."

Terry raised his eyebrows and stifled a smile. "'Cause it's good sand, man. You can't deny that."

On a humid Saturday in late August—just days before school started—our faltering two-against-one badminton match ended because, even by himself, Terry whipped us. I threw my racket in the dirt and found my yellow Whiffle bat resting in the rafters of the old shanty. I left for the public boat landing one lot over, an area hardly used by anyone anymore, though it was a graveyard for overturned rowboats and canoes. Many were smashed from downed tree limbs, or from bored children who stomped on their underbellies.

I'd been watching black-and-white reruns of *Home Run Derby* and started smacking stones out into the lake, choosing a line of ripples in the water as my fence. The round stones felt solid on the bat, blooping far out from shore into a home run epicenter. I practiced so I could challenge and beat Terry.

He followed me down to the concrete strip of the boat landing, carrying a red plastic fishing pole—a kid's fishing pole. Caleb trailed him, still with his badminton racket. Terry's fishing line was tangled, and the gears popped and ground from sand the way our teeth did when we wrestled in the circle.

"Go look for worms," he told Caleb.

"I'm not touchin' any worms. They're sick."

Terry dropped his voice so it was low and quiet. "I said go get me some worms, Caleb."

"And I said *no way*. Like you'd even do it yourself. You're all scared to even rip 'em in half, so they're too big for the hook and come off on the first nibble."

"Butt licker."

"Shut up."

"Scrotum sac."

Caleb yelled out at the lake. "Free food for fish! The worms will come right off!"

Terry struggled to attach the sinker to the line, gritting his teeth. "Midget," he mumbled.

Caleb stuck his tongue out at him. He had to keep it playful, because if he did something serious like give Terry the finger, Terry would rush him and tackle him right there on the concrete.

"You're probably small enough, midget," Terry said. "I could stick a hook in your belly and you'd probably stay on."

I kept my back to them, glancing occasionally out of the corner of my eye at Uncle Lucien. He carried rock after heavy rock across the beach to make a little dam that would redirect rainwater as it ran out of the woods, away from his perfect patch of earth. I picked up a crumbling sandstone, tossed it a foot or two in the air, and swung. It exploded, the dust stinging my eyes and sprinkling into the lake.

My mom called down to us from the deck of the cottage. "Boys, are you gonna be hungry if we eat sandwiches in about an hour?"

"We're starvin' right now!" yelled Terry, still weaving the hook through the jungle of tangled line.

I swung for about twenty minutes, until my shoulders turned sore and the bat started to fray and grow sharp barbs where stones had nicked away the plastic. Caleb sat on a tree stump, sifting pebbles through his racket. Terry sat on a smashed red canoe.

"Finally," he said, and stood up. The long fishing line swung freely. He looked at Caleb. "Let's go fish."

I wasn't interested. I dropped my bat and walked up to the cottage for a Pepsi. My mom and aunts sat on the deck drinking wine coolers and laughing. They didn't see me approaching through the trees.

"He probably has a mirror above the bed."

"Oh, stop it, Tess!"

"She said they took Polaroids."

"Damn you. I don't tell her all your sordid Friday night tales."

"Not as sordid as I'd like."

I emerged from the leafy trail, and they immediately stopped talking. I walked through the hushed voices, returned their smiles, and crossed the deck to the back door. I grabbed a can of pop from the refrigerator and drank slowly at the sink, out of their sight, trying to make out the resurfacing whispers coming from the deck. I wondered if there would ever be other men at the cottage besides Uncle Lucien.

I kept listening, but didn't hear anything. After a few minutes, I left out the side door and walked to the tire swing that hung from a maple by the shanty. I slipped my legs through the center, twisted the rope, and tried to drink my pop as I spun. I was still young enough that I never got dizzy.

An echoing chatter emerged from the lake. Down the path, Terry held the cheap kiddy fishing pole, which bowed toward the ground as he reeled in a fish.

"Holy cow, check it out!" he yelled, though Caleb was right beside him. Terry's voice squeaked in excitement—something he'd worked hard all summer to restrain. I slipped out of the swing, dropped my pop in the dirt, and ran down to the lake. He held on to the line with a blue gill at the end, its dorsal fins like needles.

"Take it off," he ordered Caleb.

"*You* take it off."

Terry saw me. "Lance."

"No way. You caught it."

He let go of the line so that the fish dropped into the dirt, its gills flapping, the hook still in its mouth.

"God, it won't stay still," said Terry. "And it's sharp as anything."

He reeled the line in slowly, the fish ascending to the end of the pole. Then Terry reached back, threw his arms forward, and cast. The blue gill—still on the line—arced over the water, smacking the surface just as Terry jerked the line back again. I ducked and covered my eyes as the hook shot toward our heads.

"Jesus, Terry!"

When I looked again, he held the line with the hook—a piece of green flesh the only thing dangling from the end. "Sick," he said quietly. And then louder, "That was sick."

"That was awesome," said Caleb.

It happened all over again about a half hour later, this time with a sunfish. Caleb held the red pole, and it looked just right in his small hands. He struggled to bring the fish ashore. Its fins were fanned in shock, and Caleb high-stepped away from it as it lay in the sand, choking on air.

"You pussy." Terry picked up the pole and started to reel in the fish, but it fell off the hook, onto the concrete boat landing. "Shit."

It flailed, turning muddy in the gravel bits that covered the concrete. I picked up the yellow Whiffle bat and started to prod the fish, flipping it toward the sand and water. The fish writhed its way down the slope of the landing. Terry shoved me aside, stepped forward holding Caleb's badminton racket, scooped the fish up, and flipped it in the air. It hit the ground like a wet shoe.

"Oh, sick, man," said Caleb, covering his mouth. But I could tell by his bright eyes that he was smiling. I probably was, too.

Terry scooped the fish up again and flipped it high enough that he had time to swing the racket and strike it on the way down. He hit it the way I hit the stones. The fish landed on the shore about a foot away. It didn't move.

"Oh, man. Put it back in the water," said Caleb, laughing through the words. It must have been the laughs that snared Uncle Lucien's attention, because when Terry tried to scoop up the fish one more time, Uncle Lucien was rumbling toward him. He snatched the racket from Terry's grip, and their shoulders struck. Terry slipped on the loose gravel, landed hard on one knee, and clumsily rolled onto his side amid the boats. The back of his head slammed against the sharp prow of an overturned canoe.

Caleb yelled, and I held the Whiffle bat with both hands, down near my waist like a sword. Uncle Lucien stooped to pick up the sunfish. He smoothed the dorsal fins down with his hard hands and submerged it in the shallows by the lily pads. It began to twist in his grip, its scales slick again with the mud washed off. It swam away beneath the lily pads, but it circled back, circled back, confused and beaten.

Uncle Lucien looked past me. He looked at Terry.

"Aw, shit," said Terry, moaning quietly in pain. His hand was pressed between his head and the canoe, and when he removed it, dark hair and blood leaked through his fingers. He stared up at Uncle Lucien. "Crazy senile fuck," he said.

But he didn't move, and neither did Uncle Lucien. The old man was alert, but not yet threatening. He was ancient and massive.

Caleb turned to run toward the cottage, but our three moms were already descending the trail. Aunt Dee Dee led them as always. Her flip-flops slapped happily, but her furious eyes were locked on Uncle Lucien.

"Goddamn you, I saw that!" she screamed, striding toward us. Her voice was sharp. She, too, had heard all the commotion, and saw everything from high up on the deck.

She kneeled and touched her son's head. "Jesus, Terry." Then, smoothing down his hair, staining her hand with his blood, she mumbled, "I told myself, If he touches him, he's gone. If he touches him, he's gone." She turned and looked up at Uncle Lucien. "I swear to God, I don't know what we were thinkin'. You abandon Dad and then you show up to keep screwin' with the rest of us. God, find another family to hate."

Uncle Lucien stayed quiet, moving only slightly to stare at her and then down at Terry. Terry started to cry, snarling through quivering lips. "Crazy fuck uncle."

Uncle Lucien turned his head and slowly scanned the family. "Uncle," he said with a strange smile, shaking his head, sickened. "Uncle." He turned his hairy back to us and began to walk up the boat landing, over the loose gravel. Then he ascended the trail toward his car, dipping into the shadows of the trees.

I heard him start the Duster and pull out onto the dirt road. When it happened, I figured he was heartbroken for having to leave. But now I think he wrote us off—wrote the cottage off—the second he started his car. Fuck the white pines. Fuck the horseshoe pit. Terry's blood? Fuck Terry's blood—it was less than the blood of a smashed horsefly.

Terry was fine, anyway. He stood, the blood already drying in rusty smears on his hand and head. The rest of the family began to wander back to the cottage for lunch, while Aunt Dee Dee and Terry kneeled on the shore, cupping water in their hands and washing off the blood. Terry protested and pushed her hand back, but then let her clean it.

A few hours later we left in our three separate cars and drove home. Even though school began that week, we agreed to return the next Saturday for the long Labor Day weekend. We'd spend two nights with the water and the beach. We'd close up the cottage for the season. We knew we'd have to rake our own sand.

And we were right about Uncle Lucien not showing up that next weekend, but he came to the cottage earlier that week—maybe several times by the scope of the work. My mom and I arrived late on Saturday, and we walked down to the shore where Terry, Aunt Dee Dee, Caleb, and Aunt Tess sat in the lawn chairs around the fire pit.

Who knows how many trips Uncle Lucien had made back and forth between Lake Tahoe and Lake Michigan that week? He probably came at dawn, filling the plastic buckets with the sugary sand and driving to Duck Lake State Park before the rangers arrived, pouring the sand back onto the Lake Michigan shore, returning it to its birthplace, depositing it for people who deserved it.

My mom and I walked down the trail, and everyone turned to look at us, to read our reactions. Then they turned back to look at the hollow where the beach had been. All the soft sand was gone, leaving a scar of roots, dark dirt, and a gaping mouth in the earth that the lake began to fill. He left us a lagoon.

We closed the cottage that day, locking doors and windows, returning the grill to the shanty, and tearing down the badminton net. We didn't sleep over. Terry, Caleb, and I stood on the edge of the fire pit.

Horseflies were everywhere, searching for blood. They landed on our necks and in our hair.

"It's like they're lookin' for him," I said.

"Fuck him," said Terry.

Caleb got down on all fours beside the lagoon, his nose almost touching it. He was quietly looking for minnows and tadpoles to see if any new life had cropped up in the new water. Terry stood behind him, and under the bright sky I could see their reflections, slightly distorted in the shallow pool. Terry's mirrored body loomed over Caleb's, out of proportion, bigger than it really was.

Aunt Dee Dee honked her car horn. We headed for the trail, where my mom stood with our suitcases and uneaten groceries. I traced the missing beach with my footsteps, walking around the perimeter and counting years on my fingers. Thirteen, fourteen, fifteen, sixteen. In four years, I'd have my driver's license. I pictured having my own car, the back end sagging from a trunkload of sand as I roared through the state park at dawn, the rangers just arriving to an already smaller beach.

This is me at age five during a family trip to Texas.
I admit I still get pretty excited about a swimming pool.

Anita Shah Kapadia's work has also appeared in *Story Quarterly*, *River Oak Review*, and *Gargoyle*. She holds an MFA from Columbia University and lives in New York City with her husband.

PLAN B

Anita Shah Kapadia

Standing over the toilet, Arjun hears Lata call to him from the kitchen: "Who washed these dishes?" Arjun peers through the bathroom window, across two duplicate squares of lawn, to the back of Maria's house. The early morning sky above is dim and blue like a painted background. Her windows are dark and Arjun wonders how, on this morning, Maria manages to sleep.

"Who washed these dishes?" Panic flutters in Lata's voice, a brief note with the shrill timbre of a dropped spoon. Zipping his fly, Arjun hurries down the hall and finds Lata standing barefoot in the middle of the kitchen. She wears a nightgown dotted with sweetheart roses, a brown wool cardigan, and one yellow latex glove. Her gray-streaked hair spirals to her shoulders. "Who washed these dishes?"

The dish drainer holds a precarious arrangement of glass and stoneware, Arjun notices now. A light touch could send the whole pile tumbling. "I washed them," he says.

"You put them in there." Lata points a shaking, gloved finger at the dishwasher.

"I washed the dishes," Arjun says. "By hand."

Lata sways side to side and her nightgown swings like a bell around her ankles. Her toes wriggle. It's as if a current is running along the pale green linoleum, sending a slight charge through her.

"I have to go today," Arjun says. His suitcase is in the trunk of Maria's car, his hotel reservations are confirmed. Lata does not respond, but

Arjun believes she understands. The doctor told Arjun that Lata's brain is severing all connections, eliminating her ability to recognize people or comprehend simple facts. Lata has never confused Arjun, though, with anyone or anything else, and he imagines a final line, thin but sturdy like copper wire, attached between them.

When the telephone rings, Lata backs her head away as if it is screaming at her. Arjun answers and speaks to their son Pravin.

"I'm sending my guy over to do your yard," Pravin says. "He's doing mine in the morning and he can do your place in the afternoon."

"I can rake the leaves myself," Arjun says.

"I know, but humor me. Plus, he'll saw down that tree in the backyard. It's rotten." Arjun hears the baby crying somewhere in Pravin's house.

"Dad?" Pravin's wife Neelam is on the phone. Arjun hears their five-year-old daughter singing in the background now along with the wailing baby. His son's house, full of this mounting chaos, is located three blocks east of Arjun's own silent home. "Dad, I've got this onion basket thing to hang up in the kitchen. Can you come over today and help me put it up?"

"Sure," Arjun says, and Neelam hangs up before he can tell her a time. Neelam looks like a heroine in modern Hindi films—thick, wavy hair and rigorously curled eyelashes, lips painted a dark plum. She has a master's degree in electrical engineering and drives an ice-green minivan.

"Dad," Pravin says, "you can expect the guy around two o'clock tomorrow." Arjun's jaw tightens. Tomorrow there will be other problems. Pravin will have forgotten about the yard work and this man will show up, electric saw in hand, and ring Pravin's doorbell. Recalling this conversation with his father, Pravin will wonder whether the old man had given him any clues. Arjun hears Pravin shuffling through papers, moving on to his next task.

"Dad?" Neelam is back on the phone. "Tell Maria thanks again for the kids' hats. These are really cute." She hangs up before Arjun can respond.

"I'll thank her," Arjun tells Pravin before setting down the phone.

Lata is still standing in the middle of the kitchen, now shaking her hand wildly, trying to free it from the glove. Grabbing the latex fingertips, Arjun pulls the glove off. Lata stares at her hand, examines her palm and the skin on each finger, as if she's checking to make sure it's all still there.

They had begun walking together in March, after Maria stopped Arjun in front of her house.

"Mr. Amin," she'd called out to him. Maria was friendly with Neelam, and Arjun sometimes saw the two of them chatting in Pravin's driveway. He wondered what Maria, with her boy-cut hairstyle and grass-stained sneakers, might have in common with Neelam. In the warmer months Arjun sometimes saw Maria mowing her lawn or climbing up to the roof to clean her gutters. "I was wondering if you would mind if I joined you on your walks. I could use the exercise." Maria tapped her stomach. "And the company."

Arjun said no, he wouldn't mind, though he did mind. Like his father and grandfather before him, Arjun had walked three miles a day, five days a week, for most of his adult life. Only exceptionally rainy or snowy days prevented Arjun from following his ritual. And for the forty years Arjun had lived in America, he had always taken his walks alone.

Maria smiled. "Neelam actually said she thought you wouldn't mind. I'll join you tomorrow. I really hope you'll tell me if it's trouble."

Arjun nodded. "No trouble."

"I hope I can keep up," Maria said.

For the rest of that day, Arjun had wondered how he could get out of his new arrangement with Maria. He hoped she might find walking boring or difficult and give it up. Arjun loved his quiet afternoon journeys, the time and space in his mind to observe and consider his neighborhood. Now Maria would ruin this silent time. What, he wondered, would he even talk to her about?

Maria had done most of the talking during their first walk, and though he missed the solitude, Arjun enjoyed listening to her. He learned she was forty-six years old and lived in a house inherited from her mother. She taught GED classes at night. "I'm a lazy girl," she said. "Absolutely hell on wheels in the morning. And I like teaching adults. I don't think I could take some sixteen-year-old big mouth seriously."

They walked uphill from Maria's house toward the high school. Maria turned her head and Arjun later learned she was checking on a corner window on the second floor, the room where she taught her class at night. She complained about the day teachers leaving the classrooms a mess for the night teachers.

"Their desks are always covered with crap," she said. "Add them to The List." The List was Maria's mental catalog of irritating persons. Drivers who tailgated, anyone with a gnome in their yard, people who left Christmas lights up until February. "Slobs and morons, mostly," she explained.

Later that spring, Maria had told Arjun she'd been married briefly. "My husband was a nice enough guy," she said, "but a complete loser. He's living in Sparta now, married to a boring lady like himself." Arjun listened carefully to the details of Maria's life, collecting them in his memory like souvenirs from a favorite trip. Maria's mother had been a nurse in England during the Second World War. Her father had died of emphysema. She drank coffee only on Sundays, and then she had two cups. She had joined the army after high school and was stationed for a few months in Puerto Rico. She relayed the stories of her life with both humor and suspense, never making Arjun feel she was confessing or troubling him.

Arjun told Maria about the year he spent in Munich with his brother before they both moved to America. He described his last visit to his brother's house in Arizona, where one morning Arjun found six tiny lizards in the kitchen. All of their tails met at one central point so they looked like a half dozen clock hands spread out on the white wall. When Arjun came closer the lizards scattered in all different directions like a bursting asterisk.

He explained Lata's diagnosis. "Like Ronald Reagan," he said. Arjun had once despised the starring role celebrities took in their diseases—the way they campaigned for research money and gave reporters teary-

162

eyed accounts of their horribly changed lives. When it came to telling Maria, though, Arjun was relieved to name a famous person and skip the brutal details of sickness.

"That's awful, Arjun," Maria said. "Unfair." They walked in silence until they reached Maria's house. "I'm so sorry, Arjun," she said. He felt grateful to Maria for her hard voice, for the way she looked him in the eye when she said *awful*. He watched her open her door. She waved one more time before closing herself inside.

After that day Maria sometimes touched Arjun's arm when she told a story. She insisted he was not *that* old. Arjun began wondering how she looked in the morning as she made her way out of her bad mood and into her day. He knew she was not beautiful, but he enjoyed the movement of her face, the line of frustration that appeared between her eyebrows, the crooked, close-lipped smile after she told a joke.

During these walks, the last forty years of his life could slip away silently, like mounds of flour shaken through a sieve. Arjun made imaginary plans that sickened him: a pair of tickets to some tropical island, a note to his son instructing him to take care of Lata, a letter to his brother asking for his understanding. To stop himself from these thoughts, Arjun imagined what he looked like to Maria—the way his scalp showed beneath his thin layer of hair, the chicken scratch of wrinkles around his eyes. He was, he reminded himself, an old man.

On the first Monday in June, Maria invited Arjun into her house for a cup of tea. The air conditioner hummed behind them as Maria poured the boiling water.

"Where should we go today?" she asked.

"Delphi," Arjun said. Maria liked to assign destinations to their daily walks and Arjun had started researching interesting places in Pravin's old encyclopedia.

"Is that in Greece?"

Arjun nodded. "The belly of the earth," he quoted from the encyclopedia.

Maria's kitchen was full of light. Through the window Arjun glanced at his own house and his own empty kitchen.

"Do they have a beach?" Maria dreamed of Pacific islands, of a candy-colored blue ocean washing onto powdery sand. She turned her face into the sun and her brown hair turned red at the ends like tiny embers.

Arjun laughed. "No," he said. "No beach at Delphi."

"I've got to have a beach." She leaned across the table, her eyes fixed on his as she approached, and kissed him. They left their cups of steaming tea on the table and made love in her bedroom with the blinds drawn. Arjun glimpsed Maria's shoulder, her breasts, and the shape of her legs through chinks of light that slipped through the slats. They continued to meet in her bedroom without any light. At first Arjun thought they chose darkness because they were old and no longer proud of their bodies. Later he decided they stayed in the dark so that when they dressed and emerged into the world for their walk, they could pretend they had not been together in that room.

Arjun reads the newspaper in the bathroom while Lata showers. After the last visit to Lata's doctor, Arjun replaced the blue and white shower curtain with a clear plastic liner.

"When she showers," the doctor told Arjun, "you should watch." Arjun stared at the doctor, feeling his suggestion somehow smacked of pornography. The doctor whispered to Arjun so Lata would not hear, making his words seem even more lurid. The doctor had given many orders for Lata's safety—don't let her use knives, don't let her plug in anything—but in giving this instruction, it seemed to Arjun, the doctor had forgotten he was speaking about someone's wife. Lata sat on the examination table in a crinkling paper gown, swinging her feet like a bored child.

In the shower Lata hums and Arjun can sometimes make out the tune. Arjun reminds her to use soap and to avoid her eyes. Pravin will have to hire someone to help bathe and dress his mother, and Arjun has mentioned this and other instructions in the letter he will leave in his son's mailbox.

"I'm done," Lata says. Arjun reaches behind the curtain and turns off the shower. Lata drapes a towel across her shoulder to cover her naked torso. The bones of her shoulders are sharp against her skin, but her slightness is nothing new. Barely five feet tall, Lata has never weighed more than a hundred pounds in her life. Arjun remembers how she used to stand on tiptoe to fix a loose lock of his hair, how sometimes he would find her standing on the kitchen counter trying to reach something in a top cabinet, and it is hard for him to believe there was ever a time she was not this frail.

Arjun pats dry her legs and arms with another towel and wraps Lata in a thin, terry-cloth robe. Her light brown skin is smooth to the touch, covered with hair-fine wrinkles like parchment that has been soaked in water. Her hands tremble like two fish pulled from the sea, shaking out their final breaths. "Cold," she says. As they leave the bathroom, Arjun sees a light come on in Maria's house.

Arjun pulls Lata's clothes from the dresser. Like a child, she grips his shoulder for balance as she steps into her underwear. Once she is dressed, Arjun hands her a large, soft brush and she sits on the edge of the bed staring into the mirror.

"Can you comb?" he asks. As if Arjun's voice has triggered a switch, Lata begins drawing the brush through her hair. Stepping out of the room and toward the kitchen, Arjun tells himself he is going for a glass of water. He pulls the phone from the cradle as soon as his feet hit the linoleum.

"It's me," he says. Through the window, he sees Maria in her kitchen, dressed in her flannel pajamas. Her back is turned to him.

"You weren't supposed to call. No walk today, no phone calls, re-member?" Fresh from sleep, her voice is still hoarse.

"I just wanted to see how you were," Arjun says. Maria scratches the back of her head. She turns and faces the window.

"Are you spying on me?" She steps out of her kitchen, out of Arjun's sight, with the phone cord stretching behind her. "You're going to see as much of me as you want in a little while."

"I know."

"Are we crazy?"

She is the only real thing in his life, but he doesn't want to terrify her with this thought. "We are not crazy," he says. Arjun turns and Lata is in the living room, watching him from the sofa. Her wet hair is neatly brushed. "I should go," Arjun says in a chipper tone.

"I'll see you tonight," Maria says.

"Yes." He hangs up the phone. He forces a smile at Lata and she smiles back.

A rainstorm in the middle of August had kept Arjun from their walks for three straight days before the sky finally cleared. In her darkened room, Maria lay naked on her back with a sheet pulled up to her waist. Arjun's eyes had adjusted to the dark and he could see the outline of her face and her long neck. For three days he had missed her and he told her this.

"How was it at home?" Maria asked.

"It was okay," Arjun said. "She's getting more confused. She told me I had to go to the bank today and she kept insisting."

"What did you do?"

"I told her I would go."

"Maybe you should ask her why she wants you to go to the bank." Quitters and easy-out takers were at the top of Maria's List.

"Maybe," Arjun said. Maria spoke as if Lata was a student in her GED class, a person who had missed the lessons of childhood and needed a special kind of instruction. "I could try that." In truth, Arjun believed Lata was undoing herself like a trail of lit gunpowder, unstoppable as it snaked backward to its source.

Arjun closed his eyes and placed his arm around Maria, grasping the back of her neck. Her skin was damp and warm. As she faded into sleep, her breathing grew louder and deeper. Arjun listened to the slight whistling sound of air passing through her nose, a sound he had not heard before.

It amazed Arjun that Maria had been a stranger to him once. Though Arjun had met Lata only twice before their wedding day, he had prepared himself for her. She was a pretty, good-natured girl, and he had decided to love her. During the days preceding his wedding, Arjun imagined Lata—the wisps of hair escaping her braid, her feet that were no bigger than his hands—and he cultivated his love. When Pravin was a teenager, Arjun had tried to explain the benefits of arranged marriage, how responsibility bonded a man to his wife far more than emotion ever could. "You can't count on love," Arjun said. Pravin laughed at his father. "Okay, Dad," he said, but rolled his eyes as if to say, *What do you know about it, old man?*

Maria startled awake. "I almost fell asleep," she whispered. Arjun took her hand and slipped her index finger into his mouth. He wanted to tell Maria she was the only woman he had ever slept with besides his wife. He held her finger in his mouth to keep himself from speaking.

She laughed. "Hungry?"

"Sleepy."

"Let's go walk then," Maria said. "We don't have time to sleep. We're going to Morocco, remember? You ever been there?"

"No, but I would like to go." He had retired on his sixty-fourth birthday, nearly two years earlier. He and Lata had planned on traveling, but took only one trip—a two-week jaunt to Italy—before Lata became increasingly forgetful.

"Morocco," Maria said. "I don't know that I'd like the desert so much. Maybe I wouldn't mind it if the hotel had a pool."

Arjun pictured himself with Maria in a hotel surrounded by palm trees. A hotel with fountains and a pool, perched in the middle of the desert like an oasis. He let out a brief giggle and tried to stifle it. He tended to laugh this way when nervous, and Maria's shoulders rose against the sound, as if she wanted to cover her ears with her shoulder blades.

"You think I'm funny?" Her voice took a tough turn, and she sounded like the teenage girls Arjun saw smoking in the parking lot of the shopping mall. *You think I'm funny*, with a rumble rising in the throat, daring you to say yes.

"No," he said.

"Ha! A hotel," she said too loudly, and her voice echoed in Arjun's chest. A firecracker, a burst balloon, a shallow pop inside of him. "I guess it is funny."

"It isn't funny. I'd like us to go there." It was the first time they'd ever talked of going anywhere together. Normally, they spoke for themselves only. *I would like to go to Switzerland. I would like to see Mount Kilimanjaro.* Now Arjun wanted her to see the desert hotel as he saw it. If they both imagined it the same way, it would be a kind of journey.

"If she wasn't sick," he said, each word tumbling from his mouth awkwardly.

"Then what?"

"Then maybe we could go."

"If she wasn't sick," Maria said. "There would be no 'we.' You'd be traveling with your wife like you planned. You wouldn't even know me. I'm plan B."

She stood and began plucking her clothes from the floor and gathering them on the bed. She wasn't plan B or any kind of plan, Arjun wanted to say, but an accident. A stroke of luck or a bad turn, he wasn't sure which, but it wasn't the same as a backup plan.

Arjun watched Maria dress in the dark and listened to the sound of her skin moving against fabric. She pushed her fist inside the sleeve of her cotton shirt to turn it right side out again. Like a strange dance, the shadowy shapes of her arms and legs struggled up and down, left and right, and slipped into the dark shapes of her clothes.

Sapna arrives at eleven o'clock in her noisy green Dodge Dart. Arjun pays her one hundred and forty dollars in cash per week to cook their meals and to look after Lata while Arjun takes his walks. A chubby girl with bulging eyes, Sapna lives in Passaic with her brother and his wife and takes night courses at a community college. After she finishes school, Sapna plans to return to her village in India to get married, and Arjun worries she will be taken advantage of for her Green Card. He pictures her future husband as a handsome, swaggering fool who will come to America and break her heart. Men can do things you can not imagine, Arjun wants to tell her.

"Who is that?" Lata asks when Arjun opens the door. She is watching *The Price Is Right* on television in the living room.

"It's Sapna," Arjun says. "You remember Sapna?"

"She's a terrible cook," Lata says as Sapna takes off her shoes. Arjun gives Sapna a look that has become his shorthand glance during the past few months. *You know how she is*, the look says. Lata, Arjun has explained to Sapna, is angry because she can not clean and cook for herself, because she feels helpless.

Sapna smiles and calls out, "Hello, Auntie," in a loud voice. Helpless or not, she won't ignore Lata's insults. Lata turns her attention back to the television. The contestants are guessing the price of an entertainment system.

"I'm going out for a little while, okay?" Arjun says. Lata's lips fold into a pout as Arjun speaks.

"I'm going to Neelam's house," Arjun tells Sapna.

"Okay, Uncle." She runs the water in the kitchen sink to wash tomatoes.

"And Sapna, Lata has a doctor's appointment tomorrow afternoon, so you should take the day off." Arjun wants to spare his son the embarrassment of dealing with Sapna tomorrow. She lifts her eyebrows high above her bulging eyes. Arjun smiles at her. "I'm sorry I forgot to tell you."

"All right," she says. Arjun knows Sapna will recall this moment, and her initial suspicion of him, when she learns the news. "I'll make extra food for tomorrow then."

Arjun nods. "Bye," he calls out to Lata. "I'll see you in a little while." Lata does not respond. She pulls the sleeves of her green cardigan over her hands. Her small fists retreat like turtles' heads into shells.

In September Maria had had a problem with critters. Raccoons or skunks, perhaps both, knocked over her garbage cans and trampled through her garden. Arjun walked to her house one afternoon and found her waiting at the end of her driveway. He had forgotten his gloves and shoved his hands deep into his pockets. Maria was better prepared for the early chill, wearing a baseball cap and a brown leather jacket that was worn and wrinkled like old skin.

"I was thinking we could walk and then you could come inside for some hot chocolate or something," she said. "It's a cold one." She inhaled the air through her teeth and then blew it out in a loud burr.

She looked like a horse, shaking her head and neck in a blustering motion.

"So I found a dead skunk in my tool shed this morning," she said as they walked toward the high school.

"Really?" Arjun hoped her story would be a short one. He had been thinking about his plan for days and was ready to share it.

"I woke up to the smell," she explained, "which is not how I like to start my mornings. God knows how long it had been in there. Maybe I trapped it in there last week when I locked up."

"What did you do?"

"Well, I pulled out the shovel and scooped him into a garbage bag," she said. "It wasn't pretty."

"Maybe you should have called someone."

"Who would I call? Besides, I needed to kill the smell. Do you know how you kill the smell?"

Arjun shook his head.

"Coffee grounds," she said. "You light coffee grounds on fire and it kills the smell of anything dead. Human or animal. I learned that in the army."

Arjun laughed. It was hard to believe that a woman he knew had fired guns and jumped out of airplanes. "That's useful," he said.

"Yep. The smell had me gagging. I ran into the house and brought out a whole can of Folgers. I poured the grounds into a newspaper, rolled it up and lit it. Poof," she snapped her fingers. "It smelled like Sunday morning."

As she spoke, Arjun saw her story. He saw her wake, blink her eyes, and shake her head at the foul smell. Stepping through her house in her pajamas and slippers, she would find her way to the problem. He imagined coffee grounds poured into a cone of newspaper and Maria standing with her arms folded across her chest as the flames licked the air around her.

"Amazing," Arjun said. "The coffee. Amazing that it kills the smell."

"I knew you would like that one," she said. "You always like the gruesome ones."

"I did like it." A brisk wind shook the trees and a few yellowed

170

leaves drizzled down to the pavement. He needed to speak before Maria started another story, or he might lose the ability to say it. "I've been thinking," he said. "I've been thinking and I don't think we can stay here anymore."

"Where are you going?"

"Not me. You and me. I think we should go to Florida."

"A runaway fantasy? Why Florida? Why not Tahiti or Japan?" Maria laughed. Arjun stopped walking.

"I'm not joking."

"Sure. And your wife?"

"Lata gets some social security—it's not much. And she can have the house. There's no mortgage and Pravin can sell it. I have two hundred and fifty thousand dollars in cash and retirement money, and I'll have to leave half of that for her. So we take the other half and get started. You can sell your house, and I get a social-security check, too."

"I forget you're a grandpa."

"I'm serious."

"I don't think you are," she said. "Listen to yourself. You're walking down your own street talking about cashing out and taking off to Florida. And what about me? What about my life?"

"We can't stay here anymore. It's not good for anyone. You can teach in Florida. We'll make friends. We'll go to the beach."

The next morning, Maria hired a real-estate agent. They would leave at the end of October and stay in a hotel near the airport. Arjun could work out the financial details with Pravin and Maria could finalize the sale of her house. The hotel would distance Arjun from his family and show them he had made up his mind. The important thing, they kept telling each other, was to have a solid plan and follow it.

Neelam answers the door wearing a T-shirt and shorts. She has the thermostat set to eighty degrees and the heat from the house rushes upon Arjun as he steps across the threshold. The baby is in the living room, wearing only a diaper. The girl, Sejal, is running back and forth along the kitchen floor in a long black dress and patent-leather tap shoes. The hot air of the house smells of warmed butter, like a bakery.

"Oh, hi," Neelam says. "I was just making cupcakes for Sejal's Halloween party." She climbs the stairs, taking two at a time, and is back in the kitchen. Her legs are thin and muscular from the three miles she runs each morning.

In the kitchen, Arjun can see that Sejal's dress is actually her Halloween costume—a full-length black robe with a white crescent moon and stars stitched across the chest. She also wears a pink knitted hat with a pompom at the top. "I'm a sorceress," she says as she taps out of the kitchen and down a wood-floor hallway.

"Aren't you supposed to wait for a couple of days to wear that?" Arjun asks.

"Maria made me this hat," Sejal replies. She looks like her mother with the curving eyelashes and the waves of hair framing her face. Arjun looks away and Sejal continues tapping.

"Dad, I'll be done with the cupcakes in a minute." Neelam holds up a butter knife covered with bright orange icing. "Why don't you have a seat, okay?"

Arjun sits in the living room where the baby is pushing a red plastic lawnmower along the carpet. Neelam's house is similar to Arjun's house in design, but Neelam's decorating has obliterated any resemblance. Oriental rugs, complex window treatments, and brightly painted walls overwhelm her home. On one wall of the living room, brushed aluminum frames hold professional black-and-white photographs of the children. The kids, barefoot and dressed in billowy white clothes, pose in complete white spaces and stare off pensively into the distance. Neelam considers the pictures artistic. Arjun thinks the children look stunned, like hungry little paupers staring through a window at a feast.

"Hello, Sajan," Arjun says as the baby crashes his plastic mower into the coffee table.

"Maria made Sajan a blue hat," Sejal says, tugging the cord that ties her robe. "Do you want to see it?"

Arjun shakes his head no. When, he wonders, did children start calling adults by their first names?

"Okay, Dad," Neelam calls from the kitchen. "Let's do this."

She holds a contraption of two wire-mesh baskets, one strung beneath the other, and she points to a corner where she wants it hung. Arjun takes a drill from her toolbox. Neelam fills the baskets with onions and potatoes while he inserts a pointed screw with an eye into the ceiling. Arjun hangs the basket contraption and gives it a gentle tug to make sure it is steady.

"Thanks so much, Dad. I wish Pravin had some of your handyman skills."

This was a simple task, and Arjun knows Neelam asks for his help to make him feel useful. Once when Arjun was driving past Pravin's house, he saw Neelam in the driveway dressed in a business suit. She was carrying a large shoulder bag, balancing the baby on her hip, and sliding the minivan door shut with one hand. Arjun had to remind himself that she didn't mean to show off.

"Dad," she says. "I saw you on your walk the other day. I was driving and I got a glimpse of you in my rearview."

"Oh," he says. Neelam is smiling.

"I'm glad you found some company on your walks. It's good to have a friend to talk to." She speaks to him, Arjun realizes, the way he used to talk to aged people when he was a young man. He wants to tell Neelam that you can't always stay on top of life, that no matter how much you think you've got it all under control, sometimes the floor will still slip out from beneath you.

"Do you need help with anything else?" Arjun asks.

She rolls her eyes to the ceiling. "No, I don't think so."

Arjun opens the door. As the cold air strikes his face, he realizes he has been sweating in Neelam's hot house. "Oh, Dad?" she calls after him. "Do you want a cupcake?"

Arjun shakes his head. He walks home and finds Sapna emptying vegetables from a pot into a plastic container. Lata sits on the same spot on the couch, as if she hasn't moved since he left.

"Auntie ate her lunch," Sapna says. "Yours is in the refrigerator whenever you're ready."

Arjun sits beside Lata and tries to read the newspaper. He has trouble concentrating as Lata changes the channel with the remote control. She keeps her finger down on the button, letting the channels flip over and over without stopping. Arjun pulls the control from her weak grip, and turns to a soap opera she used to watch before she became ill. Lata leans back in the sofa and watches.

Sapna opens and closes the refrigerator and cabinets. She cooks tomorrow's meals, which Arjun will not eat. She washes dishes and puts the kitchen back into order.

"So I put everything in the fridge," she says as she dries her hands with a yellowed dishtowel. She slips on her coat and says goodbye to Lata. Lata does not even look at her. Arjun is sorry to see her go. He appreciates her presence in his house, enjoys the clanging of pots and hiss of the gas stove as a young woman moves about his kitchen. "Goodbye, Uncle."

"Take care, Sapna," Arjun says.

Arjun knows what Sapna will tell her family and her friends—*This crazy old uncle ran off with an American lady and left his poor, sick wife.* His story will be a cautionary tale about America, about how you can live in this country and lose your mind.

After Arjun retired, he and Lata booked a two-week vacation to Italy. As he flipped through the tour books, Arjun imagined settling into a life of visiting, even living in, these old cities.

Lata vomited during the first hour of the flight to Milan, and refused to eat any food on the plane. At night in their hotel room she complained her feet ached from walking on cobblestones all day. She lagged behind Arjun in the museums and on the walking tours, even after he snapped at her to keep up. Each day she picked at her food and counted down the days until they would return home. When they came to Rome at the end of the trip, though, Lata discovered the fountains, and her gloom vanished.

On each of their three nights in Rome, Lata insisted they buy cones of pistachio gelato and stroll through the squares. She refused to go back to the hotel until she had tossed half a dozen Italian coins into different fountains. She would stand at a fountain's edge and thrust her fingers open, as if she had a bug in her hand that she hoped would fly away. The *plink* of metal breaking through water made her smile each time. Arjun did not ask her what she wished for, if anything, but imagined the places they would go and how Lata would drop her coins all over the world. For the first time since they had flown to Italy, Arjun believed they might go happily into old age.

After the doctor gave him Lata's diagnosis, Arjun wondered if Lata's merriness in Rome had been the beginning of her illness. In India when Arjun was a child, people would have considered Lata mad. In one way, Arjun thought, insanity seemed a better diagnosis. At least the world would assume she had chosen to walk into this blankness. Instead she took pills and Arjun read articles about the latest treatments for victims of her disease. Arjun liked to remember Lata stepping through the Roman squares, tossing away her change, and wished he could remember if there had been any crazed glint in her eyes.

Maria once told Arjun she couldn't stand the people who threw coins into the fountains at the mall. Arjun kept his memory of Lata in Rome to himself, unable to endure the thought of Lata on Maria's List, wedged between dogs dressed in sweaters and anyone who couldn't change a flat tire.

At five o'clock, they get into the car. Arjun slips the key in the ignition and turns to Lata.

"I'm going," he says. "I'm sorry."

She looks at him, then over his shoulder, through the window toward a pile of junk in the garage—Pravin's old bicycle, boxes of schoolbooks and records. "To the bank?" she asks.

Arjun nods. "Yes, to the bank."

"Go later," she says.

"I can't." He backs out of the garage and drives Lata to Pravin's house. Arjun has told Pravin he has a doctor's appointment. Pravin helps his mother into the house and waves to Arjun before closing the door. Arjun stops the car at the driveway's edge, steps out, and leaves the letter in Pravin's mailbox.

As he drives away, Arjun glimpses in the rearview mirror at his son's house. That was his life, he thinks, his family inside that house. All of them eating dinner, believing things about each other and about their own lives. When they find his letter they will not believe it. Later, after they come to know it is true, they will consider Arjun a stranger. Perhaps Neelam will have sympathy for him, or perhaps she will worry that her own husband has this sort of capacity, a genetic shard. Lata will not know the difference. She will ask about the bank, about going to the bank, and Pravin and Neelam won't understand.

Arjun drives to his own house and cuts the engine in the driveway. He leaves the key in the car and the door unlocked. He turns to walk to Maria's house. He checks his pockets, worried he has forgotten something, then steps back to the car to make sure he hasn't. He gets inside to escape the cold wind. His fingers fiddle with the keys and he starts the engine. This is fair, he tells himself. Lata is already erasing their life together. Because of her illness she is allowed to let all the years evaporate, so why shouldn't he have the same option? Arjun looks out the window at the rotten tree in his yard, the one that his son is going to have chopped down tomorrow. Putting the car into gear, he drives to Pravin's house. He takes the letter from the mailbox and folds it in half before pushing it into his pocket.

"I got the days mixed up," Arjun says when Pravin opens the door. "My appointment is next week." Pravin narrows his eyes as he lets his father into the house. Arjun would like to shake him and say, *I'm not going crazy too, son.*

Lata smiles a lopsided grin when she sees Arjun. They eat dinner together, the six of them cramped around Neelam's breakfast table. Neelam spoons out large helpings on each plate. "Here you go, Mom," she half-sings as she sets Lata's plate down. Sejal turns away when Lata says something to her about the food being very green.

When Arjun and Lata return home, the red light on the answering machine is flashing. Arjun pushes the button and listens to a series of blank messages and hang-ups. In one message, Arjun can hear the television in the background. In another, he can make out the hiss of Maria's breath. He has destroyed her plans. He owes her an explanation but does not know what he could say. Leaving was completely his idea and now he had run out on their planned life together. It was as terrible as running out on his real life, perhaps worse.

In the morning Arjun sees his suitcase on the front lawn. He steps across the dew-dampened grass to fetch it and wonders if Maria has cut up all the clothes inside, or spilled something all over them. He imagines her fumbling through his things, exacting her revenge. The handle is sticky from the dew. When he gets inside, Arjun finds the contents of his suitcase are untouched. That afternoon, through the window of his living room, he sees Maria walking by herself. She wears earmuffs and her wrinkled leather jacket, and she does not turn her head toward his house as she passes. Her strides are long and her arms swing at her sides. She tears across the pavement and it seems as if she is turning the earth with her feet.

*The raw, simple reality of the Israel of my childhood, especially
at home in Afridar Ashkelon, where I lived until the age of nine,
has been a life-long source of longing and wonder.*

Avital Gad-Cykman was born in Israel and has lived with her husband and kids
in Brazil for the past twelve years. Her stories have appeared in *Happy, Imago, AIM,
Salon, Mondadori, Zeotrope All-Story Extra, Carve Magazine, In-Posse, Karawane Magazine* (which nominated her for the Pushcart Prize), and elsewhere. More is forthcoming in *In a Nutshell Anthology, Raven Chronicles, Snow Monkey,* and *Yellow Bat Review.* Her work in Hebrew was a prize winner in the contest Hamegeira.

FAR FROM THE SEA

Avital Gad-Cykman

At the click-clack of many feet walking, Joshua raises his bandaged head and leans over the window to peer down. From the stone house's second floor, the red hems of the smoggy dresses look like the dark outline of translucent jellyfish.

The cook from the restaurant downstairs cocks his graying head at a full-bosomed passerby. "Marina, aren't the girls lovely today?"

"Respect, Manuel. They are going to take the First-Communion rites at the church of Fortaleza," she replies. They speak in high-pitched voices, as excited as if the Messiah has finally made up his mind to come to Brazil and see how things have been going without him.

The girls wear bride's dresses and white semi-transparent veils. Without taking his eyes off them, Joshua reaches for the red-wine bottle standing on the cement floor, and, with bony fingers, wrings its neck. The wine eases the pain his wounded head shoots to every nerve in his body. Thick like malt, it slides down his tongue, sending heat to his head. Thoughts scatter from the back of his mind, as agile as he is motionless now. He would marry each one of the girls or all of them at once. He would lay them down on his mat and conceive children the way good husbands do. There is no limit to his time, no hurry. His nights and days keep him alive between their sticky hands. A hollow in his body waits for the warm body of his son to curl into it. His strong wife should curve over them, covering both like their home's roof. Whenever he wakes up, he hears the echo of his own cry. He drags his heavy dreams toward daylight, growing tired of his breath: going on and on, trapping him the way a net holds a fish, half-dead and half-alive. Perhaps this lifeless air will transform when touched by a baby's breath. He remembers the comfort of pressing his cheek against his newborn's warm head, how the warmth and the scent calmed the first-time father's anxiety.

All the girls move with the decisive, healthy footing that mirrors high expectations. They synchronize their steps like a creature of many legs, each one a worthy, similar organ. In spite of their apparent equality, he will leave out the ones who aren't destined to carry a child, the future nuns and the infertile. He mustn't be unjust.

In the center of the festive group, a girl tilts her head nervously: a brisk movement against the delicate flutter of her bride's veil. The motion awakens a rustle of wings in his stomach, a sensation he has nearly forgotten. Her fingers pull at the veil, exposing long hair, soft and glinting in black against the white satin top cut by the shape of her small breasts. He notices her singular grace, but the distance blurs her features, or perhaps it is his sight that's going weak.

The jellyfish swim down the street, and among them, her silken black thread slips like an eel. It appears and disappears as she interrupts their lines. He forces his eyes, afraid to lose her, but he does all the same. For a brief moment he sees only a white cloud woven with red light and nothing else. He turns his head so sharply the pain becomes blazing. Just then, in a movement he feels rather than sees, she tears herself away from the group and retreats into the entrance of his building.

The other girls split and spread to all winds, chattering and tittering, but soon they give up on her and unite in their whiteness.

He hurries out, fleeing downstairs. The girl sits on the bottom step of the crooked staircase, her fingers crumpling the fabric of her dress. In surprise, he realizes that what he took for a red hem is the street dirt. The lower part of her dress has the rich color of the soil the heavy rains wash down the hill.

He coughs, polite.

She turns to him, but a sunray that bursts from the top window dazzles her. She lowers her head before he can make out the lines of her face.

"Can I stay here for a few minutes?" she asks. Her voice is girly but it rings huskier than he expected. She probably sings well. He marvels at the way she talks to him, surprisingly trusting.

"Why did you leave your friends?" he asks. Though his tone is sympathetic, she stiffens in silence.

In vain, he tries to suck his words back. As long as she is here, his own mind doesn't trouble him. He shouldn't make her leave.

"I'll wear my bride's dress when I get married. I don't want it for any other ceremony," she says in a clear display of fierce temper. But then she turns her face at him and smiles. Outside, the clouds have swallowed the sunrays, and now they reflect them in honey tones through the top window and onto her. The shape and the color of her face remind Joshua of a light brown olive, and her eyes of green olives flecked by earth. She is pretty in a strange way. She doesn't have the sweetness that makes girls lovely, but her small strong features are illuminated by her eyes and her smile.

"Is your name Olivia?" he attempts to joke.

"Huh? Only if yours is Plum."

He crinkles his face even more, and she immediately says, "I didn't mean it."

"It's the sun's fault," he says, "not yours. It makes a man in his twenties look old. But pray tell, what kind of man do you want to marry?"

"A man."

"Girls go through the Communion first. Jesus was a man."

"He's not here."

"Well…"

He descends a few steps, and sits beside her. While making a place for him, she stares at his big bandage. "What happened to your head?" she asks.

He touches the gauze, feeling the wrinkled fabric, hardened around the top of his head with his blood. His long hair strands hang down from it like a dry samambaia plant. "An accident," he says.

"What kind of an accident?"

"My boat hit the rocks when I lost control over it," he answers in a lowered voice. Bits of memories rush through him, already as natural to him as his bloodstream: dusk, high waves, a taste of salt, a scream, freezing fear, small searching arms, his own tears, water crashing onto wood and rocks, screams and more screams, pain and silence. Like an idiot, he took them with him.

She seems worried. "It looks like a serious head injury—a big wound. Does it hurt?"

"Less than I expected."

"I am sorry," she says anyway. She raises her hand up toward his head, but he avoids the contact.

"It's so dirty! Don't you have to change the bandage?" she asks, either curious or gentle.

"How old are you?" he asks.

"It looks so stiff! It must hurt! It will make the wound worse."

"That's okay," he says.

"Fifteen."

"Late for First Communion."

"Yeah, well."

"You don't look fifteen."

Her olive eyes don't give in. "Let me change this bandage for you. I bet you'll feel better."

He suddenly realizes he's already feeling better. Somehow the tough little woman spreads tenderness in this barren place. "I think you should go now," he says.

"I didn't mean to disturb you." Her words come nasal. She gets up on her feet.

182   *Glimmer Train Stories*

He looks at her upright posture, the flowing black hair over her narrow, squared shoulders. "I need to be alone."

Her eyebrows align and her eyes turn earthier. Her fingers weave through her hair. "I just offered to change your bandage. You don't have to agree."

He can't resist. "Come on up."

She jumps up to her feet as if it's been a long time since anyone has taken her in.

As he goes up, he stumbles over a step when his long white shirt, a kind of a toga, entangles between his ankles. He turns around and sees her follow, light, almost floating in her bride's dress.

He flings the patined blue door open, holding it for her to enter.

"There is almost *nothing* here!" she exclaims.

He studies his place, the way she may see it. The spacious room is clean and scarce in furniture. Beside the rough wall on the right, there is a plain wooden bed with a striped mattress and a small dresser. A square wooden table and two stools stand at the back of the room. "Fishermen's houses are like that," he says.

"But it can't be a fisherman's house. It's too far from the sea."

"Do you think they are looking for you?" he asks.

"I doubt it."

"Your mother will get mad or worried."

"My aunt thinks it's a special favor I'm doing her because she took me in. But the thing is, she did it only because she had an affair with the owner of the bar where I lived."

"You lived in a bar?"

"Yes. We were neighbors. When my mother took a job where she had to sleep over, she arranged for me to stay there and for my brother and sister to stay with relatives. I was the luckiest one."

"And where is your mother now?"

"I don't care." Her face darkens without her smile and the fresh color of her eyes.

Joshua is invaded by strong, drilling appetite as he watches her the way he would follow a fruit changing color and becoming ripe. Nobody will look for her. Won't she make a good mother? His body tightens, trembles, gets ready. But in his excitement, he stops briefly with the instinct of fishermen. "Aren't you afraid to enter a single man's house?" he asks pleasantly, his way to give her an opportunity to escape, without really doing so.

She chuckles. A trembling of the skin under her eyes, a dimple in her right cheek. "You don't look dangerous."

His son, too, was trusting, though in that innocent way of five-year-old boys. "But I am!" he says in a loud voice, against the fishermen's ritual. "You know nothing," he adds bitterly.

He closes his eyes. The pain clothes him, penetrating with fangs. It finally fills him the way nothing else does. He holds on to this persisting bond, this umbilical cord to the mother of his child and to his child. When she bent over the boy on the boat, holding his hand in hers, her light brown strands mingled with his in the breeze. From behind, their heads looked like one, as if he still belonged within her body. The breeze was growing stronger, but Joshua didn't think much of it. He was proud and vain in their presence, navigating like a beginner.

Joshua's body remembers his woman's skin, her hands, her legs. How his son crawled under their woolen blanket on cold nights. Against all his losses, at least he has his pain.

The girl approaches, touches his cheek in wonder. "You're crying."
"I am not."
She starts unbuttoning her bride's dress.
"Don't!" he shouts.
"Shush…don't yell." She giggles. She steps out of the dress, wearing black shorts and a black T-shirt.

He stands in front of her in silence, feeling big and very old.
"See? I was prepared to get rid of it," she says in triumph.

He turns his head away. She is such a child. The thought of her pregnancy becomes intolerable. What was he thinking?
"Give me a new bandage," she says.
"I don't want to be treated."
"You know what? Let's play. If I find it, I'll take care of your wound. If I don't, you'll decide what to do about it." She laughs as

if she knew no pain. And, still, too easily does she build her way to him.

"I don't know any girl who wouldn't want to wear a bride's dress whenever she gets the opportunity," he says.

"I am different from other girls."

"How come?"

She turns her head away. "I'm not a little girl."

"You are."

She retains her game: "Tell me 'cold' when I'm far from the bandage, 'warmer' when I'm closer, 'warm' when I'm almost there, and 'hot' when I'm there."

"I don't play."

"Please!" she begs. Her little tongue touches her lower lip, flowery like an anemone. Her face transforms again, maturing.

"Fine, but five minutes."

She runs to his bathroom.

"It's like a monastery here." She breathes hard.

"Cold."

She slips through the half-opened kitchen door into the small kitchen.

"Oh my. When have you last eaten?"

"Cold."

"It's empty!"

"I wasn't hungry."

She opens the door and stands by it. Her eyes are scared but searching.

"Warmer."

"Is it?" She leaps forward. "I thought you'd cheat!"

Against his will, he laughs. "I wouldn't."

"Are you hurting?"

"Not as much as I should."

She nods her head. She checks the wooden handle of the small dresser beside his bed.

"Warm."

When she pulls it out, the door hardly opens, squeaking. "There's nothing here. Just some socks and shirts," she informs.

"Oh!" He is surprised. He thought he brought a bandage from the hospital.

"Go on, go on!" she cries. "I am near, right?" She draws closer to the bed. "Yeah! There's a box here! Am I hot already?" Her round backside is more feminine in the tight shorts than it was in her bride dress. Her lean back is graceful.

He'd rather join his son and wife than stretch this torture. He approaches her. "Let's stop." He raises his hand up toward his aching head, and she moves back quickly, protecting her face from a blow. Immediately, she comes back to her senses and mumbles, "Sorry…"

His knees buckle under him and he sits down at the edge of the bed.

"Who hurt you?" he asks in grief that surprises him.

She talks fast. "Some men. Stupid junkies that hang around the slum. I told you I am not like other girls you know. I am an adult. First Communion is for little girls."

"That's why you ran away?" he asks.

"We were playing, you and I."

"From the religious ceremony."

"I told you already. Now, wait. I haven't found the bandage!"

"You didn't want to go to church but you do want to get married?"

"Yes." She looks at him, pensive, and relaxes against the wall. "My friend Leticia told me a Greek story to pass the time in the hospital. It goes more or less like this: Once upon a time people had a round shape, four legs, and four arms. Though they were happy, they were a little bored, so they challenged their gods and made them angry. Zeus, the main god, lost his patience and divided every one of them in two: a man and a woman, each with two legs and two arms. So, we all have our lost halves." Her gaze strays off toward the box beside the bed. She dives to check it, forgetting everything else.

"Your friend is very clever," Joshua tells her.

"She's my best friend!" She straightens up, his large handkerchief tied to her long hair like a ribbon. "See what I found!"

"It's ugly. You'd better leave it," he says, but he can't hold back his smile.

"No!" She moves lightly, in dancer's steps. "Come on, get it!" She laughs.

He gets up slowly, and by his side she escapes in her eel movement. She jumps onto the bed, crying, "Why don't you take it?"

He stands still to stop the merry-go-around inside his head. This time it doesn't take long to pass, but the heat spreads inside him. He takes two corners of the sheet and pulls them in the sharp way he used to retrieve nets before that kind of fishing turned illegal. He is playing now with all of his senses, and a devilish grin creeps onto his face as his mind repeats in a daze: she's an eel to catch. She's an eel. Eel.

She falls down and her hand clenches at his shoulder. Her hard breath startles him with its familiar scent. It is not an ocean fragrance but a warm, young breath.

He freezes.

"You've got your handkerchief," she says matter of factly, loosening it from her hair into his hand.

He wants to be dead. "You're not worse than anyone else. You should have gone with the other girls," he says in despair.

"I *am* different, whether I want it or not." Then she smiles again. "I am not finished here, as you know."

"There is no bandage," he says.

"Hell!" She sits back on the bed. "Don't you know how the game works? There are rules! You must have a hidden bandage. Do you have children?"

"My son liked to play hide and seek, but not with objects."

"I like it, too. Where is he now?"

"Missing."

"What do you mean?"

"After the accident his body wasn't found. They only found my wife's." He attempts to remain as detached as he possibly can, but the words weigh so heavily, he bends his body like an old man.

"Oh!" She hesitates. "You know what must have happened? When you hit the rocks, he grabbed onto one of them and climbed all the way up." She gets breathless, and her face flushes as her voice rises, self-assured. "He passed out, so he couldn't call for help, but when he woke up, he found himself on an island full of coconut trees, waterfalls of sweet water, and nice caves to sleep in. A man can survive on coconut fruit and milk alone for months. Leticia has told me that, too."

"You think?" he asks. Weakness concentrates down his stomach. He reclines over the bed. "It's not impossible." His mind races.

"With so much experience in fishing accidents, they would have found his body if there was one," she says.

He lowers his head. "No, that's impossible."

"Let me see the wound, and treat it, and I'll sail with you to find him."

He bends over, unable to refuse her anything anymore.

Her fingers at his wound send flashes of pain throughout his body and nausea into his stomach. He holds his breath.

She tries to pull a loose bit of the bandage, but stops when a moan escapes him. "Oh my God!" she says, afraid. "You must get well."

She looks around. "Got it!" Hurried, she picks her dress up from the floor. The foggy layers open up like a white rose. She stretches the dress between her hands as much as she can and tries to tear it apart.

"No!" he cries. "Wait!"

"I won't use it, anyway."

"What's your name, Olivia?"

"Isabela. And yours, Plum?" She looks up at him, waiting.

"Do you promise to sail with me until we find him?"

"He's a lucky boy. We will find him."

"My name is Joshua."

He picks up the wine bottle and balances it on his palm. Drops of red, velvety wine crawl up and down the bottle. He holds it down carefully to let red drops paint his feet. Then he pours a little wine onto his chest, over the left side of his white old shirt. Lastly, he wets the palms of his hands and stretches his arms to the sides, open. "Stay with me," he asks.

She blinks and pulls at her nose. Then she smiles.

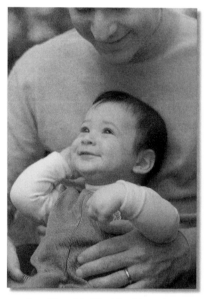

Six months old, with Dad looking down on me.

Michael Bahler grew up in Livingston, New Jersey and currently lives in New York City. His fiction has appeared on *nerve.com*, in *Hangling Loose*, and in the *New Jersey Review*, and his poetry in *Parting Gifts*. While attending law school, he studied at Boston University's graduate creative-writing program. He also clerked for the United States Court of Appeals for the Third Circuit in Newark, New Jersey.

THE DIVORCE RATE
FOR SURGICAL RESIDENTS

(signature)

Michael Bahler

It was my fourth year of med school, and time to burn all bridges but one, and decide whether I'd be happiest for the rest of my life being a surgeon, an emergency-room doctor, a pediatrician, or an OBGYN. I couldn't choose. Worse, I had little time because I'd totally pissed away my first three years of school convinced that I wanted to be a surgeon, following around the surgery attendings, grinning while I fetched them sandwiches, and it was only at the very end, after I sent away for residency program applications, when asked to write my personal statement, that it hit me like an acute anterior-wall heart attack that I might want to be something else.

There was no one to consult. The school had a bunch of psychiatry residents masquerading as career counselors and it was common knowledge that our psychiatry program sucked. My parents theoretically could have offered some good advice, but I wasn't going to go near that one; if I wound up listening to them, the choice would forever be tainted, and if I forsook the advice, I'd be tortured thinking I'd made a dumb choice out of spite. Finally, my friends were all self-obsessed bastards and I didn't have a girlfriend.

The application deadline was in seven days. I wasn't one of those kids who could crank out the essays in a night, so I had to choose right away. I unplugged the television. I killed the phone. I cleaned off the top of my desk and sat down. What was so great about surgery? Sure, it sounded good to say that I was studying to be a surgeon, but what was beneath that? What was so important about being one of the few people who could successfully remove a gall bladder? In pediatrics, I could help kids and the hours were a cakewalk. There was a shitload of money in anesthesiology, and the work was relatively easy. OBGYN, I could deliver babies. I could be a calm, friendly baby deliverer. I had to make a choice. What to do? What to do? This was the rest of my life. I was sweating through my shirt. My underarms soaked.

I decided to ask out a nurse. I reconnected the phone. In medical school, asking out a nurse was worse than joining an online dating service. It was like throwing in the towel and admitting publicly that you couldn't get a classmate to go out with you. But I didn't give a shit what people thought of me, and she wasn't just any nurse. Rosa Stein was a half-Jewish, half-Puerto Rican firebrand. She was cute but not beautiful, like a poor man's Jennifer Beals. After a few minutes of psyching myself up, I called her floor at the hospital and asked if she wanted to grab dinner after her shift.

"You're asking me out?"

"To dinner."

"I don't know."

"I'm not stiff outside of the hospital," I said. "I'm funny. But if you have other plans."

I brought Rosa to the The Flaming Pit, an upscale steak joint a few blocks down from the hospital on Michigan Ave. It was the place I'd gone with my selfish friends after we passed the Boards. I remembered it as being expansive, quiet, and clean, with bright lighting, almost—but not quite—like an operating room. I took her there because the food was good and, more importantly, I wouldn't have to make any tough choices. The menu was simple: steak, potatoes, beer. I watched Rosa pick up her fork and browse through her salad.

"I've seen heart attacks," I said. "Big ones."

"So have I."

"I've talked to the patients," I continued, "afterwards, and they said it was like an elephant was rolling around on their chest. One woman said she thought her ribs were going to blow apart. It's got to be so solitary.

192

Imagine it, the ER staff is working away on you and you're there on the table feeling like your chest is going to crack into a thousand pieces."

"My uncle had a heart attack," she said.

"Is he okay?"

"Yeah. He had to switch jobs." She stuck more salad in her mouth. "What kind of doctor are you going to be?"

"I don't want to talk about it."

"Haven't you picked?" she asked.

"This is my night out. I don't want to talk about anything having to do with medicine."

"What's wrong with you? You only have until next week to pick. Wait, I thought you wanted to be a surgeon. You're the one who operated on that kid."

"I only assisted."

"Whatever happened to her?"

"It was a meningioma in her cerebrum. Right here." I tapped the precise spot on my head. "About the size of a lemon. This big. And we cut it, and it looked like we got it all. But you never know, so we had to wait for the excisonal biopsy to come back—it took so long, and then our pathologist thought it might still be dividing. So we had to send the biopsy out to the University of Chicago and Rush and U of I. God, I was so nervous. But we got it all. Clear margins throughout. We saved her life."

"And now you don't want to be a surgeon?"

I was grinning from ear to ear. "No. Probably not."

"Why not?"

"The divorce rate for surgical residents is ninety percent," I told her. "At Duke, it's a hundred percent."

"So what?"

"I don't want to get divorced."

"You need to pick something, Alan. What are you waiting for?"

"Inspiration."

"Good luck."

"Thank you," I said.

"Well, I think you should be a gastroenterologist."

"Why?"

"The happiest doctors at the hospital are the gastroenterologists."

"Like who?"

"Kamath. Li. Kim. Rosewater."

"Rosewater's not happy," I said. "He's a grump."

"You don't eat salad?" she asked.

I picked up my fork. "If it wasn't me, I could make the decision. I just have to think about it like I'm making the choice for someone else."

"Make the choice for me," she said.

"You want me to?"

"Go for it."

I felt a shiver.

"How old are you?" she asked.

"Me? Twenty-five."

"I'm twenty-eight." She held her face forward as if to let me examine it. I spotted a couple of wrinkle lines under her eyes, and the beginnings of an actinic keratosis on her left cheek, but she didn't look old.

"I'll be twenty-six in July," I said.

She dropped her fork into the bowl. The top covering of lettuce sagged like a soft mattress. "Do you like photography?"

"Taking pictures?"

"Or looking at them."

"I don't want to be a radiologist."

"I like benches," she said. "I take pictures of benches. I'm thinking of going on a big trip across the country sometime before I turn thirty and instead of shooting the Sears Tower and the dunes in Wisconsin, I'm only going to take pictures of benches. From coast to coast."

"Yeah, I know a lot of people who take pictures of benches."

"You do?" Her eyes squinted up. "Who? What kinds of benches?"

"I don't really know."

She bowed her head. The white dash of her part glowed.

"They weren't really taking pictures of benches," I said. "It was more of just group pictures and we were tired of standing. I think it's original. Coast-to-coast benches. I don't know anyone who ever did that. Rosa?"

She looked up. "You should be a shrink."

"Really? No, I can't see myself doing that."
The steaks came and we ate.

Puru, my best friend at medical school, had already decided on dermatology. His applications were typed and proofread. He was also getting married. Except it was an arranged marriage. Puru had worse luck than me with women. He had struck out with a blond classmate from Kentucky, two Indian nurses, a homely law student, and an X-ray tech. Though I didn't dare ask, he was probably a virgin. Last summer, after being rejected by the X-ray tech, he succumbed to his parents' traditionalism and gave his mom the green light to go find him a wife. Within weeks, she rounded up a willing nineteen year old in a village outside of Delhi. Puru had never met the girl. It wasn't even one of those email courtships. I could have made sense of the arranged marriage if Puru had grown up in India and was here as a foreign exchange student, but he was from Sandwich, Illinois.

I tried to talk him out of it. We had the kind of friendship in which we were always busting on each other, but from then on I was complimentary. The better he felt about himself, the more likely he was to call it off. I also badmouthed his parents. I regretted doing it because they were always very nice to me. Whenever they drove out from Sandwich to see him, they'd take me along to the Indian restaurant on Devan. His little mom, barely five foot, would ask intently about how I got along with my family and she'd want to know the story behind Thanksgiving. Yet there I was referring to her as a bad mom who put outmoded rituals far above her son's happiness.

Puru once told me that arranged marriages were so common in India that people automatically assumed a couple had been arranged. There was actually a term in India for a couple who met on their own: *love marriage*.

I showed up at Puru's place a couple weeks ago to filibuster against the arranged marriage. I asked him how great it would be to honeymoon in India one day and tell people, "No, we're a love marriage." I thought I was being clever. I thought the allusion might trigger his romantic sensibility. After all, he was a total sap. He saved all his movie tickets, wrote two love poems for the Chinese law student our first year of school, and owned the soundtrack to *She's Having a Baby*. I was surprised when he blew up at me. Before kicking me out of the apartment, he accused me of being jealous.

I denied it, but maybe I was jealous. Maybe I, too, wanted a nineteen year old from India. I definitely wanted somebody. The other day in the hospital cafeteria I overheard a few of my classmates discussing residency programs. It was torture listening to one guy say he only applied to programs in New York because his fiancée was a PhD student at Columbia, and a woman I was sure had chosen surgery say she had picked ear, nose, and throat because she was married and the divorce rate for surgical residents was ninety percent. I felt left behind. Here I had this tremendous decision before me and I didn't have to consider anyone but myself. I wanted to sacrifice for someone, I wanted to give up surgery, or at least have that opportunity. Then I thought of Puru and his upcoming wedding, and I was so mad at him, I actually made a fist.

I called Puru after I got back from my date with Rosa Stein. "I think I am jealous of you," I said.

"Okay, Alan."

"No, I'm serious. I want an arranged marriage. I can't date. I suck at it. I'm so sick of going out with random women and having them not like me for whatever reason. Do you think it's bad if you go in to kiss a woman and she shoves you? It was a first date. God, I hate this shit."

"Who did you go on a date with?"

"A nurse. I can never go back to the hospital."

"Which nurse?"

"What's yours like?" I asked. "The future Mrs. Shah. What's her name again?"

"Sunita."

"What's she like?"

"Alan."

"I'm interested. You say I'm always being an asshole about it. Well, now I'm interested. Tell me, what's Sunita like?"

"Sweet," he said.

"How do you know?"

"Something about her voice, the way she talks."

"In English or Hindi?"

"It's hard to explain. She's…I just know she's sweet, and it's more in her voice than what she says. The same thing happened to Kandinsky. He married a telephone operator."

"Wassily Kandinsky did not get an arranged marriage," I said. "Kandinsky—and every other painter—met some woman in college, like sophomore year, and it worked out. Hold on." I pulled off my socks and threw them in balls across my room toward the open closet. "So when are you going to show me the picture?" I asked.

"You'll see her when she gets here."

"You know it's a good picture. That's got to be the best picture she's ever taken. She's not going to send you a normal picture."

"No, in India it's illegal for unmarried girls to send inaccurate pictures."

"That's so subjective. I don't mean to be a dick, but it's a crapshoot. It's a crapshoot always, but with her it's really a crapshoot. Hold on." I unbuttoned my shirt. Up on my ceiling, two white light bulbs glared down like camera flashes. I yanked my arm out of the shirt and used my hand as a visor. The ceiling light had come with my school-subsidized apartment and I had put up with it for more than three years.

"I haven't finished my applications," I told him.

"Finish. I'll look them over if you want. But you need to get everything done and postmarked by the fifteenth."

"I don't think I want to be a surgeon."

"What are you talking about?"

"I think I want to be something else," I said.

"Alan, finish your applications."

"Why do I have to be a surgeon? There's a choice here. You might not think there is, but I can pick whatever I want. I have that ability. I might want to be a gastroenterologist. I hear they're the happiest."

"You either need a psych consult or a shot of Chivas."

"I need a bride from India. Are you going to take wedding pictures?"

"Why wouldn't I?" he asked.

"Because you don't know her. You'll be strangers. It'll be like pictures from New Students Week. Wait until you at least know her for a couple of months, then take the pictures."

"You haven't heard her voice," he said.

"What's there to hear? And how do you know you're talking to the real her? Maybe it's the one girl in the village with a nice voice. She's married off the whole town."

"Why don't you shut up."

"Puru, I have no idea what to choose." I stood up off my bed. I was surrounded by my desk and dresser. "It's killing me. What do I do?"

"You're going to be a surgeon."

"Don't say that."

"Go to sleep. Tomorrow wake up early, and just get down the essays. You have to just do them. I'll come over tomorrow night and I'll help you make them pretty. Then you'll be done. It's like lancing a swollen, pus-filled furuncle. You just have to finish the essays."

"I think you're selling out," I said. "You're afraid that you're going to be single for the rest of your life."

"Shut up."

"It's going to get better. We're going to be doctors, right? Women like doctors. There's got to be some fucking truth to that. Call it off. Tell your parents no. Let Sunita find some other sucker to bring her to America."

He had hung up.

An hour later, I called Puru to apologize. I had gone too far with my last comment about him being a sucker, and I hoped he had hung up before that. He didn't answer and I apologized to the machine. Now I was going to choose a specialty. I sat down at my desk and began wading through my medical textbooks as if they were travel brochures. They all interested me—I was a medical junky—but I wasn't ready to hitch my wagon to, say, rheumatology for the rest of my life. I started flipping through the pages. Nothing was jumping out. I began palpitating. I reached the end of the book.

There was a good chance I wasn't going to be able to choose. I dropped my head on the desk. I relived Rosa shoving me back. I wasn't even going in for a mouth kiss. What had I done wrong? Too much talk about specialties. That stupid remark about knowing a lot of people who took pictures of benches. Or was it something else? Enough about that; I needed to pick a specialty. I cracked a different textbook. This one had colorful drawings instead of photographs.

I woke up at my desk. Daylight blasted through the window. It was Tuesday. I had six days to choose. In one week, it would be over. I wiped my rubbery hands over my face. I threw on a hat and headed out for some food. The mailman passed me in the lobby. I hadn't received anything in the mail since my applications arrived, except bills, but I was always hoping for a real letter from some girl in my past. There was a single envelope. It was from my school. I opened it. Dean Bernstein wanted to meet with me tomorrow. The wall of mailboxes blurred. Bernstein was the Dean of Students and no residency application was complete without his recommendation. He met with every fourth-year right before the deadline, and rumor had it that no student had ever left the meeting without a decision on a specialty. I needed to decide once and for all. I needed a specialty to just pop into my head. I didn't have a girlfriend. My best friend was getting an arranged marriage. I at least deserved a pop.

Proctology.

Great, I was getting sarcastic pops.

Surgery.

Gastroenterology.

Masters in Public Health.

Not funny.

"My mail," someone said. "I'm trying to get my mail. Hello? Can you move?"

I found Rosa in the nurses' break room. She was alone in the room, holding a piece of sandwich as she read the newspaper. A drip of mustard trickled down from the bread. In her white uniform, Rosa looked like an angel with black hair. I felt safe. It was the same feeling I got in bright elevators, when watching mindless TV, and in the operating room. Maybe I did like her. She hadn't heard me come in and

I kept quiet as if observing a deer.

"Alan, what are you doing here?"

"Did you know almost no one dies in surgery," I said.

"That's not true."

"I've had four surgical rotations and two people died on the table. Lots die in the ER before making it to the OR, or in the ICU afterwards, but no one dies on the table. It's awesome like that."

She put down her sandwich. "You chose surgery?"

"I haven't chosen anything. Do you know Puru Shah? He's Indian. This tall, my year. He's getting an arranged marriage." I slapped myself in the mouth.

"Alan, what's wrong?"

"Nothing. Nothing. You've got to promise me you won't tell anyone I told you that. You promise?"

"I'd never get an arranged marriage."

"Me, either." I took the seat across from her. "He says she's sweet, like it's not an arranged marriage. Like Sunita's just some random woman who called him. You've heard of Kandinsky and the telephone operator? He said it's just like that."

"Maybe he's right."

"I don't think we're talking about the same story."

"Kandinsky picked up the phone." She placed her thumb on her ear and her pinkie toward her mouth. "The most incredible voice he had ever heard. Two minutes of fluff talk. He hunts her down and marries her. That's an arranged marriage."

"Arranged by who?"

"Kandinsky. You can arrange your own marriage."

"No, you can't. Not like that. Your mom does all the stuff—or at least someone in your family. All I know is Puru's mom called India. Then she gave him the phone. Then, in India, Sunita's mom gave her the phone. He won't tell me what they talked about, but I know it's not that profound, because he hasn't mentioned any new theories. Then he gave the phone back to his mom. They did that phone handoff every Saturday for a month—and they're getting married. That's an arranged marriage. Do you think I'm jealous?"

Rosa finished her sandwich. "I have to go back to work."

"Wait."

"What?"

I grabbed the letter out of my pocket and dropped it on the table. "Read it. Please."

She picked up the envelope. "Why do you have two middle initials?"

"My parents suck at compromising."

"Who's Dean Bernstein?"

"I have to meet with him tomorrow. If you don't decide on a specialty by the time you get there, he puts his hands over his eyes and tells you what you're going to be. That's the rumor. Hands over eyes—boom—you're a pediatrician."

"I'm sure he'll just talk you into surgery."

"Do you think I should be a surgeon?"

"Don't ask me."

"You're a nurse," I said. "What kind of doctor do I seem like?"

"I have no idea." She gathered her garbage from the table and stood up.

I jumped to my feet. "You said gastroenterologists were the happiest. Did you mean it?"

"Alan, I'm going."

"Why didn't you let me kiss you?"

She stopped and looked at me with her brown eyes. "You're in heat. I've seen it before. Fourth-year medical students lose all direction right before the deadline for residency applications. They try to sleep with a nurse to get it back."

"Does it work?"

"Goodbye."

"No." I chased after her. "Rosa, I'm not myself. Stop." I cut her off outside the door to the break room. A tech in pink scrubs walked by. Cardiac monitors chirped away. "Remember your coast-to-coast benches idea? After graduation I have a whole month off. Let's go. I have a car back home."

She strode by me.

I followed her past the IV poles, crash carts, defibrillator. She came to the nurses' station. To my left, a white-coat attending read from a chart. The other nurses peered over at me.

"What is it you want to say?" Rosa asked.

"Not here."

"Why not here?"

I considered running off, but I needed for her to understand me. "I liked you my third year," I said. "Before any of this. When I was doing my urology rotation."

"But you waited until now?"

"I'm shy."

"Come see me after you choose a specialty," she said.

"After?" I threw up my arms.

People thought doctors were great decision makers. Decisive people. I had even heard stuff like if Lyndon Baines Johnson had been a doctor, we would have won Vietnam. That William the Conqueror was a healer. Blitzkrieg was modeled after pancreatic surgery. All bullshit. I knew lots of attendings who barked out those critical orders and later you'd see them in the cafeteria holding up the line. The grilled chicken. The chicken salad. The grilled chicken. The chicken salad.

Surgery was operations, operating rooms, procedures, unconscious patients. Non-surgery was personal interactions. The patients were awake. I would have to talk to them. Surgery was swift and certain. Non-surgery was amorphous and uncertain. I had no idea what I wanted to do. I used to think people chose careers to compensate for their character flaws. The unassuming became lawyers. The selfless went into banking. I was weak, no one listened to me—surgery. But maybe I had other character flaws that were more pressing.

I had wanted to be a surgeon ever since I could remember. In junior high school, I gave a speech in front of the whole auditorium on why I wanted to do heart transplants. But it didn't appeal to me anymore. So what if I was good at it, or great at it, or better at it than I would be at anything else—it wasn't what I wanted to do. Maybe I should go into OB. I always thought they were the happiest doctors. But I would have to do vaginals all day and STD exams. It would be for the rest of my life. I had done a six-week rotation in OB and all the residents there absolutely adored the birth. They acted like it was the greatest show on earth. But to me it was really just minor surgery, and I didn't know if I could ever get over that.

I sneaked into Dean Bernstein's office. Carpet softened the floor. Framed sketches of organs lined the walls. Not only did he have portraits of the heart, liver, kidneys, but also the endocrine glands. His white-haired secretary sat at an L-shaped desk, typing away on her computer. Luckily, the door to what I assumed was Dean Bernstein's office was shut.

"And who are you?" the secretary asked, bringing her fingers up off the keypad.

"I have an appointment with the dean tomorrow. I got a letter in the mail."

"Would you like to see him today? There's an opening."

"No."

The woman had no lips. And the skin, where the lips should be, veered up to her gums. "If you see him today," she said, "it will only be a preliminary appointment. You won't have to decide."

I tried to look like I had already picked a specialty. Which one? I turned away from the woman. "I want to change my appointment."

"You can't."

"I just got the letter today. I have to go tomorrow?"

"That's how we're doing it this year. It's experimental." I could hear her turn a page in her day planner. "What's your name?" she asked.

The shut door slapped open. Dean Bernstein appeared. He was the most famous surgeon at the hospital, and arguably the best in Chicago. While he was certainly no Dr. DeBakey, he had operated on members of the Saudi royal family, repaired a dissected aortic aneurysm on Milton Berle, and done a bypass on Shirley Temple Black. Only the residents got to round with him. I felt a charge every time I sighted the entourage rolling down the surgical floor with Bernstein at the helm. Now he was by himself and equally as impressive. Those hands had operated on Shirley Temple.

He made his way to his secretary. His hair was curled into a brown helmet. He wore clunky eyeglasses. "What's on tap?" he asked her.

"Singh canceled," she said. "Supposedly, she cut her wrists with a knife and needs stitches. This gentleman has an appointment with you tomorrow. He won't tell me his name. It's either Lee, Higgins, Farzad, or Silverberg."

Dean Bernstein looked right at me.

"My appointment's not until tomorrow," I said.

"Let's talk about it."

"No, thank you, sir."

He thumbed through the charts on his secretary's desk. He selected one and left the others. "How about this," he said to me. "I meet with you now. We try to figure out the right path for you. If you still are undecided, you come back tomorrow. It's a win win. I'm not going to cut you today, so calm down." He headed back toward his office. The yellow neck lining of his scrubs peeked up from his white coat. "Let's go, doctor," he called to me.

His office was mostly windows. The Chicago skyline met my forward glance and to my left was the lake. His desktop was cluttered with papers and coffee mugs. In a standing frame was the picture of a younger Dean Bernstein with a shaggy mustache standing at the bedside of a smiling Arab man tucked under gold bed sheets. The dean sat down at his desk and I fell into the wood chair across from him. He nodded at me. I felt incapable of saying anything intelligent.

"So?" he asked.

"I've narrowed it down to two."

"Oh, we're halfway there. Which two?"

"Surgery or OB."

"OBGYN," he said. "You realize it's going to be damn hard to be a male OB in ten years. I see it now with my daughters. I'm not saying you won't find work, but do you interact well with women?"

"I know another student you can meet with tomorrow. He's finished all his applications."

"What do you like about surgery?"

"Preciseness. The hours—it has a road-trip quality to it."

"Surgery's all concentration," he said. "See that clock. I can stare at it for eight hours and register each second. Can you?"

"You want me to—"

"No, no, it takes practice."

Dean Bernstein opened the one chart and flipped through the contents. I was positive he was reviewing my evaluations, and I felt self-conscious. It was taking so long. Beside the picture of the Arab patient was a seemingly recent shot of the dean and a young woman on a beach. The divorce rate for surgical residents—it was his second wife. Or the third wife. But it also could have been his daughter. I went feature by feature, looking for a resemblance. I thought about Rosa Stein and I regretted not asking her out last year. I couldn't pick surgery. But I wouldn't be happy as an OB. I ran through alternatives: ophthalmology, neurology, cardiology, dermatology, nephrology, peeds.

"She's pretty, isn't she?" the dean asked.

"Who?"

"Victoria," he said. "In the picture. I don't see any reason why you won't place in either field. What's it going to be?"

"I thought I had until tomorrow."

He closed the chart. His wedding ring shone. It looked brand new. "I don't think you want to be a physician," he said.

"What? I didn't say that."

He removed his glasses. "It's not too late. Yeah, you've spent four years, and a hell of a lot of money, but it's better to realize it now than seven years from now when you're in the middle of a cardiothoracic fellowship. Don't fool yourself, residency is no picnic. Thirty-six-hour shifts. I always had to choose whether I was going to eat or whether I was going to sleep. I dropped down to 130, looked like I just got out of Auschwitz. I was never home. My wife was a stranger. My kid knew how to say *Pass the ketchup* before *Dada*. It's one thing to sacrifice all that for your passion, but don't do it out of default or because your parents expect it of you. Medicine isn't the only profession out there. You're a smart kid. You'll make a living. There are so many things to do other than this. Good things."

I felt sick to my stomach.

"What's it going to be, Alan?"

"Surgery."

He nodded and I left the office. 🕴

A five-year-old me honing skills at the very first house in America (Go Buckeyes!) that I lived in. And yes, I still wear that look of intense concentration when I write…

Xiaofei Chen is a sophomore at Monte Vista Christian High in California. Her time is split between friends, homework, piano, reading/writing, and, just recently, learning to drive! She lives with her parents, sister, and dog, and wishes to live to a ripe old age before dying happily in any place with lemonade and ketchup. She would like to add that being published is unbelievably, awesomely, really, really cool(!), and that her name does not rhyme with "xylophone," and is, in fact, pronounced "Sophie."

BURYING TWELVE YUAN

Xiaofei Chen
Xiaofei Chen

To my right, in the half-in, half-out room, she packs slabs of ice into her icebox. I hear skin rub against the box's cloth carrying strap, cushioned with rags deemed unfit for scouring the gray cement floors: shredded bits of brilliant red hang like mangled flesh from under it, blue strands trickle down her shoulder, and anyway, it doesn't matter because the rest of the strap and the box wrapped in cloth want to break and tumble over while she walks through the streets hollering, "Ice cream, ice cream, ice cream, ice cream," until her voice dies from monotony and people want to buy her ice cream so they can shove it down her throat, so they can get some quiet, and, if they are particularly good hearted, so she can buy a pair of pants that fit and don't drip with yellow sweat and stick to her legs like they were glued on with ice-cream juice.

I finish my business and button my pants and pull a belt through the frayed loops, trying to straighten the crimped folds of excess waist-band puckering around my waist like I was half-swallowed by a mouth; and then I watch rotting cabbage leaves swimming in the bucket of piss-tea, bobbing up and down like they needed help.

"Dump it, dump it, dump it, dump it," she chants in her ice-cream voice, which is no longer just her ice-cream voice but her everything voice, and one day maybe I'll snap and shove the box down her throat with the strips of red rag dripping from her mouth; but maybe I won't, because she's all I have, her and the dark place we call home, and my two-wheeled wagon and bicycle that together make up a three-wheeled wagon.

I take the bucket with both hands, pinch my nose with none, and open the ripped screen door, scattering the flies hovering behind it, and I avoid stumbling over the holes in the dirt-and-rocks road as I walk. Hardly a soul living on this narrow little dirt-and-rocks road stumbles; they've lived here so long with me and I with them, and we know where the holes are, and each evening when the sun sets and mosquitoes replace it we sit on stools an inch above the dirt and rocks, and we don't smoke because such things are only afforded on New Years; and maybe this is a good thing, so the little girl that wears brown shorts, daughter of the lady three doors down and her crippled husband, won't hack and adopt a recurring pneumonia. We sit and visit with one another until we fall off our stools, numb, and disappear through our screen doors into dark little hovels.

The bucket cuts into my palms. I shift and almost overbalance, but stay on the road. I reach the corner, marked by a mean enclosure of three-foot-high walls, and empty the bucket over the flies and previous wastes within these walls. I stand for a moment and watch the contents drip out of the enclosure and slip into one of the two open ditches carved into the sides of the road, running with stagnant brown mud that might not be made of just our waste, but all the unwanted scum from everywhere, because there was so much of it and it was such a terrible mixture. Deep enough to lick at a man's ankle if he had the misfortune to step inside, and long enough so that it curved all through our alley and into the next; and the next, the hot, sour stench disappeared only in winter when it froze with our noses. So, for the other seasons, we lived in a castle: this was our moat, guarded by the repulsive things clustered thick in it, and the narrow dirt-and-rocks road our royal highway, never needing repair, packed firmly down by the perpetual rain of sweat and fatigue from the brows of those who trod over it.

When I return with the empty bucket nudging my knees, I see that breakfast is out on the table, a bowl heaped with twisted white buns. I eat, watching as she closes the box lid and puts on her black shoes, soles eaten by the ants and the miles.

"Goodbye," she says, slinging the heavy icebox over her shoulder.

"You are leaving so soon?"

"Yes."

"Where are you selling today?"

"The elementary school first. Then the Square, after the children leave for classes."

"Don't forget to bring your hat. It looks like a hot day."

"Yes, it always is."

She touches the straw hat on her back, turns away, and shuffles out the screen door, a hunched, small woman with brown wilted-flower skin and snow-pea eyes.

I turn a flat plate over the bowl to discourage the bugs and put the bowl into the cabinet. I wait a while, then get up and fill a plastic basin with water. When I plunge my hands under, the water turns brown, the same shade as the creases in my palm and around my wrist when I pull them out and wipe them.

In the mostly-out room, next to the half-in, half-out room I emptied and ate and washed in, I find my three-wheeled wagon waiting with the chilled cucumbers and watermelon and jarred sauerkraut that my wife insists on holding back in case company comes over; but I think that she keeps them there so she can say in airy tones to passersby that she has a feast of chilled cucumbers and watermelon and jarred sauerkraut sitting in the mossy mostly-out room that she'll return to as soon as she switches that shiny coin for a dirty ice-cream bar, and that she doesn't even need that coin when she has such food in her home, her ripped screen door and mostly-out room and half-in, half-out room and all-the-way-in bedroom home.

I hitch the bicycle to the wagon and tell myself to run into Jiang Xin's market to buy stuffing before the day is out, when the remaining stuffing will have already escaped from the wide gap in the right cushion. A square of cloth hangs on a wire strung across one end of the dirt-crusted wall to the other, as it always hangs. I take this and begin cleaning the floor of my wagon, because it's not my bicycle that attracts paying riders, but the cleanliness and appearance of my wagon, with its floor made of wooden boards. Two thin slats rise on opposite ends of each of the two sides (making four altogether), and are topped with two more slats to form two straight wooden benches, like a house with only a floor, two hollowed-out sides of wall, and no roof. Red cushions on the benches, fat red cushions like big sausages woven with flowers and peacocks, are my offerings of comfort to the customer. I tighten the ropes that attach the cushions to the seats, trying to press down the ends that stick into the air where the ropes cut into stuffing. While I spin the two wheels attached to the wagon, big enough to fill half the empty space between the floor and the bench, I tell myself to also pick up a bottle of grease when I get the stuffing.

Relieved to see that the bicycle itself, and the two metal rods that attach it to the wagon, are in fine working order, I grasp the handlebars and push the whole thing out the door.

It was early when I dumped the waste bucket, and it still appears to be early, eight, I think, but the sun has traveled much in those two hours. Blankets of dust rise from the road and sit on my nose in fine gray specks, as if my skin, blooming tiny gray moons, was poked too many times with a needle. The wagon floor I'd just cleaned looks mottled gray, too, diseased.

Up ahead, dumping a bucket into the three-walled enclosure, is the brown-shorts girl, buckling under the weight and looking a toasted brown, her face pinched, particularly her nose. I pedal by on my three-wheeled wagon, wheels clanking behind me, kicking up a dust tail, and tip my head to say hello.

"Good morning, Uncle," she says, almost dropping her bucket. She shies away from the smelly ditch and moves back into the doorway of her home, into the strings of beads hanging thick in front of it in place of a door.

I lean forward and pedal hard, breathe heavy, straining to crawl up the hill that rises before the alley road opens into the main paved street. A motorized three-wheeled cart passes me, a square engine fixed to the belly of the wagon, the owner's feet touching useless pedals, himself basking in the shade his red canopy affords him. If I meet enough rides today and pick up many jobs this whole week, maybe I will choose a nice canopy with soft tassels to arch over my wagon and dust away the heat.

And what fortune kisses my cheek! I am waved down on the main street as I head toward the Square to wait in a stewing pot of many three-wheeled wagons.

"To the hospital, please."

"Right away, Missus."

I pull away from the roadside and into the mostly empty street (it is still early), rays of hot dust snowing over the ground and hovering in shimmering waves. The air is heavy with moisture; I can taste it on my tongue and in my nose when I try to breathe, like breathing through a steaming, dirty, yellow sponge.

"Is she sick?" I ask without turning.

"My daughter? No, healthy as an ox, this one, but it's her grand-mother who isn't."

"Is the grandmother already at the hospital?"

"Yes. She's been there all week and the little one has been fretting."

"You're visiting her, then."

"Peaches!"

Startled by the happy new voice, I miss a beat pedaling. My too-short gray pants press against my shins as the wind blows by. Threads trail from the raw pant edges, and I squirm under the damp and sti-fling white shirt melting into my skin.

"Peaches," the little girl says again, and from behind me I hear her swinging a plastic bag: *chusha, chusha, chusha.*

"You have peaches for her? What a lucky grandmother, to have such a granddaughter." I risk turning my head to smile at the girl. The swinging bag of peaches almost hits my face, and her small mouth stretches over small teeth, giggling.

"Careful," the mother warns.

Chusha, chusha, chusha, says the bag, then, *Chushaaaaathunk!*

After a while, it becomes harder to pedal. A muffled flapping comes from the two big wheels and I push harder, panting. The hospital looms up ahead, a mound of green stone, and the flapping grows louder. I hear the mother yell for her daughter to stop, but I don't know what the daughter did, so I throw more force into pedaling because something—*something*—seems to be stuck in one of the wheels—mud?—and the hospital is so close now, and surely the mother and daughter are restless sitting on red sausages, skirt-covered knees cramped up and bare knees aching from dangling, respectively.

I hear a sob and stop pedaling.

"What's wrong?" My stomach churns, digesting a solution of uneasy foreboding. I jump off my bicycle and go 'round the back, chest thumping when I see exactly what made the girl shout. "How did this happen?"

The little girl wipes her tears, bloody hands clutching her thin ankle and shaking, and the mother holds her in both arms, rocking.

"Will you tell me, child?"

Her nose drips like a leaky faucet into her sink-mouth. "I—I thought it was fun—thought there was no h-harm, the wheels just k-k-kept turning p-past m-my heel and it f-f-felt like something just r-r-rubbing over it and it was f-f-fun and I kept my h-h-heel in and the w-wheel just kept b-brushing over it and—" She stops and squeezes her eyes shut, choking back tears. "—*honest*, I t-t-thought there'd be n-no haarrrmmm—" She howls, cradling her heel, which is slick with blood and rough with ripped skin.

"Stupid girl, stupid girl," the mother whispers feverishly, still rocking the small body in her arms.

"And it got c-c-caught and I couldn't get it o-o-o-out," the girl continues when the pauses between each sob lengthen enough to squeeze bits of talk in between. "And the wheel k-k-kept turning—with my *h-heel* still in it."

The mother nods her head at me and presses two *yuan* into my palm, ignoring my attempts to help, and picks up her daughter, disappearing into the green hospital that looks like a mammoth cloud ground to a halt over it, shadowing it, one more occupant to crowd into its hard cots in its small, square rooms bathed in disinfectant and alive with the disinfectant-resistant bacteria of disease and poverty and permanent filth.

The money weighs heavily in my pocket and I treasure it as if it were more. Two whole *yuan* earned, with the day still in its youth! Pleased, I wander up and down the streets looking for more work, circling the Square three times and pausing every quarter of an hour to rest my feet and rub muddy cracklings from the corners of my eyes.

Halfway through the fourth time around my stomach rumbles and I remember the bun in my pocket that I'd saved from breakfast. I brake the wagon and stand up, stretching, feeling in my pocket for the bun, which I find and unwrap. As I twist my neck to get a good bite, someone hollers in my ear—

"Fried strips and soymilk! Fried strips and soymilk! Only five *yuan* for a big bowl of soymilk and six strips! Come get it while it's hot! You there, on the bike—wouldn't *you* like a *nice, hot, tasty* lunch? Just five *yuan* and you can treat yourself—"

Holding the plain white bun between my hands, I can't help but look sideways at the shirtless vendor, with his white cart piled high with greasy golden dough lumps and oily plastic bowls of soymilk streaked with yellow. It smells delicious, but five *yuan*…

"Trying to decide if you want to buy? Come on now, no decision here, my strips are the best around, bowls perfect for soaking and dipping." The vendor peels his lips back, twisting his words around his tongue to make them sound enticing. "No decision, no regrets."

I tear my eyes away from the sizzling strips and look to the vendor's left. An old man with a floppy hat and skin like rice paper flicks a lighter on and off from where he sits on the ground behind his black blanket cluttered with wares. He catches my gaze and flicks his lighter on again.

"You, son! Would you like a lighter? No? Not a smoker? Try a spoon, nice and sturdy, or maybe a package of genuine ivory chopsticks? Tell you what, since you look like the nice sort, I'll sell 'em cheap, a bargain, a discount," he says loudly, to drown out the vendor's pitch, and begins pointing at several dirty items on the blanket. I am jostled from behind as people hurry by clutching their bags and children. Behind the gate, I can see that the Square has filled up, teeming with shoppers and trash sweepers and women clothed in varying shades of red, stuffing paper menus into clenched fists. A man with a lame leg and a shuffling walk scoots by, his dead foot dragging over a corner of the black blanket. The old man says something, but I don't hear, because the food vendor is yelling again.

"I'll give you a sample, then, if you're not sure of the quality!"

I begin to refuse, but my stomach groans and my fingers dig deeper into the bun, now coated with a gritty pepper.

"Yes? A good deal? See, this is the sort of generous man I am," he says, grabbing a strip with his bare hands and twisting off a third of it. He sticks the end into an open bowl of soymilk after waving away a circling fly, waits, and then gives it to me. The piece disappears quickly in my mouth, crunchy, sopping, warm, pleasant in my belly.

"Ah-ha! He likes it!" the vendor says triumphantly, licking his oily finger and plucking a plastic bag from the rack. "How much will you be taking? One serving? Two? Three?"

"I'm sorry, sir, I really can't—can't afford to take any, and it's too hot, and I already ate…"

The vendor licks his rubbery lips. "Can't *afford*? Too *hot*?" His face turns purple and his temple turns blue, and his bare chest turns black, and he looks like one big bruise.

I back away into the stream of people, spewing apologies.

"Yeah? Yeah? You wasted my time, you bastard, trying to cheat an honest man of his money! Go to hell, take your cursed mother with you! I hope that strip in you turns sour and you die a fucking horrible death, you cheat—" His face is screwed up horribly, ugly and thick and shiny. I push my three-wheeled wagon onto the street, head lowered, and pedal away as fast as I can, so fast that I almost skid sideways when a woman wearing a thick woolen coat waves me down from the sidewalk.

214

"Hello, Ma'am. Where to?" I wonder if she's planning on serving herself for dinner with a garnish of parsley over her broiled flesh.

"Underground twenty-four."

"Some nice stores down there. You'll find good things, *airier* things."

The woman sniffs, powdered nose turned in the air. "As if I'd expect to find anything decent...*here*. Why I came to visit her at all, I don't know. The weather up here is horrible, so hot, everything filthy, everyone ignorant, simply not the place for someone like me..."

I keep my mouth shut and wend my way through people and other three-wheeled wagons.

"So much difference. Travel just a bit further north from Harbin and you find this dump. I wish I hadn't agreed to stay with her, dratted sister, never knew anything—of course, that's why she turned out like this, living here in this madness. And my goodness, I've never seen anywhere so hot and dirty. How can you stand this place?"

"Most places up here are like this during the summer."

"Not nearly as stifling."

"This is my China," I reply, turning a corner onto the construction street where they're digging the foundation for a new apartment building complex. Deep holes and pits dot the ground, wooden boards and yellow machinery everywhere. A crowd is gathered tight, shouting and pointing, and occasionally one of the men sticks a hand down into the pit they surround.

"Stop," the woman says, "I want to see what's happening. Get closer."

I oblige and brake close to the crowd. The woman clambers off the wagon and takes off her wool coat. I can see globs of pink skin hanging from under her armless shirt like wings, flapping as she moves.

"Someone fell into the hole," she reports, straining her neck and shading her eyes. "They're trying to get him out."

"Would you like to go now?"

"No, no, I want to see what happens." She inches into the crowd. "Don't move. Look, that man has a rope."

"Which one?" I ask politely, prying the white shirt from my skin and fanning it to ward off the heat.

"The one in front in the blue. He's lowering the rope in, oh, they're all pulling it now, I think they've got it—"

From the pit a small boy emerges, clinging onto the rope like he was a ball of lint on a winter sweater. The crowd cheers as the boy's feet touch the ground, and I see his familiar flushed face beaming gratitude at the men who got him out.

"Stupid boy," the woman comments, climbing back onto the wagon.

"Not quite stupid enough. He's the talent here, wins every piano competition he attends. His mother says that they're saving up the prize money to send him to a school in America."

"Pshaw. That dirty little boy? A piano prodigy?"

"Have you seen him play?" I say shortly. "I have, and it's like watching…I don't know, it's like watching someone…*breathe*, the best breather in China, like he *breathes* what he's doing, and whatever he's doing it's going to get him out of here, it's going to get him to America."

The woman snorts and slaps three *yuan* into my hand. She picks her coat off the bench and waddles into the stairway leading to the Underground.

I pedal back down the street slowly, resting my prickling calves, and turn right onto an alley road, narrow and dusty like mine, and stop in front of Jiang Xin's market.

The door tinkles when I step into the room, touched by a glowing so dim it melts into the darkness. Someone, a woman, is talking in loud tones in the back, and I stand near the door, waiting and looking. I don't look for the stuffing I came for, though. I expect that to be in the back room, because the store room itself is too small to be crowded by the likes of such things. Its creaking shelves and stormy glass cases are reserved for sweets, crackers, and plastic trinkets that break two days after you buy them so you'll think that it was your fault for handling it too roughly when it was really made and timed so it would snap in half like that. I look at these toys to occupy myself: a blue whistle, and a plastic box with a plastic perfume bottle inside it that seems to have sprung a leak, because the red lining is stained darker red directly under the neck of the bottle, and a big doll with tangled yellow hair and one big button eye and a gingham dress flipped over its head, because it had fallen over on its plump arm, revealing a white bottom crossed with crude, wide stitches.

The curtain separating the back portion from the store portion sweeps open, and Jiang Xin steps out, fingers of blue cigarette smoke leaking from his mouth and reaching toward me. He tosses a box of apple juice into the air.

"On the house. You look like you need it, old man," he says, and I laugh, stepping forward in front of the counter and brushing against a set of wind chimes dangling from the ceiling.

"Just some stuffing for my cushions today," I say, paying him with a few bills, soft like mealy apple flesh. He ducks into the back and re-emerges and I take the bundle and stuff my cushions right when I get outside, knotting the loose ends so the stuffing wouldn't squeeze out again.

My next run is for a man and a woman carrying one bulging suitcase each and in a rush to get to the train station by five, so much so that they offer me five *yuan* to pedal within an inch of my life, and now I bend over my bike, gasping for breath and mopping my forehead and leaving brown streaks across my burning nose as I watch the couple lift their bags over the ground and run to catch their train. A boy wearing shredded green trousers held up by a string knotted around his waist and a red shirt that looks like crusted blood flits from person to person, hands outstretched and cupped, and from here I can hear his voice: Give me money, I need money, give me money, he says, and the man he's asking now is laughing, throwing a coin across the street and laughing again as the boy scurries to save it. There you go, boy, good boy, here you are, he laughs, and hurries into the train station while fumbling in his pocket for a smoke. A woman totters by with an icebox thrown over her shoulder like an animal carcass, croaking, "Ice cream, ice cream, ice cream," and eliciting from me a sideways look at the familiarity of the tone.

At seven, an old man asks to be taken back to his home in the alley next to apartment building thirty-two.

"Slow as you want, just before the rain starts, please," he requests, casting a worried eye at the soaking gray sky. He sits, and is so light I can feel only the slightest resistance as I pull into the street.

"So how was your day, son?"

"Fair enough, I think. Enough to buy tomorrow."

"It's what we all hope for," the old man says, and the rain falls, skipping the drizzle and plunging straight into a heavy, thick curtain. The rain is good for washing the days off the buildings and diluting the waste ditches, but it is bad for the man, who coughs, first a little cough, then a louder one, and then he's making noises like he's going to turn inside out.

"I'm sorry I'm not there yet." I pedal faster, bumping over the dirt-and-rocks road.

The man's voice bleeds into the rain and then he is quiet for a moment. "It's not your fault, son."

"I'm sorry it's raining," I say desperately, shivering from the sudden cold.

"Well, when it's raining, things around you—"

"I'm sorry you're getting wet." My voice is not my own, strange and high and pinched.

"—become wet, and it will rain around you, and that's how it is—"

"I'm sorry I don't have a canopy to cover—"

"—and everything where the rain is will get wet, too, and you will get wet, and they will get wet unless they escape, and you can't do anything about it—"

"I'm sorry I—"

"—and it could be pouring here, and just a ways west it isn't, but, son, don't apologize—"

I brake in front of a low, small house like my own.

"Thank you, son, done in good time."

He brings out two *yuan* and pays me, and I watch him walk into his home and close the door tight, and the rain still pours around me, but lighter, and I look up into a small circle of blue sky above me and peer at the darkness around me, and I am seized by a thundering claustrophobia that dissolves and slips into the mud as my twelve *yuan* and I pedal away, lost in the pit bottom, going nowhere.

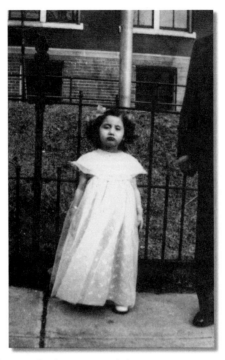

*It was only recently that I noticed this was not just a picture of a
little girl. The presence on my left must be someone close to me,
but I no longer know who—this figure is what the story is about:
I am dressed up to be in a wedding, and he is the funeral.*

Ioanna Carlsen's poems and stories have appeared in *Poetry*, the *Hudson Review*,
Nimrod, Poetry East, Café Solo, Chelsea, The Quarterly, Field, Apalachee Quarterly, the
*Marlboro Review, Quarterly West, Alaska Quarterly Review, Columbia, Solo, Luna, Whis-
key Island, Prairie Schooner, Confrontation*, and *Mondo Greco*, and is forthcoming in the
Hollins Critic. One of her poems has been chosen to be a part of Poetry 180, an
online program of the Library of Congress.

GOING HOME

Ioanna Carlsen

At the airport I have to make a phone call for someone to pick me up because my mother is at the hospital with my father, who has had a stroke. Next to me is a young woman also making a call; she turns to me, the phone dangling, "The ticket agent screwed up the connections—I'm missing my mother's funeral," she says.

I nod. "Maybe it's for the best," I say.

"No," she says, "I want to be there."

"You'll get there," I assure her, "don't worry."

As I turn away I see other women, ages thirty to fortyish, dressed in black, probably going to funerals, too. I glance back at the young woman talking intensely into the phone. I imagine her name is Charlotte and the funeral is somewhere in the deep Midwest. Afraid of missing it, she will not. And although she dreads arriving at it, she will attend it all the way there, and back.

Driving myself to the airport that morning I had my new blue truck in cruise control. As I was trying to figure out how it worked, it seemed to me that cars on a highway were like emotions—sometimes, in the left lane, they were going faster than I was. Sometimes, in the right lane, they were going too slow; sometimes they would come up on me, out of nowhere, sometimes I would see them up ahead and approach them for a long time. Sometimes the other cars seemed like other people's emotions, but mostly the cars were my own emotions—some of the cars were old and banged up, and some of the cars were shiny, expensive, or cheap and new. Manifesting outside these windows on the surface of this blacktop, the cars appearing out of nowhere, the high-way itself, were parts of me.

It didn't take long to figure out that in order to stay in cruise control I had to gauge the situation and change lanes ahead of time. The instant I got reactive, I was out of cruise control. The closer I got to the city, the harder it got to stay at the same steady speed because there were more cars.

The closer I got to home, the more emotions I had. When I got to the hospital, my father did not know me, although my mother pretended he did. "He's dying," I said to my mother. She looked at me across his body in the hospital bed: he seemed already in his casket, sleeping so deeply she had to bring him back from long distances to force him to eat—I could see how far back he came and I was amazed.

"He won't die," she said, "I won't let him."

The hospital room became our home. The home I had just left had its children and its husband, its wife and mother, who were me. But here, again I was the child; my intervening life barely existed; it seemed more like a dream. My father was her child now, too; my mother was still my mother, but also his—as a mother or a wife, I was imaginary, and as a father so was my father.

No, he didn't die. How could he? She and I fought over it. You've got to let him, I would say. She would just ignore me. People would come in to test him for rehabilitation possibilities and she would prompt him the way she used to prompt me from the back of the room at spelling bees, forming the letters with her mouth.

Now when I go home to see him, one more time each time, I'm glad she saved him; it gives us time to get used to it. I walk into the kitchen and put my bags down on the same green linoleum with the white swirling. The oven is new, and they have a dog; we never had a dog when I was growing up because my mother thought animals were dirty. But now that my brother and I are gone, they have animals. I know the drawers are full of things she never uses that are as familiar to me as the photographs in the box with the broken hinge that she keeps in the closet. I know there is money in the bags of clothes there. I know there is jewelry hidden in other boxes under the bed. I know the altar is still in their bedroom with baskets of unironed clothes next to it because she keeps the ironing board in there next to the exercise bike she is always nagging my father to ride. She doesn't have to because she has high blood pressure. The kitchen radio is on like always; the TV, like always, is on in the living room.

I set down my bags. My mother opens the dishwasher—which hasn't worked for ten years and which she never replaces because since we kids are no longer at home she has no reason to entertain—and throws in another plastic top from a margarine container. She never throws anything away anymore.

My father is sitting at the kitchen table fluttering in and out of the present like a leaf blown about by wind.

There are times when he just isn't here at all; the question is where, at those times, he is. Lost in the past, I think, as if it were a place—a room within this room, like Russian nested eggs.

When I am home he tells me stories from that place. In his particular case, it's an island, Greek. He sees the skirts of the old men swaying—he remembers being a little boy, teasing the old men who wore the Turkish-style trousers, called *vrachia*, that ballooned out at the hip; he's throwing pebbles at an old man, and then he sees the dirt road, the black skirt of the trouser swaying—suddenly, he tells me, it's as if he is actually there.

Whereas we can go out to dinner with old friends and the rest of us are chatting and he is not. He eats his food very slowly, head bent over his plate, as if engrossed not in eating, but contemplating it.

My mother, twenty years his junior, gives things to him, a glass of wine, a piece of bread. He ignores the wine, takes the bread and looks at it, turning it over, looking at her, as if to say, what is this?

Afterward someone asks him if he enjoyed his dinner. He looks up, startled. "No," he says.

Later we are at our friends' house, chatting, and suddenly he enters the conversation. We all look at him, the way you look at a person just entering a room.

The next day I say to him, "Why did you tell George you didn't enjoy dinner last night?"

"Did I say that…," he says. "I wonder why."

"Well, you didn't seem to really be there during dinner," I start to say, and then suddenly, I get it, and I start laughing, saying, "but of course, no wonder you didn't enjoy it—you weren't there—it makes perfect sense, how could you enjoy it…"

We're both laughing now; he finishes the sentence for me, "…when I was someplace else."

We find this excruciatingly funny. My mother tries to pretend that it is not; she is annoyed with us and does not want to laugh. She cannot help finally smiling, because is it funny, but she doesn't like it. She doesn't like me getting into his oldness, she doesn't like me encouraging him to give in to being old.

It took him a long time to get old. But now he is being old with a completeness that takes my breath away. He reminds me of my grandmother, who was so old she died, twenty years ago.

He takes his teeth out and doesn't like to put them back in. My mother pushes them at him across the table. He reminds her of my grandmother when he does not put them in. We call her the sergeant. "The sergeant wants you to put your teeth in," I tell him, and he laughs and discreetly slides them under his napkin.

She is fighting the whole world, the laws of the universe, of life itself. He reminds me of my grandmother, and she reminds me of the Spartans at Thermopylae, doomed but resisting to the end; her love for my father is an idea she still has. One day I see him hobbling to their bedroom in the middle of the day. "I can't go on," he says to her, naming her name. "I can't," he repeats in the language they speak to each other, the language of their parents, their past, their lives branching off around it with all the things that are private between them, all the things I can't know.

But now I know something new. I know that just as she does not allow him to die, he lives only for her. It's a love story, the love story of the century, two merely human beings defying, for each other, for as long as possible, death.

I try to get the story out of her, their story; she has always been reticent, letting it out in little bits and pieces. I ply her with questions: Tell me when was the first time you…, tell me how did you know that…, tell me. "Why do you want to know," she says. "Maybe I'll write about it," I tease her. "How can I make your story into a best-seller if you don't tell me?" She gives me a long look across the kitchen table which she is now leaving to go in and see how he is.

"Use your imagination," she says, and goes to him.

The young woman at the airport made it to her mother's funeral just in time. I can just see it—her father in a black suit, one of the pallbearers along with her brother. It is a hot day in early October in the Midwest. There is a haze over everything, and the small town her mother lived in before she died is far from here; only the family will go there to bury her on the farm where her people are buried. But her father is ill, her father is having some kind of attack, her brother stays behind with him and takes him to the hospital—they will follow later in the car, but she drives the hearse with her mother in the back up to the farm at Oscola; when her brother and father arrive, they will bury her together. The cat will watch from the window, the dog will be locked in so it doesn't sniff the coffin. At the church she took the diamond earrings her husband had given her for Mother's Day and put them in her mother's pocket before they closed the casket. The diamond in her mother's pocket glittered in the dark like living eyes as she drove her mother, in her casket inside a hearse, along the highways of southern Illinois, each farmhouse farther from the next in the dry October heat and the glazed sky.

At the farmhouse that she had grown up in, she had not the courage to open her mother's casket and look at her once again, alone now in this bleak Midwestern landscape she had always been trying to escape. She left her mother and found the key in the place it was always hidden, and let herself into the dark house.

Those few hours with the coffin in the car, between the church and this house that now was her mother's gravesite, drove a wedge between her ordinary life and the present. She felt exposed, on some new threshold of her life, in an old house that was a new house. The furniture in this one was as good as sold, the contents of its drawers piled up in the center of the living room in boxes ready to be taken away, the walls already showing holes where the paintings used to hang, the flowers already dying of neglect in the garden. She remembered her mother the last time she had seen her, standing here, just inside the doorway waving goodbye—her mother, grown stout, but still pretty, waving goodbye in her robe and wearing socks with her slippers.

Fear struck at her like a weapon; her legs were weak and she felt as if she had to go to the bathroom. She walked inside the house and let its emptiness ring through her as if she were a room with no one in it, loneliness ringing through her like a phone.

This empty room held her past. It was empty and yet full. It had all the familiar plates and chairs and tables and lamps she had grown up with; only the people were missing. Only the life was gone.

It was like stepping into an old dress, being back here, alone with her mother dead in the driveway. It was like the dress didn't fit right anymore; she wanted to take it off, sell it, give it away, but even if she could do any of those things, it would still be with her, in the closet of her head.

She sat down in the room. She sat on the couch as if she were testing it. If they did sell the house now, it would be empty for a while, then someone else would live in it. All their things would be dispersed: were the things their life, where was their life? Was it inside these walls, was it in the cloisonné vase on the coffee table? Was it in the photographs in the box in the right-hand drawer of the kitchen chest? Was it in her, was it that now she was her mother?

Then she realized the phone was actually ringing, and it was her brother; they had taken some tests at the hospital. Their father would be all right, they would both be up next morning.

She sat back down on the couch in the house, in the complete darkness that had now overtaken it, and the night was like a coffin closing over her face.

In the morning when she woke, she was her mother. She was her mother and she was making eggs in the same pan her mother always used, only wearing different clothes that were her own. Her hands went unerringly to the right places for everything she needed, her thoughts on the woman in the hearse in the driveway. She was quick to notice how fast the fire leapt into blueness and made the butter melt its heart out on the stove; she touched the silkiness of the glaze on the plate sitting attentively next to the stove.

That plate had all the time in the world, she thought.

She felt so alone it was like being in the Himalayas: the air was lighter than usual; she could just breathe it in. She was a dream, breathing.

The house was just the same as they had left it, the same plaid plates she still liked, the same green linoleum streaked with marbled white, the same dog bowl in the same corner, although many of the dogs who had used it were dead.

Outside the window she saw how the driveway curved around to the back meadow, where down below, at the foot of a small hill next to a pond, a little graveyard lay with the remains of three bodies: her grandparents, and a child born dead to her mother before she had been born. She saw how that road was her road, a road she was now on, that had no side roads; that now that she was on it, she would have to take to the end. She heard how a bird outside the window was singing it's your turn, it's your turn, over and over again. She heard how another bird answered at intervals, It's my turn, it's my turn, again and again. She saw how you can make birds say anything you want, and so she said to it, "Don't be afraid. Say, 'Don't be afraid'; say it again."

Her father looked so pale in the black suit. "You can take that off, Dad," she said, "it's only us now." "No," he said, "not till after," and he burst into tears. She tried to comfort him, but he kept her away. She brought tea and bread and butter to the table with some ham; she was angry. He gave way to his grief, ignoring her. Her brother opened a beer, ignoring him. She watched her father, saying nothing, seeing how separate from him she was.

He pushed away her food, he pushed away her drink, he hung his head and his hands, looking down, toward the side. Then he put his arms on the table like a protection and dropped his head down inside them and stayed that way, finally falling asleep there, grieving as if the world had begun and ended with his wife, ignoring his children— grieving for her as if she had been his life.

The next morning they buried her. They drove the hearse down to the place where they had paid a hired man to dig the grave. It was in line with the others. Her father insisted on opening the casket one last time. They had rolled it off the casters and it sat there beside the rectangular bed of the hole. They opened the casket and their father leaned into it, kissed his wife, and stayed there so long they had to pull him out. And when they did, he sobbed, a choking sound came out of him, and he fell back in, dead.

They couldn't believe it at first. At first they were furious, like orphans abandoned at a crossroads. Her brother kept slapping his father's face, but she saw it was no use. "Terry," she said, "calm down. He's gone, they're gone, they've left, it's over." They sat down beside the coffin, him still leaning into it, and they held each other and cried. They stayed there until they were both quiet.

"Let's go back in the house, Terry," she said, "and call the doctor."

"Why," said Terry.

"We need a certificate of death."

"Then we're going to go through all this again—right?"

"Oh no, Terry," she said, "no, we're not. I'll tell you what we're going to do."

How she explained it to him on the way up to the house was how they did it. After the doctor came, the hired man came again with his son, and they buried her and put him in the ground next to her, the way he was, buried him like that, in the fetal position.

There was something comforting about the way the ground took him in. In this ancient, time-honored way, I imagined the woman, whose name I thought must have been Charlotte Irons, put her father into the ground beside her mother.

My father is older now than it is possible to be and still be, but he is. My mother brings him to visit us, old as he is. She will go nowhere without him, and he is upset if she is not around. His hands shake when he brings his fork to his mouth. Food spills down his shirt. He almost totters over every time he gets up from a chair. Getting him into a car is a drama, each leg lifted separately, the cane, the handle of the door, the door, each thing having a speaking part.

He shuffles when he walks, bent at the waist as if listening to something underground. The altitude is too high for him here and he does not feel well. One day he comes in from being outside and sits down heavily at the kitchen table where my mother and I are shelling peas. He looks pale and waxen; something has happened to him. "I feel death coming closer," he says.

We all look at each other. I tell my mother to give him a glass of wine. She thinks I drink too much and encourage him to drink more than he should, but this time she gestures to me to get it.

"I don't want it," he says. "Drink it," she says—the sergeant. I rub his shoulders, because he is crying, then I cry. My mother doesn't like it when we cry, but she cries, too. He drinks the wine; my mother and I start making dinner, chopping, peeling, frying. My husband comes in and wants to know why we are all crying.

"He was outside and something happened to him," I say. "His death is coming closer, getting to know him like a friend."

"What does that mean?" My husband sometimes reminds me of my mother.

"He doesn't feel well," I say. My mother laughs.

"What was he doing outside?"

"Looking for things, he's always going in drawers looking for something. Sometimes he goes outside looking," says my mother.

"What is he looking for?" I ask.

"Money," says my husband. This is very funny because my father has always been a gambler, and one who lost a lot of money in his day: horses, poker, the stock market—he probably was looking for money. With one foot in the grave, he's still looking for money, and it makes us all laugh.

My father finishes the wine and he feels better. Nothing happens, again. Before they leave, my mother wants to know when I will be coming home again.

I am always going home, that's what she doesn't understand. I'm always just going home, driving to an airport, using cruise control for as long as I can, and then getting there, gaining on my parents, who are moving very slowly as I come up on them. He has a cane, she is smiling, and then, in no time at all, I see myself enveloped in the arms of the past.

The Last Pages

Blanche Howland with her children Dorothy and George Jr.

This is my daughter Grace, our dog Fielding, and me. My wife took the picture. We are in the kitchen, which is an all-purpose room. We cook, eat, listen to music, gather with friends, do art projects, set up train sets, have tea parties, do homework, grade papers, practice yoga, prepare bills, play games, watch television, and, of course, write in this room. For years, I thought I had to have a special place to write—a place that was all mine, that was somehow sacred, quiet, inviolate. Over time, I realized that I did have such a space—and that I shared it with my family. The kitchen is often messy, cluttered, and noisy. I usually do dishes before I write. The space is ever-shifting. "The Small Side of Large" was written at the table just out of sight in this picture. Over the course of the last two years, Willard Dix's story underwent many changes, just like the room. Although Willard and I are about as different as can be, I did, in fact, propose to my wife in the movie theater. My thanks to her for the picture, and for sharing her life with me.

—Clark E. Knowles

It's me. It's her. It's us together, each in her own corner. It's home with two rooms.

It's the story. It's the way it was, is, and will be.

It's you I love, her I loved, it's over, it's always.

It's a house with spaces for more than one. It's going home.

—*Ioanna Carlsen*

I wrote "Victor's Bird" during an intense summer of drought in Colorado. To the near northwest, a wildland fire burned out of control. The little village where I live was on preliminary evacuation. We woke each day to the smell of smoke, and we watched the far ridge line for flames. We were packed and ready to go. Meanwhile, the usual mountain jays squawked at the usual complaints of crows. And then there was the unlikely song of a tropical bird and a blue chair, and the baked earth didn't look so dead, and the dying trees didn't seem to be dying. The fire burned 137,000 acres but never reached the village. The evacuation order ended, and the firefighters disappeared overnight from their camp at the edge of town. Not far away stands a blackened forest, beautiful and haunting at once. I think it is sometimes the big dramas that hold the little stories, dozens of them.

—N. Nye

In 1998, my friend Ted was a fourth-year medical student, considering surgery. He called me up one night with an unbelievable statistic: ninety percent of married surgical residents got divorced. Even though Ted wasn't married, dating anyone, or afraid of hard work, the high divorce rate was causing him to rethink surgery. It struck a chord with me, even though I wasn't married, dating anyone—or in med school (I was in law school, and had no idea the commensurate divorce rate for young litigators). I proceeded to write the first draft of this story. Three years and more than thirty rewrites later, I hopefully got it right.

—*Michael Bahler*

I'm usually pretty good with titles. It's a trait I got from my mother, who once helped me name a seventh-grade history report, "What's So Great About Catherine?" But this story, which finally became "Fighting with Fire," had me stumped. For a long time I called it "The Great Valley," but that sounded too much like a TV Western. Here are some of my other attempts. Feel free to cringe.

—*Frances Lefkowitz*

Some Seek Pleasure
in the GV

✓ Waiting for Rain
The Promise of The West
The Great Valley
Finally the Rain
Down Comes The Rain
✓ Continental Drift
Earthquake Weather
✓ Living on The fault line
fertile
floods
extremes of drought + flood
—————— Valley → a twist on it
✳ Stopping in the Valley
Leaving the Valley

the grapes of wrath
Transients

A crack in The Earth
Sometimes the Earth
gives in
the House on the Hill
Where i come from

This piece was inspired by a trip to China to visit my relatives in 2001, and was actually written the following summer. And although it doesn't sound like a place that would rival the Bahamas as a desirable vacationing spot, it is. And even if you don't have relatives living there that you hadn't seen since you were seven, it still would be. There are so many people to observe when you think that they're not looking, so many open-air marketplaces smelling of clean dirt or shipments of clothes to wander through, and more than enough exposure to new ways of thinking, and interesting people to change your perspective on… well, lots of things. Sure, it's hot, and sure, you'll sweat, but you'll always find a small family-operated market stocked with frozen confections. Sure, the plane ride is thirteen-plus hours, but then you'll find yourself in a thirty-story hotel looking down at the flaring lights of a massive city and feeling very small—but not in a bad sense. Anyway, I think that wraps it up for me. I have lots and lots of bizarre and intriguing incidents that I would share, but hey, look, my two hundred words is up.

—*Xiaofei Chen*

Glimmer Train Stories

© Lord Snowdon / Retna Ltd.

William Trevor

Daniel Villasenor

In this picture, taken by my father, I am sitting in my mother's lap at my third birthday party. To the left are my brother and sister, who are nine and ten years my seniors, respectively. I was born a year after my family moved to Queens, New York from Bombay, and I often wonder about the life my family led in India before I appeared—the people they knew, the home they lived in—and how difficult it must have been for each of them to leave that life and come to a completely foreign place. My fascination with their ability to leave has contributed to several of my stories. With "Plan B," I started off writing about this character who encounters a chance to walk away from his difficult though familiar life into a free but uncertain future. As I wrote, I found that I was most interested in the process by which Arjun considers his current situation and his potential future, and how he weighs one against the other.

—*Anita Shah Kapadia*

My wife and I are a cult of two, devotees, only in a playful sense, of Harold Pinter's film version of his backward play, *Betrayal*. In it, the Ben Kingsley character tells his friend that he went to Torcello in the dawn and read Yeats. And he was happy there; "such a rare thing." So, once, on the spur of the moment, we decided to go to this little island near Venice packing our Yeats. And we were happy there; such a rare thing.

—*George Fahey*

Glimmer Train Stories

"Sand Thieves" stemmed from a eulogy I gave for my grand-father, including recollections of a perfect beach he had made. I have vivid memories of him raking crisscrosses into it, and another of him sitting there in his chair and showing us kids how a horsefly could draw blood.

My grandfather *was* a bit of a sand thief, but only in the noblest sense. He also shared the same unique perspective of the natural world as Uncle Lucien, and perhaps some of his physical characteristics, but thankfully little else. He shared most of Lucien's best traits.

By the end of this story I had reason to love and hate all the family members, including the narrator. None of them are ever worth wholly condemning… sort of like real family in most cases. And the kids are like most kids: on the verge of simultaneous goodness and badness. On the verge of adulthood. I began to like this story when I no longer knew whom to root for.

—*Adam Schuitema*

My grandfather, Peter Rozycki, and his sand.

The schizophrenic identity of the short story has an exceptional attraction for me. When I read a story, I am moved both by its fictitious lives and by the discreet sheets from which I imagine the writer reaching out at me. Each story unfolds its obscure aspects that write their own imaginary tales, and beyond these stories lies the author's spirit.

In such a generous opportunity to speak my mind, I would rather cut through the labyrinth of fiction and admit to the truth of my storytelling. When I write a story, I cling to it, breathing a bit too loud, secretly hoping to put my heart in the reader's hands. This is a way of making friends. I have seen worse.

—*Avital Gad-Cykman*

For some reason, I take great comfort in the fact that I'm just a blip on the geological radar. This guy Parker from the story needs some of that comfort, too, before he ultimately buckles, turning his daughters into teeny anxiety cases along the way. So if I've gotten it right, "Vast Inland Sea" concludes with a sense of "hopeful transcendence"—the sense that despite great pain or confusion, a small move has been made toward an eventual peace or joy. I first heard of the idea at school from a professor named Richard DuPree. It stuck with me. Here was a man coming to class every day throughout his chemotherapy—a man who would die only months later. He taught us of the modern-day happy ending right up until the very end.

—*Jonathan Kooker*

Windy Hill, Bath, New Hampshire

Dorothy Grace, circa 1928.

COMING SOON

Say, we're just trying to get out of childhood in one piece, all of us.
from "Hiram the Desperado" by Robert Olen Butler

The cotton candy was too sweet, the popcorn too salty, the petting zoo full of nothing but farm animals. "Where are the pandas?" she cried. "Why can't we go dancing?"
from "The Words Honey and Moon" by Jennifer Tseng

Pascual's father started to die in March. By summer, it was nearly complete. It came upon him all at once, a summer storm brewed from a cloudless sky, and rendered him—in quick and cold fashion—a ghost, a negative image, weak and formless, a fourth cup from a single bag of tea.
from "A Strong Dead Man" by Daniel Alarcón

One of the things I do with my fiction students is to get them to try to consider that every family has a way of doing things. Then you bring your friend home from college and they say, "Why do you put the Kleenex in the piano bench?" You say, "Everybody puts the Kleenex in the piano bench." Your friend says, "No, they don't."
from an interview with Mary Gordon by Charlotte Templin